"But it's not his baby, Floretha. I just know it's…Red Jannik's."

Trent's heart stopped at Harper's words. Every rose-colored dream he'd had the past week died.

"Oh, lordy, child, how on earth did you get things into such a state?" The housekeeper's mournful voice broke through Trent's rage.

"That's a real good question, Harper," he said.

He heard the sharp intake of her breath. "Trent, no—"

"Save it," he snapped. The last time he'd felt this crushed, this betrayed, this much the damned fool, had been the day Freddie Benton told him what his mother really did with Farrell Landen up at the big house. That day he'd felt murder in his heart. And he felt it now, too. He wheeled and stalked out of the house, ignoring Harper's tortured voice as she called after him.

Harper rose to her feet and walked toward the door. She had to explain. She reached the parking area behind the barns in time to see the cloud of dust left behind as Trent's Chevy roared toward the lane. She ran after it, calling his name, mindless of the dust on her new graduation dress.

The dress that was to have been her wedding dress.

ABOUT THE AUTHORS

Leigh Greenwood is an award-winning historical author, perhaps best known for his highly acclaimed Seven Brides series. *Only You* is his first contemporary romance. Leigh, who is involved with the Romance Writers of America, was also a teacher and musician for several years. He was born in North Carolina, where he still resides with his wife, Anne, and one of his three children. Anne and Leigh are no strangers to long-term romance, having recently celebrated their twenty-fifth anniversary.

Peg Sutherland is also an award-winning author and has been writing for Superromance for the past seven years. Her critically acclaimed books have made her one of our most popular authors. In an interesting twist, in *Only You* Peg has written the historical parts of the story. Like Leigh, Peg is also involved with the RWA. She lives in Charlotte, North Carolina, with her husband, Mike.

Books by Peg Sutherland

Don't miss any of our special offers. Write to us at the following address for information on our newest releases.

Harlequin Reader Service
U.S.: 3010 Walden Ave., P.O. Box 1325, Buffalo, NY 14269
Canadian: P.O. Box 609, Fort Erie, Ont. L2A 5X3

ONLY YOU
Leigh Greenwood
& Peg Sutherland

Harlequin Books

TORONTO • NEW YORK • LONDON
AMSTERDAM • PARIS • SYDNEY • HAMBURG
STOCKHOLM • ATHENS • TOKYO • MILAN
MADRID • WARSAW • BUDAPEST • AUCKLAND

ISBN 0-373-70754-1

ONLY YOU

Copyright © 1997 by Harold Lowry and Peg Robarchek.

Printed in U.S.A.

ONLY YOU

PART ONE: SPRING

CHAPTER ONE

Collins, South Carolina, 1968

HARPER WEDDINGTON wasn't his type. But she was exactly what he was looking for. Trent knew that the first time he saw her.

Fender backed up to a fire hydrant on Broad Street, he sprawled in the front seat of his bondo-and-rust-colored '61 Chevy with its cracked vinyl seat and dangling left headlight. With part of the twenty-dollar bill in his back jeans pocket—his last folding money—he'd bought a soft drink and a bag of hot, greasy fries at the drugstore lunch counter. He was wondering whether he could make his fortune in Collins, South Carolina, when a black-and-white police car purred to a stop beside him.

Frowning, Trent took a long swallow of his drink and watched over the rim of the paper cup as the local cop approached. The cop wore that same distrustful expression Trent inspired in everyone over the age of thirty.

"Howdy," Trent drawled.

The cop nodded, but barely. "See your license."

It wasn't a question and Trent didn't like orders. But he studied his opponent and the patrol car that blocked his retreat. Anchoring his cup between his thighs, he slipped two fingers into his back pocket. He took his time opening the denim wallet his mother had bought him for Christmas, then let the license dangle from his fingertips.

The representative of Collins's official welcoming committee studied the photo, then studied Trent's face. "Gordon Elliott Trent, outta Whitlaw, South Carolina. You a long way from home, son."

"Yep."

"You got business here in Collins?"

Measuring his reply, Trent took another swallow of the watered-down soft drink while the officer peered into the back seat at the windblown pile of jeans and T-shirts.

"I reckon I'm looking for work," Trent said.

The officer clicked Trent's license against his knuckles. "Not many employment opportunities in front of a fire hydrant, son."

Trent feigned an innocent gaze. "Am I parked illegally, Officer? Now that sure was careless of me."

"Maybe it'd be better if you went elsewhere for…"

The roar of a souped-up engine muffled the officer's words. A candy-apple red convertible had careened into the middle of Broad Street and paused beside the black-and-white. Psychedelic rock polluted the air. The ragtop was crammed full of teenage boys who had *trouble* stamped all over their smirking faces. Hoods, Trent's mom would call them.

But the only passenger Trent noticed was the driver.

She knocked a hole in his gut, that's how beautiful she was. Her jet-black curls were cropped short in a style that was nothing like the stiff flip every small-town beauty queen in South Carolina was wearing this year. Her skin was like white china at the big house where Trent's mom worked, touched by spots of color high on her cheeks and a bow of dark red on her lips, also unlike the death-mask pink most girls were copying out of fashion magazines.

The volume of the music came down.

"Afternoon, Officer Monk," she said, her voice a sugary, taunting drawl that grabbed Trent by the crotch and throttled him breathless. "Did you realize by any chance that you are obstructing traffic here on Broad Street?"

All the boys in the convertible laughed, and Trent hated each and every one of them.

"You run along, Miss Harper. This here is official business."

She peered at Trent then, pursing her lips until a dimple appeared in her right cheek. "He looks dangerous to me, Officer Monk. I'd lock him up if it were me."

Then the laughter rolled over Trent again, the music cranked up and she vanished in a V-8 rumble. She wasn't his type—Trent leaned toward the sweet, freckled type who were so darned easy to lead astray—but he knew exactly what the quickening of his pulse meant.

"Who was that?" he asked without meaning to, without stopping to think that his arrogant smirk had disappeared.

"That's Miss Harper Weddington, son. 'Bout the

only one in town likely to be more trouble than you.''

Weddington. Trent barely listened as Officer Monk lectured him about illegal parking and told him that Collins had no place for him. Trent murmured, "Yessir," and pulled away from the curb while Monk watched in silent satisfaction. But the cogs in Trent's mind whirred noisily, spinning fantasies about Miss Harper Weddington.

He'd seen the sign on his way into town, a massive wooden sign over the entrance to a long, winding drive, all of it bordered by an immaculate white picket fence, leading to a house that couldn't be seen from the highway. Weddington Farms, the sign had read. He'd seen the name once again after he passed the town limit sign, this time etched in the massive granite marker directly across from the row of shops along Broad Street. Weddington Textiles.

Yes, Miss Harper Weddington, with her candy-apple convertible and half the town named after her, was exactly what Trent was looking for.

HARPER KNEW IT WAS half-past dinner when she wheeled to a stop behind the house, spitting gravel and dust on the farmhands gathered by the paddock fence. She had a moment of unease until she remembered she wouldn't be seeing Red Jannik. He was gone; her daddy had seen to that.

Probably the only thing Sam had ever done that pleased her was running off Red Jannik.

She killed the engine, ran her fingers through her tangled curls and stepped out of the car. She paused by the hood, waiting to capture the attention of all her daddy's hired hands. When she had it, she smiled and wiggled the tips of her fingers at them. "Hey, boys!"

Some of them called back. Some of them grinned. Some of them, who knew what had happened to Red Jannik and didn't want it happening to them, ignored her.

Harper laughed and marched toward the house, letting her hips sway more than was decent. Her smile faded as soon as her back was to them.

Her heart wasn't in that particular little game any longer. But she'd been acting as long as she could remember. What was a little more? Just enough to see her through to graduation. Then she was out of here. Collins, South Carolina, could kiss her fanny goodbye.

Floretha looked up, shook her head in disapproval but didn't speak when Harper walked through the kitchen. Harper stopped and leaned her hip against the big wooden table and plucked a slice of peeled apple from the bowl Floretha was working over. The tiny woman's dark head was sprinkled with gray, although she wasn't yet forty.

"Apple cobbler?" Harper popped the apple into her mouth.

"Apple muffins for breakfast." The woman's velvet voice had the hard edge she reserved for new kitchen help and the bad child she'd had a hand in raising. "Which you wouldn't be getting into if you weren't late for supper."

"Dinner," Harper corrected her, studying the brown chapped fingers of the older woman. "You know Leandra would be mortified to hear you talking about supper. 'They eat suppah in the trailah pahks.'"

Harper giggled at her exaggerated imitation of her mother, but Floretha gave no sign of amusement. "You show a little respect, child."

"Yes, ma'am," Harper said, all hint of mockery banished from her voice. "Guess I might as well get it over with."

"Reckon you might as well."

On her way out of the kitchen, Harper gave the big-as-a-minute servant a hug and drew a deep breath before shoving open the door to the butler's pantry. She stood in the narrow passageway, surrounded by shelves of silver serving trays and crystal candy dishes, and listened for voices in the dining room. Silence.

That won't last long, she thought.

She looked down at the amount of leg showing below her miniskirt, at the rib-knit top clinging to her generous curves, and knew she would not be considered dressed for dinner. She also knew that anyone who came close enough would get a whiff of corn liquor on her breath—a touch she'd added by design. All but the single swallow she'd taken was still in the mason jar beneath the seat of her car.

Ready or not...

She tossed out her smile as she sashayed into the dining room and took her seat. "Mother. Daddy."

Her first thought as she took them in was how pathetically predictable they were. But she supposed the same could be said of her. Predictably outrageous.

Leandra Harper Weddington, however, was predictable in a way that left everyone around her feeling frostbitten. Still lovely, Leandra looked every inch the society matron. Her choice in clothes leaned to cashmere twin sets and double-strand pearls. She had recently asked her hairdresser to soften the color of her ebony hair—more suitable as forty approached. Her makeup was soft and her body starved to slender grace. A pillar of the community, she buried herself in charities and church committees.

Harper wondered, however, if anyone in all of Collins *liked* her mother. If so, she'd missed that particular rumor.

Then there was Sam. Big, ruddy Sam with the slash of a dimple angled across his right cheek. Sam, who had a smile for everybody but his daughter. Sam was so homely anybody who didn't know how rich he was would wonder how he'd landed a beautiful wife like Leandra.

Sam couldn't seem to get it through his head that his daughter couldn't be controlled as easily as his lovely wife. He seemed to believe that his daughter, after seventeen years of being headstrong and disrespectful, would miraculously blossom into a sweet-tempered, easily led young debutante. A freshman at a fancy, deadly dull girl's college in Atlanta.

"Well, missy," Sam said before Harper could transfer a roll from the silver bread basket to her bread plate. "Can't be bothered to get home in time for dinner, I see."

Leandra passed the platter of stuffed pork chops.

"Sorry, Daddy." Harper flashed the smile that no longer had the power to charm Sam Weddington, but at least he paid attention now. At least there were no more long, silent dinners when her voice seemed to startle both her parents, as if they had forgotten her existence.

No, when Harper reached her teens, she realized she had the power to capture her father's attention. Leandra remained too cool to get down in the dirt with her daughter, but Sam was a scrapper.

Like his daughter.

"Sorry? That's all you've got to say?" Sam sounded incensed. "Push me too far and I'll take that fancy red car away. You'll have to ride the school bus with the country riffraff. Then you'll be home in time for dinner."

Harper buttered her roll. She knew he wouldn't take the car again, because he'd learned the last time that Harper would simply take to riding in jalopies with all the town's most notorious white-trash boys. Now, at least, they rode with her in style.

"I was at the library, Daddy," she said, knowing he would realize she was lying. "And I got so caught up in...in the life of Karl Marx that I lost all track of time. I was thinking I might become a Communist when I grow up."

Sam shook his fork at her. "Don't mock me, girl."

Harper could play the simpering little girl with Sam for only so long before she lost her temper.

"I'm not a child any longer," she argued, digging the stuffing out of her chop and nudging it to one side on her plate. "I'll be eighteen in a few months. Old enough to do whatever I please."

And what pleased her was to blow this joint. As soon as the stupid graduation exercise was over in May, she would hit the road. She had her savings and her car, and the only other thing she needed was a road map from Tolly's Texaco on Broad Street. She might go to New York and become an actress. Or maybe to New Orleans and become a stripper—why not get paid for letting stupid men make fools of themselves?

Most of the time, though, she thought of San Francisco. There, she would find other people like her, people who were tired of the hypocrisy of grown-ups. The idea of being a flower child held great appeal for Harper. She just hoped everyone wouldn't give up and go home before she got there.

The daydreams kept her going.

"When you're eighteen," Sam was saying, "you'll go on up to Agnes Scott and get an education. And until then—"

"I'm not going to that stupid girl's college and you can't make me," Harper said, realizing too late how much like a ten-year-old she'd sounded.

"Amanda, stop provoking your father." Leandra was the only one in the world who still refused to call Harper by her middle name. With everyone but her mother, Harper had almost lived down the first thirteen years of her life, when the world had known her as Mandy.

"Mother, who are you talking to?" she asked, trying to match her mother's frigid tone and knowing she would never be that good.

Sam flung his linen napkin onto his plate. "That does it! Missy, I—"

Not to be outdone, Harper jumped up from the table before he could dismiss her like a child. "If you'll both excuse me, I think I'll retire for the evening."

Then she sashayed out as provocatively as she had sashayed in, ignoring Sam's outraged bellows. All the way up the winding staircase, she heard the heated rumble of Sam's voice, followed by the empty silence that would be her mother's aloof presence. She closed her bedroom door behind her, shutting them out, the way they had always shut her out.

She thought of calling Annie Kate. But sometimes Harper thought that even her best friend disapproved of the way Harper carried on around town. Sometimes Harper thought the only reason Annie Kate put up with her was because the Weddingtons were the richest people in town.

She thought of crawling into bed and crying herself to sleep, but Harper no longer believed that tears helped even a tiny little bit.

She thought of climbing out the window and going to the car for the jar of white lightning. But even corn liquor didn't make things less ugly anymore.

TRENT POKED AROUND the musty room and figured it was no worse than the other places he'd stayed since he left home.

And it had the added benefit of being a few hundred feet behind the barn at Weddington Farms, which was just a few hundred feet behind the big house. A rush of excitement sang through Trent's veins. His plan was off the ground.

"Don't expect you'll be here long, anyway," said the leather-faced farmhand who had introduced himself as Nigel. "Sam don't like the hands livin' on the place anymore, so we've all got rooms in town. Expect you'll find somebody in the gang to bunk with before long."

"Sure." But Trent had no intention of looking too hard.

Nigel was passing him the key and offering to help him bring things in from his car when voices drifted in the open front door of the one-room cabin. Nigel froze and so did Trent.

"I don't know who told you that ugly old story, but it's just plain mean of you to believe it," grumbled the sweet, petulant voice of Miss Harper Weddington.

Trent hadn't been able to get her off his mind since laying eyes on her the afternoon before. With her so vivid in his memory, his plan had crystalized quickly. He could see it all unfolding, and it was perfect.

This one's for you, Mama, he thought.

The next voice thrust itself into Trent's reverie like the grunt of a bulldozer upending concrete and gravel. "Missy, I've got the jar right here. Came right out from under the seat of your car. So don't think you can sweet-talk your way out of this one."

Her laughter trilled through the spring air. Trent felt himself stir at the sound.

"Oh, Daddy, anybody could have put that there.

One of your farmhands probably did it just to set you off."

Where her voice had warmed Trent it now sent a chill through him, hardening his heart and his jaw. No matter how sweet the voice, no matter how soft the skin, he couldn't forget she was from the big house. And he knew what the people from the big house were like.

Trent couldn't afford to forget that he had a purpose here: to make them pay for all the times people like them had dumped on people like him and his mother.

They were gone now, their voices fading as they passed. Nigel cleared his throat and dropped the key to the cottage into Trent's palm. Once through the screen door, they paused again, both of them watching the barrel-chested man and young woman as she swished off. From the neck down, she was as stunning as she had been from the neck up the day before. Not tall, but all curves in a pair of tight jeans and a skimpy halter top. Trent felt the chill in him melt at the sight of her.

"That's the young miss of the house," Nigel said. "Miss Harper. You'd best stay away from her. That's how we lost our last foreman. Mr. Sam don't cotton to the hands messing around with Miss Harper."

CHAPTER TWO

ANNIE KATE THUMBED through a picture book of sex techniques called the *Kama Sutra* that her cousin from San Francisco had sent.

"This is what all the hippies are doing." Leaning against one of the beams in the loft of the barn, Annie Kate pointed to an illustration that Harper felt certain was anatomically impossible. "Exploring their freedom."

Harper propped her chin on her fists and stared out the window. She wasn't interested in the explicit illustrations that so intrigued her friend. They made her feel queasy, but she was too cool to say so. "Big deal. Like you have to be in San Francisco to have free love."

"Well, if you have free love in Collins, every horny boy in town will know about it in forty-eight hours," Annie Kate retorted. "You can ask Rowena Kudrow about that."

Harper used to look down on Rowena Kudrow, the way all the other girls at Collins Senior High did. Sometimes, these days, Harper felt less inclined to judge Rowena. But she was too cool to say that, too.

"I've only got three more months in this hick town, anyway," she said instead.

Annie Kate slid across the bare wooden floor, closer to the narrow window overlooking a freshly tilled garden plot. "You're really going to do it? Run away?"

Harper frowned at her best friend. "It's not running away if you're grown. It's splitting."

"And you're not even scared, are you?"

"Scared? Why should I be?" She hadn't been afraid until recently. Harper had always figured she could handle anything. Now she wondered.

"How will you support yourself? Where will you live? Will you have to find a job and—" Annie Kate leaned closer to the window and pushed her wire-rimmed glasses higher on her long, sharp nose. "Who is *that?*"

That was what Harper had been waiting for, lying here staring out the loft window.

Sam had hired him two days ago, and so far Harper hadn't been able to find out a thing about him. Nigel said his name was Trent. "That's all any of us need to know," the older-than-dirt farmhand had said when pressed for more details.

Harper wasn't even sure why she pretended an interest in him. He was just another grubby farmhand. He probably had bad teeth and worse manners, just like the rest of them. But she had always chased after them and flaunted it under Sam's nose. It wouldn't do to change her game a few months away from total freedom.

Trent had taken off his shirt and hung it over the low rail fence bordering the garden. His faded jeans hugged narrow hips, and his smooth chest was already slick with sweat. His hair was dark with perspiration, kinked into tight, damp curls. He hefted a shovel and began to work manure into the sandy earth.

"He might have bad teeth," Annie Kate said, having heard her friend's judgment of her father's farmhands many times, "but there's not much else about him that's bad."

"He's probably stupid," Harper said. "Why else would he be working on a farm?"

"Like Alex DeLong's a genius," Annie Kate retorted.

"I don't like Alex DeLong, either." She did like the steady rhythm of the new farmhand's labor, however. The muscles along his sun-browned back and his upper arms bunched and swelled in exactly the same way at exactly the same pace, over and over again. Watching him soothed her, made her feel calmer than she could ever remember feeling. She envied his being a man. Harper had always suspected things would have been different between her and her father if she had been born male. Besides, men could do whatever they wanted and nobody harped at them.

Annie Kate was still going on about that DeLong nitwit. "But you hang out with him," she said.

Harper gave her friend her most withering look, the one she usually reserved for her mother's back. Annie Kate and Harper had been best friends since elementary school, and Annie Kate knew perfectly well why Harper hung out with hoods like Alex DeLong.

All her life, Harper had rebelled against being the daughter of Collins's most prominent family. Even as a child, Harper had mostly wanted to run wild with all the little boys in town when they skinny-dipped in the creek or gigged frogs.

Worse, even, than being simply rich had been the

fact that the Weddingtons were also the town's main employer. To some minds—especially Sam Weddington's—that gave Sam power over most everyone in Collins.

And that further set Harper apart from her playmates.

Harper hated her father for making her different. But even more, she hated him for making the mistake of thinking she was one of the people in town he could control.

Harper had been showing him all her life that she had no intention of dancing to his tune. Toying with the town bad boys was just one way of doing that. But right now, she was more interested in the way the new farmhand stopped to rub his palms along the denim covering his thighs. She grabbed the pulley cord dangling overhead and swung her legs out the narrow hayloft window.

"What are you doing?"

"Going down to introduce myself."

"Harper! Are you crazy?"

Harper shoved off and went spiraling out and down.

"I thought you said you didn't want anything else to do with people like Red Jannik!" Annie Kate called out the window as Harper's feet touched the ground.

Harper smiled up. "Well, we don't know that he is until we check, now do we?"

"Harper, you're crazy!"

"And that's what you like most about me, isn't it?"

Annie Kate stared down at her, then tugged on the

pulley rope to return it to the loft. "*I'm* coming down the ladder," she announced primly.

Harper started toward the lone man in the garden. She could hear a muffled grunt signaling his exertion each time he tossed a shovelful of manure from the truck onto the garden plot. Drawing closer, she saw the way his burnished skin glistened in the soft spring sunlight, the way perspiration trickled along the valley of his spine and collected in a dark V at the waist of his low-slung jeans.

She had started out with a taunt in the back of her mind, but the words momentarily stalled, stuck in her dry, tight throat.

He must have sensed her presence, for he suddenly stopped and looked down from the truck bed. He leaned on his shovel and drawled, "You must be the boss man's little girl."

Stung, Harper found her tongue quickly. She raised her chin. "That's right. And I suppose that makes you the new manure shoveler?"

He chuckled. "I hear there's a ton of it around here."

She laughed along with him. His sparkling blue eyes made it hard to do anything else. They seemed to jump right out of his deeply tanned face. His smile revealed even, white teeth and emphasized his lean and chiseled features. His jaw was touched with a dusting of golden stubble. He didn't look as old as most of the drifters who made their way through Weddington Farms. Barely out of his teens, she guessed. He looked like a smart-ass.

She liked that.

"I'm Harper," she said, putting out her hand.

He didn't move a muscle for a moment, just stood

there staring at her, a near grin still touching his lips. Then he stared down at his right hand, which was streaked with grime and sweat. He squatted in the truck bed, took her hand in his but didn't let it go. He just held it, softly but firmly. His palm was hot, and she felt grit rubbing off onto her skin. She shivered as he released her but saw no hint that he had reacted to the touch at all. And if there was one thing Harper had already learned to calculate, it was her effect on men.

"Trent," he said, standing. "Pleased to meet you, Miss Harper."

She gave him her dimple; that always worked. She sensed that Annie Kate had walked up behind her. "What big dreams you must have, Mr. Trent, to have worked your way up to—" she gestured toward the truck "—all *this*."

Annie Kate groaned softly.

"Yeah," he said, hefting his shovel and giving nothing away. Those incredible eyes didn't linger over her body; he obviously wasn't struck dumb by the invitation in her big eyes. "Today rich people's manure, tomorrow the stars."

He rammed the shovel into the manure again and put his foot on the back of the blade to sink it deeper.

Annie Kate put a hand on Harper's shoulder and whispered, "Come on, Harper. Leave him alone."

Harper ignored her friend.

"Where are you from?" she asked, determined to end the conversation when she wanted and not because he was ready.

He paused but didn't look at her. "All over."

"I see. And I suppose you've left a string of broken hearts around the world."

"Now where would a young thing like you get ideas like that? I know that's not what they're teaching in school these days."

Harper felt herself bristle. Was it only her imagination or was this Trent fellow treating her like a child? "What brings you to Collins?"

He tossed a shovelful dangerously close to her feet and said, "Well, I'm not here to baby-sit."

Pure, black fury clouded Harper's vision for a moment. She heard Annie Kate's snicker and wanted to kick the dirt right back into his face. She stood still and willed the moment to pass. When she knew she could keep her voice from quivering with suppressed anger, she said, "I'd watch myself if I were you, Trent. Sam's been known to run men out of town when he doesn't like the way they treat his daughter."

"That's what I hear," Trent said softly.

EVEN IF SHE HAD BEEN old enough to legally enter the place, The Stallion would have been off-limits for someone with Harper Weddington's pedigree. That's why it was her favorite place to party when she had a foul mood to dispel.

And that's why she found herself sitting on a barstool at The Stallion the night after she met Trent.

The Stallion was a hellhole of a dive just across the county line. A private club where almost anything you wanted could be bought and sold, it was grimier and smellier than any of the barns or sheds or compost heaps at Weddington Farms. It reeked of spilled beer and worse. Cigarette smoke hung in the air, and the country-music juke box could barely be heard over the buzz of belligerent voices and the

sharp clack of billiard balls slamming against one
another. The other women in the place favored
bleached hair and black eyeliner.

Harper loved it for the attention she generated and
the sure knowledge that being discovered here would
give both her parents a fit of apoplexy, whatever that
might be.

Tonight, she wanted to forget that Trent had
treated her like somebody's kid sister. That he had
blown her off as if she didn't matter.

Doesn't he know who I am? The inward cry of
outrage had filled her head most of the day.

She ordered a beer and let a man wearing denim
and a gaudy turquoise belt buckle pay for it. She
moved around the room, swinging her hips and running the tips of her fingers along the edge of the pool
table to catch the eyes of those who were playing.
She smiled at every man who had the gumption to
approach her, successfully playing them off one another so that no one could get possessive.

She didn't want any of them. She just wanted all
of them to want *her.* But she was getting bored with
the game, wondering where you went when The Stallion no longer gave you a charge. Then her answer
walked through the door.

Trent.

SHE MIGHT AS WELL have been under a spotlight. She
stood out that much in this crowd.

Harper Weddington was the last person Trent had
expected to see when he'd decided on a night at The
Stallion to celebrate his employment. The Stallion
was noisy and it was cheap, and company could be

had here if it was company you needed to keep your head empty of unwelcome thoughts.

Tonight most of his thoughts were about his mother, but they were good thoughts, for a change. He imagined setting things right for her, making men like Farrell Landen pay for robbing a good woman of her self-respect and dreams. Men like Sam Weddington, who was just another version of the Farrell Landens of the world.

And he thought about Harper. Even before he walked in and saw her through the smoke, he'd been thinking of her. Yes, she was arrogant. Spoiled. Everything a rich girl was supposed to be. But she was also beautiful and sharp-tongued and spirited.

If he possessed her, he would have all the revenge any man could ever want.

He meandered through the crowd, headed for the bar. He would make her come to him. That much, he knew.

Trent knew about women. He'd spent most of his twenty years in a cramped rented duplex inhabited by his mama and her two single sisters. Every Friday night for as long as he could remember was Gals' Night at the Trent home. Their friends poured in, bringing chips and soft drinks and pints of vodka, with boxes of permanent-wave solution or hair color or a magazine with the latest, hottest hairstyles guaranteed to disguise an oversize nose or make beady eyes look luminous.

Trent had sprawled on his bed in his room those nights, sometimes reading his comic books but mostly eavesdropping on the talk of how foolish men were and all the mistakes they made and their downright cussedness.

Trent knew about women. And he knew the only way to win a woman like Harper was to make himself unavailable. If she thought she couldn't have him, she would move heaven and earth to get him.

He ordered a beer and ignored the way his heart was thumping. He bought a vodka and grape juice for a woman who didn't yet know that beehive hairdos and go-go boots were no longer all the rage, even in rural South Carolina. She brushed against him and he pretended to listen to her aspirations of putting an above-ground pool behind her mobile home.

Then the air around him changed, suddenly felt charged the way it did sometimes when he knew it was his night at the poker table. She had found him.

He kept his attention focused on his friend with the grape juice and vodka, waiting. He heard *her* voice over his right shoulder, clear and cultured and unlike anything else a body might hear at The Stallion. She ordered a beer.

"Can I buy you another?" he asked his friend with dreams of a pool.

"Sure, darlin'. Aren't you the perfect gentleman?"

He ordered the drink. It was then that Harper spoke. "You weren't lying, I see."

He turned slightly in her direction. "About what?"

She looked across him at the woman with the beehive. "You definitely aren't baby-sitting."

He was grateful the noise level was so high that his companion couldn't hear Harper's veiled insult. "You shouldn't be here, you know."

"Whyever not? Do you think I don't know the score?"

"I doubt if you even know which numbers to add up, Miss Harper," he said, although the message in her violet eyes said otherwise. "Does your daddy know where you are?"

She paid for her beer and took a sip. Trent thought he detected the barest wrinkling of her perfect, up-tilted nose.

"Why? Are you planning on telling him?"

"Anybody here check your ID tonight, Miss Harper?"

She flicked foam off her upper lip with the tip of her tongue. Trent felt sucker punched, walloped in the midsection by a teenage vixen who probably needed paddling worse than she needed kissing. He had to remind himself he was waiting for her to do all the seducing.

"Everybody here knows I'm plenty old enough to do whatever I please," she said in her low, soft voice.

Then she raised her beer mug in salute, turned and walked the length of the bar. He watched her. He'd liked her in jeans this afternoon, but he had to admit miniskirts were made for legs like Harper Weddington's. Walking slowly and provocatively, she settled on a stool at the end of the bar, directly in his line of vision.

He paid for more grape juice and listened to stories about a hateful line supervisor at Weddington Textiles, a sorry so-and-so who couldn't understand that women sometimes had perfectly valid reasons why they couldn't clock in precisely on the button at 7:00 a.m. But from the corner of his eye, Trent watched Harper.

She struck up a conversation with a grease monkey

masquerading as a cowboy. She smiled for him and
tossed her curls for him, but her eyes kept flickering
in Trent's direction. Trent pretended he didn't notice.

"Darlin', are you payin' even the least little bit of
attention to me?"

Trent focused on his companion. Looking her
squarely in the eyes after being so close to Harper
was an exercise in disappointment. She probably
wasn't ten years older than Harper, but the years had
been hard on her. Too much peroxide, too many
nights in smoky bars, too many free grape juice and
vodkas, too, and all the paybacks that implied in a
place like this. Trent fought back a sigh. Why had
he gotten himself into this?

The problem was, he *liked* women. *Sincerely* liked
them. Blame it on all those Friday nights immersed
in the problems of his mama and his aunts and their
friends. But Trent thought most women got a raw
deal, and he was always getting himself into things
he ought to stay out of by trying, just for a moment
or two, to make them think their lives weren't so bad
after all.

He had to remember that buying them a drink and
getting their hopes up wasn't doing them any favors.
Not when he had bigger plans than ending up in a
trailer park up to his ears in debt for an above-ground
pool.

He downed his beer, cut his eyes fleetingly in the
direction of Harper—Bronco Bill had his arm draped
possessively around her shoulder—and said, "Truth-
fully, miss, I can't seem to keep my mind off other
things tonight."

That was another thing. Trent didn't believe in lying to women. Fudging the truth when necessary,

maybe, but out-and-out lying was something he tried to avoid.

She patted his hand. "I knew it. You got all the earmarks of a broken heart, darlin'. Why don't you tell old Sherri all about it?"

Trent eased off his bar stool. "Sherri, you're an angel. You deserve better tonight than listening to me cry in my beer."

It took another few minutes to extricate himself, and when he looked once again toward the end of the bar, Harper and her cowboy had disappeared.

Trent cruised the bar, growing uneasy when he didn't spot Harper or her new best friend. The joint had grown more raucous as the hour grew later, the crush of people making it hard to get around. Trent knew it would be easy to miss someone in such a crowd, but he also knew he wouldn't have a bit of trouble finding Harper if she was still here. She drew him like a porch light drew bugs.

He told himself if she'd left, it didn't matter. He should let it go. Let *her* go. Wasn't that part of the plan? To act as if he didn't give a damn, to make her come to him?

Still, he kept thinking of what could happen when a headstrong girl like Harper walked out of a place like The Stallion with a man she didn't know. A man who thought he'd bought and paid for her with the price of a draft beer.

Unable to ignore the uneasiness in the pit of his gut, Trent pushed his way to the door.

Outside, Trent peered around the parking lot, checking out the collection of rattletrap pickups and souped-up jalopies, finally spotting a candy-apple red convertible on the dark edge of the lot.

Harper's friend had her backed up against the hood of the car, his body pressed against hers. The sight set Trent's blood to boiling. It shouldn't have. He knew what rich spoiled brats like Harper Weddington did when they went slumming. He wasn't naive. Not by a long shot.

Sticking to the shadows, he eased closer. Close enough to realize that Harper was leaning backward, pushing the man away. Trent tensed. Was this all part of her game? Or was it something uglier?

"Stop it," he heard her mutter, then heard her little squeal of protest as the man forced his lips to her face.

Before Trent could react, he heard a thump and a grunt, followed by the man's growled response. "Why, you little—"

Trent sprang into action, grabbing the cowboy by his plaid shirt and yanking him back just as Harper jerked her knee upward in a strategically planned defense maneuver.

Trent flung the cowboy aside. He stumbled against a nearby car, clenching his fists and glaring.

"Listen, pal," the cowboy said, "this is none of your business."

"That's right!" Harper said huffily as she smoothed her skirt and brushed her short hair off her face.

Trent gripped Harper's arm and put on his best smile for the man with revenge in his eyes. "I just wanted to thank you for finding my baby sister. She's always running off and stirring up trouble. You know, my daddy's fit to be tied right now. He swore the next person who laid a hand on Susie here was going to spend the rest of his life behind bars."

Through narrowed eyes, the man looked from one to the other. "She's *jailbait?*"

Trent nodded. "Fourteen."

Harper tried to jerk her arm away, but he held fast. "Why, you—"

"Her next birthday," Trent added.

In a matter of seconds, Trent and Harper were alone in the parking lot. He let go of her arm, but she was so clearly furious that he kept a careful eye on her knee. She backed against the door of her car and glowered at him.

"I had everything under control," she snapped.

Trent chuckled. Now that he knew she was safe, he felt fine again.

"Only if you were planning to change that 'no' to a 'yes' any minute," he said.

"Well, if I was, it's none of your darn business."

He heard a tremble in her voice, a tremble she tried to hide with her anger, and he felt his good humor slip again. Harper Weddington wasn't as tough as she liked to pretend, and somehow that troubled him. He didn't want to start thinking of her the way he thought about other women. Women he liked because they, too, had gotten the short end of the stick too many times.

This is Harper Weddington. The rich *Harper Weddington,* he reminded himself. *She doesn't need—or deserve—your sympathy.*

But she stood there with her arms wrapped tightly around herself, her dark hair atumble and shadows accentuating her pale, perfectly sculpted face. And Trent had trouble remembering she was everything he hated. That he planned to use her, the way the rich had always used the poor. Poetic justice, he thought they called it. But he saw the bruised look of those tender lips, which had settled into a pout that was as lovely as her smile, and found it hard to remain resolute.

"How old are you, Miss Harper?"

"Eighteen." A slow grin overtook her pout. "My next birthday."

He laughed lightly.

"So I don't need a protector." She moved a little closer, close enough to raise her leg and caress the inside of his thigh with her knee, reminding him of her earlier plan of attack. "I can protect myself. And I certainly don't need a big brother."

Her knee drew dangerously close to the part of him that was vulnerable to her in more ways than one. He recalled again exactly how much trouble a girl like Harper could get herself into. Suddenly angry, he took her thigh in his hand and held her tightly against him.

"You let yourself get picked up by guys like that, you drink their beer and follow them into the parking lot, you remember one thing," he said. "They think you're bought and paid for."

He ran his hand up her thigh, forcing himself to concentrate on his anxiety when she had been in danger and not on the silky feel of her warm flesh. But before he could stop himself, he'd slid his hand all the way up her thigh, stopping only when he cupped his palm over her heat.

"They think they own this. And they won't give a damn how rich your daddy is."

He expected her to cry out, to shove him away as she'd tried to shove away her cowboy. But she didn't. She stared up at him with confused, glittering eyes. And she moved against the palm of his hand with such subtlety he was certain it was involuntary.

He jerked his hand away.

They stared at each other in the darkness. Trent feared he might explode with a sudden, powerful longing. He tried to remind himself of all the reasons he didn't really want her, the reasons he only had to pretend to want her. But his mind was empty of everything except the heat that still seared his palm and the soft glitter of longing in her dark, wide eyes.

"Go home," he said gruffly. "I'll follow you."

She didn't move.

"Get in your car and get out of here before Bronco Bill comes back with his posse."

She put her hand on the car door then, moving in slow motion. He waited until she was behind the wheel and had the engine running. As he turned to walk away, she said, "I don't belong to anybody. And I don't need anybody's help."

She almost sounded her old, flippant self. But Trent heard the soft plea beneath her words. He thought of turning south on the highway, heading in the opposite direction and never looking back. But he followed the taillights of the candy-apple red convertible and wondered what it would be like when he finally owned a woman like that himself.

He ignored the tiny voice that said no man *ever* owned a woman like that.

CHAPTER THREE

TRENT WAS making her crazy.

Harper wasn't used to thinking about anybody but herself—unless, of course, she was steaming over something Sam had said or done. And it was driving her nuts to realize she couldn't keep one arrogant farmhand out of her mind. She even started going home after school, finding reasons to be in the barn or the corral or anywhere else she thought he might be. She hated him for doing this to her.

"So, how old are *you*?" she asked one day as she dangled her legs over the edge of the loft and watched him muck out the stalls. "I mean, you know how old I am."

It was as close as either of them had come to mentioning the night at The Stallion.

"Twenty." He grinned up at her. "On my *last* birthday."

"I guess I'm supposed to be impressed," she said, returning the mockery in his smile. "A real grown-up."

"You don't have to be impressed. But a little respect does seem to be in order."

She laughed. He made her laugh a lot, which was good because it took her mind off the way she'd felt that night when he touched her. She hated thinking about it. Every time she did the same thing happened:

she grew hot and soft inside, as if she had simply melted away to nothing. She'd never felt quite that way before.

"You have sisters?"

"Nope."

"Brothers?"

"Nope."

It was always like this. She dug for answers, he hid them. And the more he hid them, the more determined she became to get at them. Funny, she almost liked the game. After the way most guys fell all over themselves to get on her good side, Trent's indifference was refreshing—and stimulating.

"You've been disinherited, right?"

He snipped open a bale of hay. "No, that's your goal in life, not mine."

"Then tell me yours."

He gave her a funny look and quit smiling. "Nothing you could understand."

This wasn't the first time he'd said something like that, something to remind her that she was too young or too rich to be a part of his world. To cover her pique at being dismissed so easily, she took a flying leap and landed in the middle of his neat pile of hay. She surfaced with a squeal, brushing hay out of her hair and eyes.

"Try me," she said. "You have to talk to somebody."

"I'll talk to Nigel."

"Oh, pooh! Nigel's an old goat."

He tried to hide his grin. "At least Nigel doesn't come along behind me messing up my work."

"Okay. Then I'll tell you my goal in life." She jumped to her feet, grabbed a pitchfork and started rearranging the pile of hay she had scattered. "I want to get as far away from Weddington Farms as I can. I want to go where nobody knows who I am and nobody tells me what to do and people will like me just because, not because of who I am."

When she finished she saw that he was leaning against a beam, studying her with those crystal blue eyes. Just talking to him made her feel elated. She felt understood for the first time in her life, in a way that even Annie Kate had never understood her. She didn't quite know why, but she knew that Trent was more like her than anyone else she'd ever met.

He couldn't see that yet. But he would.

"Good luck," he said, turning back to his work.

She felt the bite of his dismissal. But she still couldn't stay away.

She saw him the next day, because she walked out to the creek after dinner. He'd said he went there sometimes, and sure enough, he was backed up against a scrawny pine, staring into space. She sauntered up and plopped down beside him.

"Well, I know you have a mother," she said without preamble. "Everybody has a mother."

He didn't turn to look at her, didn't even turn his eyes in her direction. "Yeah," he said at last, so softly it was almost drowned in the chorus of crickets tuning up for dusk. "I got a mother."

"What's she like?" She studied his face. She loved looking at the sharp angles of his face and trying to read what was behind them. Most boys were so transparent, you could read their every thought. Trent wasn't like that. She supposed it was the difference between men and boys.

"Never mind what she's like," he finally said.

"Is that why you ran away? Because of her?"

One of his cynical chuckles escaped. "No, Miss Harper. Say, what kind of name is that for a girl, anyway?"

She laughed and slid down to lie on her back and look up at the sky. "My mother's name. She was Leandra Harper before they married. Of the Camden Harpers. She always says it that way, like it means something because they've been there since seventeen hundred-something. Big, hairy deal. But—"

"But what?"

She hesitated. "But that's only my middle name."

He leaned forward, put his elbows on his knees. "It is? What's your first name, then?"

"You'll laugh if I tell you."

"Yeah, probably."

She laughed. "Amanda."

"*Amanda?*"

"Is that gross or what?"

"No. I kind of like it. It sounds like you."

"It does not."

"Sure it does." He affected the kind of old-money drawl she always heard at Harper family reunions. "Mandy, won't you please accompany me to the cotillion?"

"Oh, hush. Don't you ever call me that again." But she smiled. Somehow it didn't bother her when Trent teased her. Not anymore.

She found a way to see him every day. Even a few minutes in his company made life easier. Her mother's coolness and Sam's preoccupation with other things didn't matter so much once she realized that somebody liked her company. And Trent *did* like her company. She saw it in his eyes, heard it in his voice when he teased her. *Truly* liked her, too. Not because she was rich, or because he hoped she might put out.

Her classes zipped past in a blur of anticipation and remembered laughter. Harper even discovered she didn't want to spend her time after school hot-rodding around with the losers she had once collected like prize seashells. Most of the time she went home, sat by the window in her room and did her homework with one eye on the lookout for Trent.

Until Sam said something about it, Harper didn't even realize how much things had changed.

"I'm pleased to see you're settling down," he said one night at dinner.

Harper looked up from her gilt-edged plate. She found his gray eyes trained on her and looked back to her plate.

"I haven't had a single report on you this entire week," he said. "Floretha tells me you've been coming straight home from school every day, so I guess you're not up to anything."

She took perverse pleasure in knowing that he would have a conniption fit if he heard the reason for her changing behavior. But not as much pleasure as she might once have had, for the thought occurred to her that Sam could run off Trent just as easily as he had run off Red Jannik.

The notion chilled her. For the first time in her life, she didn't want to flaunt her indiscretions under Sam's nose.

That was why Floretha's words on Saturday morning cast such darkness over her spirits. She had been looking forward to the day, having suggested that Trent meet her for a long ride in the country after he finished his half day. But as she rummaged through the refrigerator for leftovers she could use for a picnic, the housekeeper fixed her with a piercing gaze from warm, chocolate eyes.

"You keep on, you're going to get that boy in trouble," Floretha said.

The words struck sharply at Harper's heart, but she feigned innocence and unconcern.

"And don't give me that look you use on Mr. Sam. Floretha is no fool, girl. I may be nothing but a housekeeper, but I see things others don't want to see."

Harper placed the covered bowl of fruit salad on the counter and turned to fling her arms around Floretha's neck. The familiar comfort of those thin arms, the fragrance of honeysuckle dusting powder that she had associated with feelings of comfort and security since childhood, reminded her that her petty rebellions probably hurt this woman more more than they hurt her own parents.

"Oh, Floretha, you're not just a housekeeper," she said, hanging on to the hug as if she would never let go. "You're...you're..."

Floretha gave her a pat on the backside. "I know. I'm the one who wiped your nose and kept you from breaking every piece of crystal in the house."

They laughed and pulled back to look at each other. Harper knew Floretha was only a little older than her mother, but there was a lifetime of difference in the faces of the two women. Leandra was like one of her Chinese vases, smooth and flawless, with nothing to hint at how long it had been around. Nothing to invite a touch, either. Floretha, on the other hand, showed all the fine cracks and chips that came with years of being dragged down off the shelf to be handled, to be useful, to be part of somebody's life.

Harper ducked her head to hide the tears that welled up with the knowledge that she loved this woman the way you were supposed to love family. And that she was loved back.

"So, are you going to listen to your old Floretha or keep acting like you know it all yourself?"

Shrugging, Harper said, "I promise, I'm not doing anything wrong."

"You can be as innocent as that passel of new kittens out in the barn, girl. But if your pa comes down on that boy because you won't stay away from him, the fault is yours and that's that."

TRENT CAME OUT of the makeshift shower to find Nigel sitting in the single chair in his one-room cabin. The old man leaned against the wall, boot heels hooked on the cross brace of the chair, dusty hat on his knee.

Surprised and a little apprehensive at Nigel's appearance, Trent gave his hair a quick swipe, then wrapped the towel around his waist. "Anything wrong?"

The old man studied him for a moment. "Guess you're not having much luck finding a room in town."

Trent went about dressing so he wouldn't have to look Nigel directly in the eye. He liked the old man who was serving as foreman until Sam Weddington found somebody else. Nigel was fair, but it was also clear he didn't like being the man in charge. Trent felt the niggling concern that he'd taken advantage of that by failing to look for a room. But it suited Trent's purpose to stay here. As long as nobody pushed, he planned to stay.

"Sorry, Nigel. Guess I forgot."

"I'd be right grateful if you'd put your mind to it."

"I will."

Come to think of it, maybe that wasn't such a bad idea. Now might be just the time to make himself a little less available.

Guilt tainted his satisfaction. Trent cast it aside. Harper was using him, wasn't she? Where was it written he had to be the noble one here?

He pulled a clean T-shirt over his head and sat on the bed to pull on his boots. Trent stood and tucked his shirt into his jeans, then reached for the watch on the unpainted nightstand. He had forty-five minutes. Nigel still hadn't moved.

"I been thinking, son. Maybe I forgot to mention this when you first showed up."

Trent's uneasiness grew.

"About Miss Harper—"

"You told me."

"I did?"

"Yeah."

"That's good. I wouldn't want you gettin' yourself in dutch just because I'm a mite forgetful from time to time." Nigel eased the front feet of the ladder-back chair to the wooden floor and slowly rose to his feet. "Yep, you're a damn hard worker. Want to make sure you stick around awhile, you know."

"Thanks, Nigel."

He followed the old man to the door, his mouth dry, wishing he could fool himself into thinking

Nigel didn't remember warning him. But Nigel remembered. And that meant Nigel had his suspicions.

He felt uneasy, too, because he wondered what had happened between Harper and that foreman, Red Jannik. Trent hated to admit it, but the idea of her flirting—or worse—with this faceless man gave him a sick feeling in the pit of his stomach. He had to remind himself that, no matter how vulnerable or how lonely she seemed to him, she was still nothing but a spoiled rich kid. A user.

But remembering that was so damn hard, especially when he saw how hungry she seemed for somebody's attention, affection, approval.

He had to speed to get to the park in the next county on time, and he liked the feeling of wind rushing through the open windows, the slight shimmy in his old car when the speedometer inched past seventy and the feeling he was pushing everything to the limit.

Like this thing with Harper.

He was ten minutes late and she was waiting for him, impatiently pacing up and down the bank of the oversize pond everybody called Foxtail Lake. The color was high in her cheeks, and her legs, in cutoff jeans, were already golden, even this early in the spring. Her slight pout disappeared the minute she looked up and saw his car.

"I thought maybe you changed your mind," she said, so young—and apparently so trusting of him—that despite her tough veneer she didn't know any better than to let him see her uncertainty.

There it was again, that voice deep inside him that said she didn't deserve to be dragged into his problems. Because he would hurt her. He knew that. That was the plan, to wreak as much havoc as possible in the lives of the rich. And wasn't Harper one of the rich?

Then why was he starting to think a better idea would be to find a way to protect her?

"Changed my mind? About a picnic with Mandy?" he said. "Wouldn't miss it."

She laughed and linked arms with him. He liked the way her soft curves snuggled so easily against his body. He liked her warmth. He liked the way she leaped from girlish to guileful with no warning. He liked the three pale freckles dusted along her right cheekbone, just below her eye. And he liked her straight, even teeth, because he liked imagining her in the braces she must have worn a few years back. He didn't want to like so much about her, but he did.

"You know you're the only one who gets away with calling me that," she said, her coy mask almost entirely gone. She plopped onto the blanket she'd spread on the creek bank and he dropped beside her, admiring the taut swell of her hip.

"How'd I get so lucky?"

"Must be those wicked blue eyes."

"Wicked? My mother always says I have the eyes of an angel."

Wistfulness flashed through her eyes for an instant, then vanished. She began drawing things out of an enormous basket, like a child setting the table for an imaginary tea party. Trent's emotions rioted as he watched her. In so many ways, she was that child, from the peanut butter and jelly sandwiches and iced chocolate cookies she'd brought for their picnic to the unabashed delight in her dimpled smile as she chattered about preparing everything herself.

Then there was the part of her that tempted him despite himself, the part of her that was all plump hothouse bud, restless to burst into full bloom and petulant at being forced to wait a moment longer. Amanda Harper Weddington was an endearing woman-child, and fully as dangerous as that implied. Just looking at her made his blood pound, made his fingers ache to brush the cookie crumbs from the corner of her mouth. She licked them off herself with a knowing flick of her pink tongue. She captured his gaze with hers as she finished the cookie.

"Does your mother like you a lot?" she asked, lying back amid the bread crumbs and the pile of cookies that had spilled out of a paper bag.

"Of course she does," he replied automatically, realizing only when he saw her expression that his answer wasn't necessarily true for everyone.

"Tell me about your parents," she said, groping at her side for one of the cookies.

A part of him wanted to tell her there was no father, not since Donald Trent walked out after supper a dozen years earlier and never made it home. But he didn't like to talk about that. "That's old news."

"But you still love them, don't you?" She licked the icing off her cookie, but this time only the little girl in her made an appearance. "Even though you ran away."

"I didn't run away."

"Then tell me why you left." Her request was delivered with the dimple she seemed to know precisely when to produce. She propped up on one elbow and looked at him so eagerly that he thought he might just tell her.

"I won't tell," she said softly. "Not even Annie Kate."

All he knew about her was that she was spoiled and self-centered and immature and probably sexually precocious. But he believed her when she said she wouldn't tell. He believed Harper Weddington was honest, and he supposed that made him a fool.

The way his mother had been a fool, believing Farrell Landen all those years.

"I left because..." He thought of the dozens of reasons that had tied him in knots for months, and wondered which ones to tell her. He chose the reason that was at the center of all the other reasons. "Because I couldn't stand watching some man make a fool of her."

She didn't say anything, and Trent found himself longing to spill out the hurts he had bottled up.

"We were broke after my old man ditched us," he said. "Mom went to work at the big house."

"The big house?"

The question in her voice drew a bitter smile. "Yeah. The big house that belonged to the big man around town. Farrell Landen. Owner of the tobacco farm and all the people who worked there."

"Like Sam." The edge in her voice matched the sharp feelings in his heart.

"Yeah. Like Sam." He rolled over on his stomach and began picking at the grass. Their shoulders touched. "He told her all kind of lies. And she believed him. And—"

He couldn't say it. As many times as he'd heard the other kids snicker about it and use it to tear his guts out, he couldn't voice the truth himself. Trent had learned early to resent the rich man who seemed to own the very souls of the people who worked for him. But that resentment grew when he learned from his buddies, at the age of ten, that rich Farrell Landen also owned the heart of Carlene Trent.

"They were lovers," Harper said, leaning into him.

A bark of bitter laughter escaped him. "That's nicer than anything anybody back home ever said."

"People are mean. Especially when they get a chance to take a shot at the people who have all the stuff they think they want."

Trent looked at her, aware that she spoke from her own experience.

"I can understand that," she went on. "People like Sam, they just do what they want. They don't think much about other people."

"She always said he would marry her. That he would divorce his wife and make her the queen of that big old house she cleaned every day."

"But it was a lie," Harper said.

"Yeah. I knew that a long time before Mom did."

He turned to Harper, studied her profile with its upturned nose and the chin that was just sharp enough to remind everyone that Harper Weddington would have her way.

"Sam is just like that," she said. "He told me for years that if I studied hard and got good grades I could have all my friends over for a big sleep-over birthday party. But every year he always had some reason why I couldn't. Then I figured it out. It was just because he didn't want the people who worked for him sending their grubby little brats up to sleep in his big, fancy house."

Something opened in Trent's heart when he realized that a rich kid like Harper could end up feeling just as left out as he'd always felt.

"He did it to Mother, too," Harper said, her voice low. "Whatever she wanted, he ran over it like a bulldozer. She wanted to work for the Kennedy campaign, but he told her to stick to church work. She wanted to volunteer at the hospital, but he told her it wouldn't look right. One day she just quit wanting anything."

She looked at him over her shoulder, and he could see in her eyes that she had already learned what it had taken his mother a half-dozen years to discover. When it comes to rich men, their promises are meaningless and their affection comes with strings attached.

He rolled over and pulled her close. Her soft curls whispered like silk against his chin and cheek; her breasts were soft and heavy against his chest. They lay like that a long time. He listened to her breathe, felt her heart against his ribs, her thigh curved intimately around his thigh. And he marveled that this young woman who had grown up in the kind of big house he had always hated had learned to hate it, and all it stood for, as much as he did.

He wanted to save her from it. Just like he wanted to save his mother.

"I'm going to go back there one day," he said at last. "I'm going to work hard and get rich and I'm going to buy that bastard's big house and throw him out of it. Then I'm going to move my mother in and set her up like a queen."

"Wow." Harper's soft whisper fluttered against the hollow of his neck. "I wish I could go with you."

Trent's heart lurched. He wanted to tell her right

then, but something held him back. He wanted to tell her she could go, because she was going to make all his big dreams possible. Because that was the plan, to marry money. Then he could buy his mother all the respectability she'd never had. Sticking it to some rich muckety-muck in the process just made the plan more appealing.

Especially now that the one he would stick it to was Sam Weddington. Wouldn't that mean Trent was paying the old man back for everything he'd ever done to hurt his daughter, as well? Wouldn't it?

Ignoring the doubt gnawing at his conscience, Trent touched his fingers to Harper's chin. Her lips parted as he lowered his lips to hers. He kissed her gently and was surprised to find her response so shy and tentative. She wasn't the hellion she liked to pretend she was. Her kiss was innocent and trusting, and it tore at Trent's heart.

When he stopped it was because he knew it would be too easy to keep going. Later, he told himself. Soon. But not quite yet.

Yes, Harper Weddington would be easy to lure into bed. And in a small town like Collins, a rich man like Sam Weddington would be willing to do anything to avoid a scandal involving his only daughter. Even embrace the ne'er-do-well who'd knocked up his heir.

Trent touched the soft, firm slope of Harper's upper arm and squelched the uneasiness in his chest.

CHAPTER FOUR

HARPER CAUGHT a spring cold that left her feeling tired and dragged out, but she told herself that was only because it kept her from seeing Trent for two whole days.

On the third day, she could barely sit through her classes for wanting to see him. As soon as the final bell rang at the end of seventh period, she broke every speed limit in Collins delivering Annie Kate to her front door.

"You're going to see him, aren't you?" Annie Kate said, gathering her books up from the floorboard of the car so slowly Harper thought she might just scream.

"Well, what do you think, slowpoke?"

"I think you're asking for trouble. Harper, what if you end up ruining your life just to get back at your father? This is—"

"This is different." Harper thrummed her fingers on the steering wheel.

"Different?" Annie Kate sounded dubious. "How is it different? He's just another guy who's passing through, working for your father, and he's got one thing on his mind, just like—"

"That's not true! Trent is kind and sweet and he really cares about me."

Annie Kate rolled her eyes. "I know what he cares

about," she said, opening the car door and stepping to the curb. "But I can't say, because ladies don't talk that way."

Harper laughed, relieved to be rid of her friend. She popped the car in gear, said, "Ladies don't have any fun, either," and peeled away from the curb. Annie Kate called after her, but the rumble of the car engine and the blare of music from the eight-track player drowned out her words.

Harper roared back down Broad Street to the other side of town. She wouldn't be going home early today.

Trent had moved, but it hadn't taken her long to wheedle out of one of the other hands where he had gone. He was renting a room in one of the identical cottages that backed up to Weddington Textiles. Two generations ago, the cottages had belonged to the company, and they were still called the mill village by everyone in town. Harper had never been inside one of the mill cottages. But she planned to be there today when Trent got home from his day at the farm.

Ten houses lined up on each side of the long block, and Harper selected the third one on the left. The clapboard was more gray than white, she noticed, and the rain gutter sagged forlornly in the middle. She tried the front door and wasn't surprised to find it unlocked. Not many people in Collins locked their doors; not many had much worth taking, especially here on Spindle Court.

The house smelled funny, kind of stale and musty. What little furniture the living room held was either faded with the years or coated with a film of dust. She peered into each bedroom, hoping for some sign one of them belonged to Trent. One was a disaster area of rumpled clothes, and Harper decided Trent hadn't been here long enough to create such havoc. In the second, a pair of jeans the size of South America was looped over a straight-back chair, dripping dry onto the bare wooden floor.

Harper entered the third room and closed the door behind her. A cardboard box sat on the end of the narrow bed, filled with a jumble of jeans and T-shirts. A comb and toothbrush were on the bedside table, half hidden behind a black-and-white photograph in a cheap metal frame. Harper picked it up. The woman in the photograph was pretty, but her eyes and her smile, even her limp curly hair, looked tired. The little boy on her knee had an impish grin, and he looked as if he were ready to burst after sitting still long enough to have his picture snapped.

Harper traced her finger over the glass.

Seeing the little boy smile out at her gave Harper the sensation that she was being drawn even closer to the man. And since Saturday, she had felt entirely too close already—yet not nearly close enough.

Harper placed the frame back on the nightstand, then moved the suitcase to the floor and lay back on the bed to wait. She wondered, as she lay there, what it would be like to have nothing more to your name than a car, a few pairs of jeans, a toothbrush and a photograph of your mother. She tried putting herself in Trent's place and began to wonder how he kept from despairing.

By the time she heard Trent's car rumble up, she was dozing. She didn't bother to sit up or straighten her skirt or smooth her hair. She lay there with her eyes closed and listened for his footstep on the bare floor, waited for him to close the bedroom door behind him.

"You shouldn't be here," he said softly.

She peeked at him through half-closed eyes. He leaned against the closed door, his clothes streaked with Weddington Farms dirt. "You ran out on me."

"It was Nigel's idea."

Harper told herself that didn't necessarily mean that Nigel or anyone else had caught on to them. "Did you think I wouldn't find you?"

"They said you were sick."

Good. He didn't sound sure of her, either. "Did you miss me?"

He walked over to the bed, sat beside her and started pulling off his boots, then his socks. "Your old man will raise hell if he finds out you're here."

"Who's going to tell him?"

"Some kiss-up down the street who works the line."

"Nobody likes Sam enough to tell him. They'd rather see him look like a fool."

"So how'd he know about Red Jannik?"

The name struck her like a slap. She could only hope she hadn't flinched when he said it. "Forget about him."

He studied her; she avoided his gaze.

He stood and stripped off his shirt, dropped it to the floor. Harper's throat contracted at the sight of his bare chest, smooth but knotted with muscles. She wondered how his bare skin would feel, and an ache started in the tips of her fingers.

"I'll shower."

He took a fresh pair of jeans from the suitcase and a well-worn towel from the back of a chair and disappeared down the hall. She listened to the hum of water in the pipes and wondered what would happen if she took off her skirt and her knit top and the little scraps of underwear to greet him when he returned.

Her nipples grew tight and hard thinking about it, the way they had when he kissed her.

But a part of her remained frightened by the thought and shrank away from carrying the vision any farther.

TRENT KNEW THE RISK he was running by allowing her to come every day. But he was beyond saying no to her. Being with her every day, talking to her, sometimes kissing her and sometimes knowing that kissing her would mean going all the way, these were things he needed more than he needed food or drink or sleep.

Sometimes, when they sat in his room and talked about their childhood and their parents and the ways they felt alike, he asked himself how he had lost control of his plan so quickly. The plan was now nothing more than to be with her as often as possible. But often during the workday, when he stared up at the big house and fancied how cool it must be in one of those high-ceilinged rooms, or on payday, when he saw how little his sweat was worth, Trent still felt the hunger that had nothing to do with the way he felt about Harper. It was simply buried deeper now.

But feeding that hunger would mean betraying Harper, taking advantage of her, treating her no better than her old man had treated her all her life. To-day, Trent no longer felt so sure Harper deserved that treatment.

So he stopped at the diner and bought take-out

burgers and fries for them on his way home. Sometimes they talked late into the evening. Once, they
drove to the next county for a '50s sci-fi movie at
the drive-in and laughed so loud the management
threw them out. She taught him to waltz and didn't
mind that he had two left feet. He beat her at poker
over and over and over again until she grew bold
enough to bluff, and then he didn't stand a chance
against her.

But mostly they talked. Trent had never talked to
anyone the way he could talk to Harper. He marveled
at how much he trusted her. Her of all people, the
hell-raising daughter of the man who owned Collins,
South Carolina.

"What's your greatest fear?" she asked one night
as they crumpled up the wrappers from their burgers.
She was always talking about things like that, things
nobody he'd ever known talked about.

He wasn't sure how to answer, but that was okay.
Harper, he'd learned, would sit quietly in the dim
light and let him think about his reply.

"I...I guess my greatest fear is that I'll end up
like my mother. Being some rich person's fool."

Harper nodded. "But if she loved him, really
loved him, maybe she wasn't the fool. Maybe *he*
was."

Trent didn't believe it, but he had begun to like
the way Harper always made him see things in a way
he never had before. "Ask anybody in my hometown
and they'll tell you who the fool was."

"Nope," she said, tossing one of the balled-up
wrappers toward the floor lamp. She sank it, banking
it off the rim of the shade before it rolled in and fell

through, the perfect basket. "I learned a long time ago that what people think doesn't mean squat."

"Easy for you to say," he countered, wondering if she would be so ready to spit in the eye of public opinion without her old man's fortune to back her up.

"Easy for anybody to *say*," she said. "The hard part is learning to mean it. To feel it in your gut."

"And do you?"

She rolled to the floor and put her head in his lap. Sometimes she seemed so innocent it was all he could do not to pack up his car and drive straight out of Collins. He couldn't bear the thought of being the one who destroyed that innocence.

"Sometimes I do. And sometimes I don't."

"And when you don't?"

"Then I need you to kiss me."

He didn't even ask if now was one of those times. He simply cupped her head in his hands, lifted her to him and kissed her. He drank in her sweetness and her courage and the tough exterior that didn't run nearly as deep as she wanted everyone to believe. He coaxed her lips open and taught her to welcome his tongue with hers. He let his palm drift down her side, over her hip, back up to her breast. He heard the soft moan deep in her throat and told himself his plan was never going to work at this rate.

But the plan didn't seem so important at the moment. He sent her home and spent another restless night.

HARPER PASSED her mother's bedroom door on her way to her own room. The door was ajar, and she caught a glimpse of Leandra sitting at her dressing table in a circle of rosy light. Her footsteps slowed. The image of her mother giving her long hair its nightly one hundred strokes threw her back to her childhood.

Once she had loved to sit at her mother's feet and watch this ritual. Sometimes she had asked if she could do the brushing, but Leandra had complained when Harper tugged too hard. In time, Harper had been encouraged to retire a half hour earlier.

Harper studied Leandra now, her back still straight and slender in her silk robe. She still wore her hair long, but it had been years since Harper had seen it down around her shoulders. She felt an ache to go in and take the brush from her mother's hand and say, "See, I can do it now. I'm bigger now. I won't do it wrong again."

Watching her mother, she thought about how Trent had been so close to his mother that he wanted revenge for the anguish she had suffered. Harper wondered if she should want revenge for the sterile life Leandra lived, and felt sorrow at realizing she didn't care.

Still, a part of her hungered for that closeness to her mother everybody but her seemed to enjoy. She wondered what made her so unworthy of love.

"You look beautiful," she said, startling herself and Leandra.

"Good gracious, Amanda, you frightened the wits out of me. Must you skulk around so?"

"Sorry. I just... I saw you and stopped to watch. Remember when I used to help?"

"Did you? Heavens, that must have been years ago."

Harper told herself the coolness meant nothing; it was just Leandra's way.

THEY WALKED IN THE RAIN. Harper insisted, Trent gave in.

They wandered to the woods bordering the south end of Collins, and Harper held her face up to the warm spring drizzle. It clung to her eyelashes and made her hair spring wildly around her forehead. It washed away the heavy feelings that had been with her since the night before, when she had spoken to her mother.

"You're nuts," Trent said, hunching his shoulders against the damp.

"Maybe. Does that bother you?"

"No."

"It just feels good to me, that's all. Free." She stopped and faced him in the misty dusk. "Sometimes I think I'd give anything in the world to be free. Do you know what I mean?"

He smiled his crooked half smile and took her hand. "Yeah. I think so."

She sometimes thought he was the only one who accepted her just the way she was. Leandra wanted her to be a simpering fool, and Sam wanted her to be silent and invisible. Her teachers wanted her to live up to her potential, and all the guys she knew just wanted her to put out. Even Floretha wanted her to behave, to cause a few less ripples.

But Trent liked her fine the way she was. And that, too, felt like freedom.

"But we're going to get soaking wet," he said.

"Wet clothes," she said. "So what?"

And with that, she stepped out of her shoes and ran along the damp ground in her bare feet.

He picked up her shoes and followed. "You *are* nuts."

She laughed at him and, on a whim, yanked her knit top over her head and threw it at him. The mist immediately began to seep through the wispy fabric of her bra, but she didn't care. She ran ahead, deeper into the woods. He called after her, but she didn't stop.

"Officer Monk told me you were trouble," Trent called out. "That first day."

She stopped on the path, eased the zipper of her skirt down and let it slither to her feet. Still laughing, she darted ahead, turning in time to see him staring down at her skirt.

He looked up and said, "He was right."

At the look in his eyes, Harper's laughter died in her throat. A moment of apprehension clutched her as she realized she stood in the woods alone with him, wearing only skimpy bikini panties and a scrap of a bra that hid nothing.

She whispered his name, to remind herself that this was Trent.

He dropped her shoes and her top onto the ground beside her skirt and started walking toward her. Their eyes locked, and that was all the promise, all the safety she needed.

With barely a touch, he stripped her of her remaining garments. She expected him to grab her then, to clutch her against him and give her the kind of hard, demanding kiss he hadn't yet given her. Instead, he began to touch her with the tips of his fingers. They slid along her wet skin, tracing the heavy swell of her breasts, the aching tightness of her nipples, the inward curve of her ribs. Harper feared her legs wouldn't hold her up any longer, but the truth was she couldn't move, not even to slide to the ground.

He flattened his palms against her belly, then raised one to cup a breast and lowered the other to entwine in the damp curls at the juncture of her thighs. Harper thought she gasped, but she realized no sound had escaped her throat. Then, when she believed it impossible to feel any more inflamed than she already did, he lowered his hand yet again and slipped it between her thighs.

This time he touched her the way she now realized she had wanted him to touch her in the parking lot outside The Stallion. His thumb played over her almost imperceptibly, while his forefinger parted her, tested, slipped inside her.

Now she truly could stand no longer and she leaned into him, sagging against him as he continued to caress and probe. He held her in the circle of his arm and lowered them to the ground, never ceasing to touch her the way that was driving her to an aching madness she'd never known before.

Mindless of the wet leaves, the cool ground, Harper clung to him. She fumbled with his shirt buttons but found her fingers didn't function. In fact, she seemed to have disappeared, except for that tiny area where Trent was touching her. Emotions welled up inside her, too powerful to suppress, and she cried out like a wounded animal. But in truth, Trent's touch seemed to heal the wound that had been festering deep in her spirit.

He robbed her of his touch only long enough to

unzip his jeans, then she felt him hard and hot against her inner thigh. He kissed her, still tenderly, his lips brushing her cheek, her neck, her breasts. She looped a leg around him, urging him closer.

He grew still and pulled back to look her in the eye. "This isn't...you've done this before, haven't you?"

His words barely registered. All she could think was that it was important for him to know this was nothing like anything that had ever happened to her before. "No," she murmured. "No."

"I'll be gentle," he said. "I won't hurt you. I promise I won't hurt you."

And he eased into her slowly, gently, filling her. And when he had filled her completely, he lay still against her body, looked into her eyes and said, "I love you, Harper. No matter what, you have to know I love you."

The naked emotion in his silver-blue eyes told her the truth of his words. A truth that echoed in her own heart, revealing what she hadn't realized until that moment.

"I love you, too, Trent. I never knew I could love like this."

Wrapped in the tenderness of their feelings, their bodies rocked gently together, oblivious to the rain, conscious only of the way their emotions soared, erupted, then drifted gently back to earth.

CHAPTER FIVE

THAT SPRING was the happiest Harper could ever remember. She couldn't imagine the euphoria ending.

Passing algebra and finishing her senior English term paper paled in importance to afternoons spent in Trent's arms. They made love in his tiny room, shades drawn, a tiny transistor radio providing bubblegum rock as mood music. They fed each other black cherry milk shakes and ketchup-doused french fries from the drug store. They walked in the woods and drove down the highway with the top down. They learned each other's bodies in intimate detail.

But as consumed as they were by physical pleasure, it was the emotional closeness that fed most of Harper's hunger. And Trent never left her wanting. It was as if, with the declaration of love, he had opened to her and could no longer close the door.

They lay on the floor in his room, feet on the bed, fingers interlaced, and talked about growing up in the fishbowl of a small Southern town.

"It was like everybody had a right to tell me what to do," he said. "I always thought it was because my old man left and they thought I'd go to hell for sure if they didn't keep me straight."

She squeezed his hand. "And did you?"

"Naw, I was the model kid."

Glancing at him, she saw his teasing grin.

"Well, at least on the surface. I was good at that, hiding what was really going on."

"Not me," Harper said. "What you see is what you get. And if you think that didn't set a few tongues wagging, you don't know much about people in Collins."

He kissed her then, one of his hungry, desperate kisses that always left her breathless and throbbing and led to more lovemaking.

Afterward, she said, "What'll they say about us?"

"They're not going to know."

"Eventually they will, won't they? I mean, this summer after school is out, I can get a job and be on my own. Or we could leave together, find a new place where... What is it, Trent?"

He had looked away, stared at the ceiling instead of at her. "Maybe that's not the right thing, Harper."

"What do you mean? Of course it is. Why wouldn't it be?"

"You ought to go to college, the way Sam wants you to."

She drew out of the circle of his arm. "You don't want to be with me."

"That's not it. It's just... I want what's best for you."

"Being with you is what's best for me."

"But first—"

"I know what I want and I know what I need. And I don't need some snooty girls' school where all I'll learn is more math and history junk I'll never use. Oh, Trent, you don't really mean that, do you?"

And he pulled her into his arms again and whispered softly against her ear, "I only want you to be happy."

"Good. I'm happy."

She smiled against his bare chest, telling herself she only imagined that something troubling continued to darken his voice.

SAM WAS WAITING UP for her when she got home that night, sitting on a screened side porch puffing on a cigar. The sweet, heavy smoke landed with a thud in the pit of her belly, nauseating her.

"Where you been, missy?"

As if he cared.

"Out."

"None of your lip," he growled. "I want to know where you've been. That's that."

Harper's stomach did a nasty flop. She turned away, gulping lungfuls of fresh air from beyond the screen.

"Studying," she said as defiantly as she could manage, given her reaction to his stinky tobacco.

"Studying, my fat rear end."

"I have a lot of finals coming up," she said. "Haven't you ever heard of cramming?"

He let out a heavy sigh and stared at her from beneath heavy brows knitted together in a fierce frown. "I heard from my friend at Agnes Scott today."

She groaned. The girls' college he was determined to shove down her throat. "Oh, Daddy..."

"I don't want to hear it. Everything's set. All you have to do is pick up that diploma in four weeks. You hear?"

In four weeks, Harper hoped to have talked Trent into leaving with her. "I hear."

"In the meantime, your mama and I would appreciate it if you could keep yourself out of fracases that'll mess up any chance you have for a decent future."

She almost smiled, thinking of his rage if she told him what she had been doing—and with whom— every night this past month. But getting a rise out of him was no longer her goal. All she wanted was to be with Trent, where she felt the love she'd craved all her life. The love everybody else was too busy to give her.

"I'll try," she said.

"You do that."

She turned and went into the house. The parlor was dim except for the small Tiffany lamp on the library table. She saw Floretha, her forehead pressed against the mantel. Harper stopped, knowing the housekeeper had heard everything.

She had never seen Floretha look so dejected or so alone. Floretha looked up at that moment, and the sorrow in her eyes stopped Harper. Without a word, Floretha shook her head, turned and left the room. Startled by the housekeeper's strange actions, Harper followed Floretha down the entrance hall toward the kitchen.

"Floretha! Floretha, what's wrong?"

Floretha paused at the kitchen door and looked back at Harper over her shoulder. "When are you going to learn, child, it's not all a game?"

The words from the woman who had all but raised her gave Harper a chill. "Wh-what do you mean?"

"I mean this is all just fun for you, keeping everybody stepping to your tune. Well, I want you to understand, child, that what you are doing is breaking some hearts."

Harper tried to put on her flippant smile, but it wouldn't come. The urgency in Floretha's voice touched something within her, made her question herself.

"One of those hurting hearts is mine," Floretha continued. "But I know that all the concern you have is for yourself, and I understand how you got that way. But you're near grown now. It's time you started acting it. Unless you figure out that Harper Weddington isn't the only person in this world, the next broken heart is going to be yours."

"But—"

Floretha touched Harper's cheek, drew one leathery fingertip along the path of a tear Harper hadn't even realized she'd shed.

"It's all right, love. Your old Floretha will be here for you. Your old Floretha will love you no matter what."

HARPER AND TRENT drove to the beach on Saturday. It was a chill, gray day, not typical for May. But it suited Harper's mood. Even the steady, in-and-out rush of the surf didn't soothe her. She walked in the sand in her bare feet, holding her shoes instead of Trent's hand, cold water rippling over her toes, tickling her ankles, the wind whipping at her short hair.

Floretha's words hadn't left her.

"Am I selfish?" she asked, knowing Trent would tell her the truth.

So would Floretha, admonished the voice in her head.

"What makes you say that?"

She glanced at him. "Just answer me."

"Of course you are. You've had to be."

Her heart gave a little twist. Floretha had said she would always love her, but that didn't mean Trent would. Not if he saw her as selfish.

He put a hand on her shoulder and they stopped walking. "Don't you see, if there was no one else to take care of you, you had to do it yourself. You'd be nuts not to be selfish."

She recognized a certain truth in his words, but she discovered that it hurt nevertheless to think of herself as selfish. Which was foolish. She'd created that reputation for herself, the spoiled rich kid. So why complain now?

"But what if I don't want to be that way anymore?"

Trent pulled her close. "Just be who you are, Harper. I love you just the way you are."

"But—Floretha said I was going to break everybody's hearts."

He grinned. "Now, I could have told you you're a heartbreaker. You didn't need Floretha to tell you that."

She smiled a little. But the idea that she needed to change still nagged at her. What if she could become kind and loving like Trent and Floretha? Wouldn't it be nice if someday that was the way people thought of her?

But making the change seemed so overwhelming. She decided not to think about it today, to just enjoy the salt air and the sea breeze and the reassuring roar of the surf.

They bought a Frisbee and threw it until Harper grew too tired to run up and down the beach. They bought hot dogs at the amusement park; Harper ate half of hers and gave the rest to Trent.

"You hardly eat anything these days," he said.

She wrinkled her nose. "Nothing tastes good."

"You've lost weight, too."

She shrugged. "I haven't felt too good lately."

"Maybe you're sick again."

"I'm not sick," she said, but she had wondered that herself. Had wondered and set the worry aside.

"Maybe you ought to go to the doctor."

She thought of old Doc Forstman, who gave Sam his blood pressure medicine and Leandra those little pills she sometimes used when she was feeling nervous. "I don't need a doctor."

Then what little bit of the hot dog she had eaten threatened to come back up. After that, there was no dissuading Trent. She would go to the doctor.

HARPER DID HAVE one thing her way. She didn't go to Doc Forstman. She picked a doctor two counties away, where nobody had ever heard of the Weddingtons of Collins. At least, she hoped not. Just to be sure, she gave them a phony name, although she told herself there was nothing she needed to hide.

"You don't have to do this," she told Trent as they sped across two counties in his shabby old Chevy. He had insisted on driving her himself. "I'm fine, you know."

He looked over at her and said, "Fine, huh? And all this time I thought you could act."

"I *am* fine," she said, realizing she must've said the same thing a dozen times in the two days since they returned from Myrtle Beach. Two days in which she had continued to feel pretty lousy. "There's nothing to worry about."

Seventeen-year-olds didn't get sick and die, did they?

Dr. Hurbert Allenbrandt's waiting room was dark

and dingy; the vinyl seats were cracked and uncomfortable. The only other people waiting were over sixty.

"We ought to go," Harper whispered to Trent, who was thumbing through an issue of *Progressive Farmer* magazine. "I'm not sure he's licensed to treat people my age."

"Sit still," Trent whispered back. "Read your *Reader's Digest.*"

Only through sheer willpower was she able to sit without wringing her hands until the nurse called her. Through dry lips, she explained how she'd been feeling. She took her clothes off and lay back on the examining table, heart thumping, wishing she had a mother to be here beside her and hold her hand. The exam was uncomfortable and embarrassing, and she shivered as she put her clothes back on and waited for the doctor to return.

If she hadn't been seventeen and way past such things, she would have felt like crying. Her breath shuddered in her chest, and she gulped to regain control of it.

The examining room door opened, startling her. She couldn't quite look at Doctor Allenbrandt, who was the approximate shape and color of the pumpkin Annie Kate had carved into a jack-o'-lantern last fall.

"Well, Miss, ah, Porter. It is 'Miss,' I presume."

"Yes." The word was the barest of whispers.

"Well, then, let me see." He studied the chart in his lap. "Of course, we won't know for sure for several days, but my best guess is that you are pregnant."

Harper felt the way she'd felt the one time she'd fallen off a horse. She had landed on her back, driving all the air out of her lungs. All she could do was lie on the ground and wait for the world to stop whirling.

"Pregnant?"

He nodded. "Every indication."

She wanted to argue, to tell him it couldn't be. But she realized, as she sat there in the chilly, dank examining room, that she had somehow known all along. From the very night Red Jannik had caught her in the barn...

She had brought it on herself. She knew that. Knew from that very night that she had no one to blame but herself.

Red Jannik was almost as old as Sam, but he was hard and tapered and good-looking, with his coppery red hair and spring green eyes. Harper had flirted with him mercilessly from the moment he set foot on Weddington Farms. He had ignored her at first, the way most of the hands did. But finally he had given up pretending she didn't get to him.

That, of course, was when she took to ignoring *him.*

She'd been in the barn with the litter of two-day-old kittens. She was so engrossed she hadn't realized she wasn't alone until the stall door creaked. She looked up and saw Red.

"Well, if it's not the princess," he said, closing the stall door behind him.

The stall suddenly felt too close. Harper backed up against the wall and gave him her best daughter-of-the-boss-man look. "Well, hello, Red."

"Oh, is the royalty feeling friendly tonight?"

He dropped to his knees beside her. She knew it was silly, but his presence felt menacing.

"Not especially," she said.

"That's too bad, princess," he said, sliding even

closer, so close his thigh pressed against her.
"'Cause I'm feeling real friendly."

"Cut it out, Red."

But he hadn't. He'd pinned her down, explained
how her cries would do nothing but bring more of
the farmhands, all of whom would no doubt like to
join the party. Harper knew he was right. She struggled silently, swallowing her screams. But he was
too strong for her.

Now, almost three months later, that night came
rushing back to Harper, causing her heart to thump
painfully. She had fought so hard to forget, but now
she knew that forgetting would be impossible.

"When... I mean... How long?" she asked.

"Well, that's hard to say," Doctor Allenbrandt
said. "We'll know more in a few weeks."

But Harper couldn't wait weeks to confirm her
worst fears. "Three months?"

"Three months along, you mean? Oh, quite likely.
Have you been feeling poorly for a while?"

"I had the flu a month or so back."

He nodded. "Yes, flulike symptoms are common.
Three months is certainly possible."

Harper wished with all her heart that she had been
struck with some fatal disease. Anything would be
better than having Sam and Leandra find out she was
pregnant with Red Jannik's baby.

The only thing worse would be explaining it to
Trent.

CHAPTER SIX

THE RIDE BACK TO Collins passed in a blur of dazed confusion and sharp-edged guilt.

"He didn't say *anything?*" Trent pressed her one more time. "You're sure?"

"That's what I said, isn't it?" Harper snapped, realizing only too late that she had never before used that tone with Trent. He didn't deserve it.

You're the one who's getting what you deserve, she told herself.

Trent patted her hand and spoke soothingly. "Okay, okay. But you have to tell me as soon as he calls about those tests."

She promised to do just that, but as she drove the few miles from the mill village to Weddington Farms, Harper felt as if a committee of judgmental, angry, self-righteous voices were holding court in her head. Some of the voices said she had played with fire too often and, just as Floretha had predicted, people were now going to get hurt. Others said she didn't deserve this, that no one deserved what Red Jannik had dished out. A few loud voices that sounded like Sam's raged at her for ruining her future, shattering her dreams.

And one tiny voice suggested that there was a way out. Trent.

The very idea of using Trent in that way made her

sick enough to pull off to the side of the road until the nausea passed.

As she dragged herself upstairs, Harper couldn't help but think how much more bearable this whole situation would be if only the father of this baby was Trent.

She crawled into bed and pulled the covers up, but the committees did not adjourn.

It *could* be Trent's. They hadn't used protection every single time, had they? So what if the doctor had said she was likely three months along? He had also said he couldn't be positive.

But Harper knew. The black certainty that she would pay for her mistakes had burrowed into her heart from the moment Red Jannik had cornered her in the stall. The certainty had grown, filling her with fear and anguish that nothing could diminish.

Until Trent.

He loves you, the tiny voice said. *Just as much as you love him.*

But it's wrong.

He's the only answer you have.

THEY SAT ON THE HOOD of her car beside Foxtail Lake. It was the first time she had agreed to see him since they returned from the doctor's. She had been avoiding him.

His heart had been leaping happily ever since she came out to the barn earlier in the day and asked to meet him after work. But now that they were here, face-to-face, he knew that whatever was wrong still troubled her. She looked drawn, and she refused to meet his gaze.

"What's wrong?" he said. "You're driving me nuts, you know."

"I'm sorry," she said. Even her voice sounded different.

"I'm imagining all kinds of stuff. Like you're dying or something. Tell me you're not dying, Harper."

"Maybe it would be better if I were."

He took her hands in his and clutched them desperately. "Nothing's that bad."

She finally looked him in the eye and searched for whatever reassurance she needed. Finally, she said, "I'm…expecting. A baby."

Relief was quickly followed by elation. A baby! His and Harper's. Oh, thank you, God, it could all come true. Then cold, hard reality set in. Yes, it was coming true, but it wasn't just his sunny dreams about being together with Harper forever and always. No, what was happening was his ugly little plan. The one he'd devised to use Harper, to dupe her, to ruin her life.

It had worked.

And look at the expression on her face.

Despite the guilt creeping into his heart, he pulled her into his arms. "You know it's going to be all right, don't you? You know we'll make everything right."

She struggled against his embrace and looked at him. She didn't look reassured. "It's not that simple, Trent."

He touched her face. "Sure it is."

"No, no, no!" She covered her face with her hands, so distraught it pained him to watch her. "Please, Trent, you can't fix this. It's all wrong!"

"Harper, please don't feel so bad. I promise you,

I'm right here with you and...and..." Her shoulders were beginning to shake. "Please, baby, please. Trust me."

"I do. But..." Her protest dissolved into sobs.

"I know your old man will raise holy hell, but—"

"No, it's not just that. It's—"

"You leave Sam to me. Besides, he won't even have to know until it's too late to do anything about it. We can leave next week, right after graduation. Your folks'll think you're in Myrtle Beach with all the other kids."

Her sobs began to die. Still, she shook her head and her voice remained thick with tears when she spoke. "Oh, Trent, you just don't understand."

He hated seeing her look so miserable. He pulled her close again, and this time she stayed. "We'll be married before anybody knows a thing about it. Okay?"

He held his breath, waiting for her response. He made a vow to himself that if she married him, he would do everything in his power to make it up to her for ever thinking of using her. Because it wasn't that way now. Now he loved her. He only wanted to make her happy and safe. He wanted nothing more than to be the father of her baby.

"You're sure?" she said at last in a voice so soft and uncertain he barely heard it.

"I'm positive," he said, smiling against her soft curls. "You'll see. We'll have the prettiest baby in the whole world. She'll have your dimple and your black hair and my blue eyes and sweet disposition."

Tears trickled silently down her flushed cheeks. Trent held her. He would make it up to her. She would never have to know the truth.

HARPER WALKED THROUGH the week leading up to graduation like a zombie. Annie Kate knew something was wrong, and nagged her about it constantly. Floretha knew, too, although she kept quiet.

Sam and Leandra, of course, noticed nothing.

Trent treated her like a precious porcelain doll. His attentions, which should have made her feel treasured and special, merely aggravated her guilt. The committee in her head rarely fell silent these days, nagging her with a million different opinions as graduation day grew nearer.

But Trent's apparent joy over the situation paralyzed her, making it impossible to tell him the truth. He talked of nothing but his plans for their elopement. He talked about buying a ring she knew he couldn't afford. He talked about a wreath of flowers for her hair and the honeymoon suite at the best hotel in Myrtle Beach.

"Don't, Trent," she had said one night, her guilt gnawing at her. "Quit trying to make this sound like a real wedding."

"It will be a real wedding," he declared. "Better than a real wedding."

He had been patient with her moods and unfailingly good-humored about everything, which made her love him all the more. And hate herself.

The morning of graduation, Harper woke in an agony of indecision. Could she really go through with this? Could she betray Trent, the one person determined to stand by her? Should she give in to the inevitable and tell her parents? She cringed at the thought.

At times, the thought of a living being growing inside her actually calmed her. This would be her baby. It would love her just because she was its mother. And she would love it. This baby—her baby—would never grow up thinking no one had time for it. It would never think it was just an inconvenience in other people's lives.

Those calm, reassuring feelings came and went quickly, but they made it possible for her to get through the day.

They hadn't, however, helped her figure out what to do.

Trembling, she picked up the phone on graduation morning and dialed Annie Kate. Her best friend was always so levelheaded; maybe today some of it would rub off.

"Oh, Harper, aren't you excited?" Annie Kate's voice was almost a squeal. The squeal of a child, and Harper knew *she* was no longer a child. What, after all, could Annie Kate do to help her? "How many swimsuits are you taking? If you aren't going to use it, can I borrow that little dotted swiss cover-up Floretha made you last summer?"

"Sure," Harper said. "Whatever."

"Well, you sound like this is the worst day of your life instead of the best. Is this the same Harper Weddington who's been counting the days till graduation since October?"

Harper lost the urge to confide in Annie Kate. She got off the phone quickly, finished dressing and went down to a breakfast she wasn't sure she'd be able to eat. She learned from Floretha that both Sam and Leandra were gone already, Sam to the mill and Leandra to the church.

"They said they would meet you at the school," Floretha told her.

"Oh," Harper said, taking a biscuit from the pan on the stove and sitting at the old kitchen table. She was glad to miss a meal with her parents; she liked eating in the cozy kitchen with Floretha and her daughter. "Will you and Sandra be there?"

Sandra looked up from her heaping plate of eggs, bacon, biscuit and gravy. "Will we, Mama?"

"Of course we will," Floretha said, pouring two glasses of juice and placing one beside each girl. "Why, I wouldn't miss my girl's big day for any amount of money."

Harper nibbled at her biscuit, brought her juice glass to her lips but couldn't swallow. Sandra chattered away about her own graduation, still six years away. But Harper barely heard a word. When Sandra headed to the laundry room to iron her best dress, Harper hadn't eaten half her biscuit.

"What troubles you, girl?" Floretha asked, dropping into the chair her daughter had just vacated.

"Nothing."

Floretha sighed. "After all these years, I had hoped you trusted me a little more than that."

Harper looked up long enough to see the genuine concern—and love—in the housekeeper's eyes. It came to her that she would find no better confidante than Floretha. Suddenly, the idea of unburdening herself sounded like pure heaven.

Impulsively, she flung herself into her old friend's arms and said, "Oh, Flo, you were right! I've messed up everything!"

"Now, sugar, you tell me what's wrong and we'll figure out what to do about it."

"I think I know what to do," Harper said, realizing it would take courage to tell Trent the whole story. But she knew it was the first step toward no longer being selfish. She would tell Trent the truth, even if it drove him away forever.

She had no doubt Floretha could tell her what to do about having a baby and raising it all on her own. After all, Floretha was doing the same thing herself. But could the housekeeper tell her what to do with her broken heart, for it surely would be broken after she told Trent what had happened.

But at least he would hear it from her and not find it out the hard way sometime down the road.

TRENT KNEW THAT approaching the back door of the big house was a foolish risk, but he had to see Harper today. He needed some kind of reassurance that she wasn't going to back out. With a trumped-up excuse for Floretha's benefit, maybe he could catch a glimpse of her, even catch her eye.

He had never in his life been happier than he'd been these past few weeks, and not because he believed that marrying Harper would gain him any of the things he'd once hoped for. No, he now felt pretty sure that Sam Weddington would send them both packing when he found out about him and Harper, but somehow that no longer mattered. All that did matter was that he and Harper would share a life and that he could make it up to her for all the misery she had suffered at Sam Weddington's hands. He would make a good life for her and their baby, no matter how much hard work and sacrifice it took.

He walked toward the house, trying not to grin, trying not to whistle. He paused at the screen door, screwing up his courage to knock. Then he heard her voice and paused.

"But it's not his baby, Floretha. I just know it's...it's Red Jannik's."

Trent's heart stopped. And every rose-colored dream he'd had the past week died.

CHAPTER SEVEN

"OH, LORDY, CHILD, how on earth did you get things into such a state?"

The housekeeper's mournful voice broke through Trent's rage.

"That's a real good question, Harper."

He heard the sharp intake of her breath and the low groan from the older woman as he opened the screened kitchen door. They were sitting at the big wooden table, the old woman's hand covering Harper's. Harper stared up at him, stricken.

Seeing her like that, he had to fight to hold on to the rage that had enveloped him when he heard what she'd said about their baby. No, not their baby. Not his baby. Hers and the last poor fool she'd sucked in with her poor-little-rich-girl routine. His first instinct was to ask her why, so he could hear the excuses that might soothe the ache that had already started in his heart.

But he couldn't let that happen. He couldn't allow himself to be any more gullible than he'd already been.

"Trent, no—"

"Save it," he snapped. The last time he'd felt this crushed, this betrayed, this much the damned fool, had been the day Freddie Benton told him what his mother really did with Farrell Landen up at the big house. That day, he'd felt murder in his heart. And he felt it now, too.

But just as he'd wanted to blame everyone but his mother, he now wanted to blame everyone but Harper. And that made him angrier than anything else. What a fool he was.

"I don't want to hear any more of your lies," he said with a sneer, all the bitter blackness in his soul tumbling out. "They won't help. I see you for what you are now, Harper. I can see now this whole routine of yours was one big scheme to give you someone to take the blame for your little bastard brat."

"No, I—"

"At least I have the satisfaction of knowing you'll rot in hell for it."

He wheeled and stalked out of the house, ignoring Harper's tortured voice as she called after him.

HARPER FELT AS IF all her vital signs had shut down the moment she heard Trent's voice and realized what he had overheard. Her heart must have stopped, her blood must have frozen, her brain went on hiatus and her limbs ceased to function. And now, all she could do was watch him disappear out the back door, disappear with all her hopes and dreams.

Just as she had known it would be once he heard the truth.

Why, oh, why hadn't she told him herself? Maybe... But no, that was foolish. The result would have been the same no matter when or how he heard the facts. He would still have believed exactly what he'd said to her. That she'd used him.

He was right.

"Girl, you love that boy?"

Harper looked at Floretha. Still unable to talk, she simply nodded.

"Then get after him. Make him listen."

"But—"

"*Now*, child, before he does something foolish."

Harper rose slowly to her feet and walked toward the door. By the time she reached the yard, urgency gripped her. Floretha was right. She had to explain. He couldn't stop loving her just like that, could he? And if he still loved her, even a little, she could make him understand. She could...

She reached the parking area behind the barns in time to see the cloud of dust left behind as Trent's Chevy roared toward the lane. She ran after it, calling his name, mindless of the dust on her new graduation dress.

The dress that was to have been her wedding dress.

She stood in front of the big, columned mansion until the cloud of dust died and the angry sound of the car's engine faded in the distance. Floretha came up behind her and put an arm around her waist, murmuring something comforting. But Harper knew with certainty that she had gotten exactly what she deserved.

If anything, knowing it made the pain even sharper.

PART TWO: AUTUMN

CHAPTER EIGHT

Collins, South Carolina, 1997

THE SOUNDS AND SMELLS of WedTech's spinning room enveloped Harper Weddington. The deafening clatter of the equipment, coupled with the sharp scent of processing cotton, had become her life.

Some women craved mood music and twenty-five-dollar-an-ounce perfume. For Harper, Wed-Tech was her love.

Earplugs firmly in place, she nevertheless distinguished the shouted greetings of the workers who depended on her to keep their families in shoes, supper on the table. As Harper yet again examined the aging, inefficient equipment, she wondered how much longer she would be able to keep her end of the bargain. But she smiled at her co-workers and kept her worries to herself.

"How's that grandbaby?" she asked one of the grizzled women who worked nonstop to feed the spinner.

Ollie Hunt shook her head. "Not so good. They say he needs another operation if he's ever going to see right. But…"

Ollie shrugged and Harper knew what the gesture meant. But who had the money for another operation? These days, lack of money was a frustration Harper understood all too well. She put her hand on Ollie's stooped shoulder. "You come see me after your shift. We'll work something out."

"Oh, Miz Harper, I couldn't—"

"No arguments, now. If that baby needs something, we'll figure out a way to see he gets it."

Ollie pursed her thin lips, then nodded. Harper smiled at her and continued her rounds. She didn't have the foggiest notion how to help Ollie's grandbaby, but she would do something. Call that doctor friend of Sam's in Charlotte, maybe, and see if he knew an eye surgeon with a big heart.

If she weren't already robbing Peter to pay Paul, she would take the money out of WedTech's coffers and pay for the operation herself. But she was barely meeting payroll as it was. And her personal finances were even worse. The garage had already waited two months for the money for the brake job on her old station wagon. And she'd talked to Dillon twice about renting out the stables. The last thing she wanted was another head-butting session with her son.

Harper sighed, feeling the weight of the financial problems that had started before her father died and hadn't let up in the half decade since.

Preparing to chat with another worker, she spotted her office manager waving at her from the catwalk leading to Harper's office. Harper nodded and headed for the stairs, wondering what was up.

The expression on Dessie's face was grim when Harper reached her office. Dropping the earplugs onto her cluttered desk, she asked, "What?"

"You'd better get out to the house."

With a start, Harper thought of her granddaughter. Or Floretha. The very old and the very young. "What's wrong?"

"It's that SOB Burton Rust over at the bank," Dessie said. "He's sent some woman out to Weddington Farms."

Another start, this one for a very different reason. Guilt, maybe? "What woman?"

"Some rich woman who's looking for a farm to buy."

Rage washed over Harper, the old rage that had been so unmanageable when she was younger. She managed it better these days, but this was too much.

"Who gave him the right to do that?" she said, snatching her blazer off the back of her chair. "I never told that...that..."

"SOB."

"Exactly. I never told him I was ready to sell." Although she knew, in her heart, that she was up against the wall. "I told him to put out some feelers. That's *all.*"

Harper was out the door and headed for her car, all the way calling out instructions to Dessie for the rest of the day. But her mind had already left WedTech behind, was already zipping down the highway to the farm.

She could only pray she could waylay this rich woman before she ran into Dillon. There would be hell to pay if he met the woman who wanted to buy his home before Harper could get to her.

"MRS. STUART DOESN'T want you to help me!" seven-year-old Christine Winthrop shouted at her father. "She doesn't like you!"

Clutching a very large Madame Alexander doll to her chest, she backed away from Dillon and the pair of riding britches he held out toward her. Her agitation caused her blond pigtails to gyrate wildly. Her sky blue eyes glistened with the hint of tears, but Dillon could also see fear in their depths.

"You can't dress yourself."

"Mrs. Stuart doesn't want to go riding. She hates horses!"

Christine backed away from Dillon, around the huge four-poster bed in which she slept, around the table holding her dollhouse, around a chair crowded with dolls, until she backed up against the front window of her corner bedroom.

"Mrs. Stuart isn't going riding," Dillon said, trying to sound patient and calming. "You are."

He fought to control the hopelessness that nearly overwhelmed him every time he was around his daughter. He kept reminding himself she hardly knew him, that she'd never seen Harper until he moved back home. When Evelyn divorced him, her lawyers had managed to whittle his annual visitation down to two weeks. Determined not to repeat his own personal history, Dillon had taken a job close enough to see his daughter every day.

The effort had been futile. Evelyn wouldn't allow him five extra minutes with Christine.

When Evelyn died a year ago, Christine told him she wanted to live with the Stringfellows, Evelyn's parents. That had hurt, but he refused to let it show. Instead, he'd put as much distance as possible between him and the Stringfellows' divisive influence by moving himself and his daughter from California to South Carolina and the farm where he'd grown up. He'd been certain it was only a matter of time before they developed a warm, loving relationship.

But no matter how he tried, he couldn't seem to break through the barrier the child—with the help of her mother and maternal grandparents—had erected between them. She grudgingly accepted her new grandmother, but she flat-out didn't like her father.

"We don't have time to argue," Dillon said. "Mrs. Owens will be here in fifteen minutes."

"Mrs. Stuart wants Floretha to help," Christine said.

Dillon wanted to jerk the doll from her hands and rip it into a thousand pieces. Christine never defied him directly. She let her dolls do it. She looked ready to cry. If he forced her now, she'd probably run away again.

"Okay, but if she's busy, you'll have to let me help."

Hoping Floretha was up to her elbows in cake batter, Dillon called downstairs.

"Hold on. I'll be there in a minute," she called back. "These old bones don't climb stairs like they used to."

The old housekeeper never was too busy. She had watched over mother, son, and now granddaughter. Dillon wished he knew some of what she seemed to know by instinct. He wondered if all men lacked such instincts.

Or maybe it was heredity. His own father hadn't stayed around for Dillon's birth. He'd just disappeared without a trace twenty-nine years ago. Maybe Dillon's failure with Christine proved he was like his own father.

Dillon directed a foul curse at the faceless man he'd hated for so many years. He also cursed the guilt he felt at being forced to allow his own daughter to be reared by a mother who changed lovers with the calendar.

But all of that was over now. Despite a battery of lawyers hired by Evelyn's parents and a custody challenge that had depleted every penny of his own savings, he had his daughter, and he meant to keep her. He didn't know what it would take, but somehow he would learn to reach her. He wasn't going to do to her what his father had done to him.

"Now what's wrong that I had to leave my kitchen and climb all those stairs?" Floretha asked from the doorway.

Christine emerged from behind the curtains and threw herself at Floretha. "Mrs. Stuart wants you to help me get dressed."

"Why can't your daddy do it?" Floretha asked as she took the pants Dillon handed her and held them for Christine to step into. "No sense in old Floretha having to climb all those stairs."

She gave Dillon a questioning look. He shrugged and turned to the front window. "I see dust up the lane. It must be Mrs. Owens."

Christine thrust her arms into her shirt, tossed Mrs. Stuart on the bed and reached for her hat.

"I'll never get these buttons done up if you don't stand still, child," Floretha said.

"Hurry," Christine said, dancing with impatience. "I'll be late."

"There," Floretha said as she handed Christine her hat. "You look pretty as a cotton blossom."

But Christine was gone too quickly to hear the compliment. Dillon turned back to the window to avoid staring after her.

Floretha began to pick up and fold the discarded clothing, stopping to pat his shoulder. "She'll come around. She's still missing her mother."

Dillon hadn't meant for the housekeeper to see how much he hurt. "That's not Mrs. Owens's car," he said. "Who the hell is it?"

"You shouldn't be cussing," Floretha scolded as she folded a pair of bright pink shorts. "That's no kind of example to set for Miss Christine."

"She's not here."

"I still don't like cussing," Floretha said. "It's not right for a gentleman to go around using dirty words."

"They're just words, Floretha. They're not dirty."

Floretha favored him with the intractable expression he knew so well. "They were dirty when my mama was bringing me up almost seventy years ago, and they were dirty when her mama was bringing *her* up."

Dillon didn't respond. He'd spent the first eighteen years of his life under her benevolent dictatorship. But after living away from home for nearly ten years, it was difficult to adjust to being viewed

as one of her wayward children again. He turned
his attention to the black Mercedes careening up
the long drive, hitting every pothole dead center,
no doubt sending the driver bouncing against the
roof.

"Are we expecting visitors?" Dillon asked.

"No, and it's a good thing, with you dressed like
a field hand. When I started keeping house here,
your grandfather never came out of his room without a coat and tie and a freshly ironed white shirt.
Starched." She smiled at the memory. "Mean as a
snake, Mr. Sam was, but he sure looked like a
gentleman."

Floretha left the room, but Dillon's gaze followed the car as it emerged from the lane and
reached the long, curving drive that led through
a lawn dotted with overgrown azaleas and rimmed
by a row of pines. After disappearing behind a
group of towering magnolias, the dust-covered car
came to a stop before the front steps.

A tall, slim blonde wearing a cream-colored,
smartly tailored suit got out. Dillon was certain he
had never seen her before. A man didn't forget a
woman who made his body tighten at the mere
sight of her. He didn't know why she was here,
but he hoped she wouldn't leave right away.

He started for the stairs, and before he was halfway down, heard Floretha answer the door.

"I'm Angie Kilpatrick," the woman said. "I have
an appointment with Mrs. Weddington."

Her clipped speech told him she wasn't from
South Carolina. Somewhere in Pennsylvania, he'd
guess.

"I'm sorry," Floretha said, "but she's not at the

farm today. Did you mean to meet her at the mill?"

"No, I spoke with Mr. Rust on the car phone fifteen minutes ago. He assured me she would be here."

The mention of Burton Rust's name gave Dillon an uneasy feeling. He didn't like the man and didn't trust him. While Floretha called WedTech to see if Harper had been held up, Dillon came down the stairs. Angie Kilpatrick was on the porch staring at the grounds when Dillon reached her.

"There's no need to wait for my mother," he said, trying to keep his mind off the enticing way her suit curved over rounded hips. "You can talk to me."

Angie turned. "Who're you?"

The woman was coolly confident, unruffled by his presence or appearance. She had the look of a woman very much in control.

"I'm Dillon Winthrop. Harper Weddington's son." He waited, edgy, for the question everyone asked. The one he had no good answer for. Why would a woman go back to her maiden name, abandoning her married name, her only son's name? Dillon knew, of course, but damn if he planned to satisfy anyone's curiosity.

Angie Kilpatrick quietly studied him a moment, something else Dillon was used to. But she didn't ask the question he expected. "Did she tell you I was coming?"

"No."

"Then I'd rather wait. Do you mind if I look around?"

His temper flared instantly. "What for?"

Angie regarded him with a slightly puzzled look. "I'm considering buying the place."

Dillon felt a knot form in his stomach. All physical interest in this woman vanished. "It's not for sale!" he barked.

"That's not what your banker says," Angie replied. His flat denial had done nothing to disturb her cool confidence.

Cold fear squeezed him like the coils of a giant constrictor. He told himself it was ridiculous to panic. His mother wouldn't put the farm up for sale without telling him. Burton Rust must've gotten his wires crossed.

"Look anywhere you damned well please," Dillon said.

He hadn't meant to snap, but he didn't feel like being polite. He watched as she headed for her car. He would straighten this out pretty quick and get this woman off his land.

Off his *mother's* land, a mocking voice in his head reminded him.

Fear curled more tightly in his belly. Damn, it was that mill! It had to be.

THE MOMENT CHRISTINE rounded the corner of the house, she slowed to catch her breath. Even here under the dogwoods, the air was close and heavy with moisture. It wasn't a thing like California, and Christine hated it.

Well, maybe not *really* hated it. She liked being free to wander around by herself. She couldn't do that in California. Mommy had always worried somebody would snatch her.

But she didn't like living with her father. He never laughed like her mother. He didn't stay up late or have lots of men friends over, either.

She missed Grandma and Grandpa Stringfellow. They never made her do anything she didn't want to do. They told her to call them the minute her father did something awful and they'd come get her.

But he never did.

Christine entered the barn. She saw her pony's head over the stall door. "I'm going to saddle you all by myself today, Eddie. Daddy says I'm too little, but I'm not."

She didn't really mind learning to ride. She just said so because Mrs. Stuart didn't like being left behind.

Living here wasn't so terrible, even if her daddy didn't give her lots and lots of presents like Grandpa and Grandma Stringfellow. He was always watching her and telling her what to do, but he never forgot to pick her up at school. And she never had to eat by herself or go to bed without a story.

But sometimes he looked so fierce he scared her. She was afraid to climb into his lap and hold on tight like she could with Grandma Stringfellow.

Even if she wanted to.

Which, of course, she didn't.

Most of the time.

AFTER THE JARRING RIDE down the lane from the road, Angie drove more slowly toward the barns. She was irritated at Mrs. Weddington's failure to meet her. She was even more irritated by her son's reaction. He obviously didn't know the farm was for sale and didn't like it a bit, but that was no reason to take his frustration out on her.

Angie didn't know why Dillon's surliness should bother her. Usually she would just shrug it off. Most men were quick to realize she was in the driver's seat and adjusted their attitude accordingly. Not Dillon Winthrop.

Her initial reaction to him was the same as her reaction to any handsome man. She'd experienced a distinct tug of animal attraction. She usually tried to pretend it didn't exist, but this time she hadn't succeeded.

From the scuffed boots to the tight jeans that hugged his hips and thighs to the shirt that molded itself over his shoulders, Dillon Winthrop looked as if he'd stepped out of one of those magazine ads about men who go nuts over trucks. No bulging muscles, no rippling pecs, just well-shaped, firmly packed manhood.

Despite looking a little grungy, he conjured up thoughts of secret weekends and torrid sex on hot summer nights. Nights that felt a lot like this one would, despite the fact that September was almost over. Angie never had gotten used to the South.

Angie's thoughts surprised her. Dillon must have made a deeper impression than she'd realized. Maybe she wasn't as much in control as she thought.

Impatient with herself, she cast thoughts of Dillon from her mind. She had come here to look at a farm. Indulging in idle fancies about the owner's son was neither professional nor useful. She should keep her mind on her work, get it done and get out of here.

Weddington Farms wasn't on her short list of properties that best fit her requirements, and she didn't really want to look at it. She'd only come here to please her stepfather. When she'd decided to leave the family bank to open an equestrian center, she intended to buy a ready-made operation. Meticulous research had turned up several on the east coast. She had narrowed the field to six when her stepfather heard about Weddington Farms. He was certain the place would be perfect. Angie doubted it. But it seemed to matter to him, so she agreed to look.

As she pulled her car to a stop between two large long-leaf pines, Angie glanced down at the folder lying on the seat next to her. She knew every bit of information inside the folder by heart. The farm belonged to Harper Weddington, a widow who had resumed her maiden name when her son went away to college and she went to work at the family textile mill. Her young husband had been killed before the son was born. She was in financial difficulty because of declining productivity at the mill, the only employer of significance in Collins.

Angie changed into boots and stepped out of the car.

The barns suffered from the same lack of maintenance as everything else. The first one didn't seem to be in use. The grass had been cut, but it grew close to the barn and showed no sign of being cut by horses' hooves. The second barn stood open.

The eerie quiet of the place made it feel long deserted. After living most of her life in busy, noisy Pittsburgh, the silence was unnerving. Even Charlotte, North Carolina, where her stepfather and the family bank were now based, bustled with traffic. Angie had always thought she would enjoy living in the country. Now she wondered. The feeling of isolation made it all that much more unexpected when she looked inside the open barn to see a little girl in formal riding clothes struggling to saddle a pony.

Angie's first impulse was to offer help, but she held back. She remembered her own impatience to be grown-up enough to ride her horse without having to wait for someone to saddle it for her.

The child adjusted the saddle cloth with meticulous care. But when she tried to put the saddle on the pony's back, the trailing straps and buckles knocked the cloth out of place. The pony sidled nervously, making it impossible for the child to right the saddle or the cloth. The little girl stamped her foot, pulled everything off and prepared to try again.

Angie stepped into the barn. "Would you like me to give you a hand?"

It took Angie's eyes a moment to adjust to the darkness inside the barn, but she could sense as much as see the child's fright at the appearance of a stranger.

"He's a really beautiful pony," she said of the blond chestnut gelding. He had four white stockings and a blaze. A little too flashy for her tastes, but just the kind to appeal to a little girl. "What's his name?"

The child didn't answer, but she did peep from under the pony's neck to get a better look at Angie.

"I have several horses of my own," Angie said. "None as pretty as yours. My favorite is called Ring. Actually his name is Spring Run, but I feel stupid calling him that."

"Who are you? Are you a friend of my daddy?"

"No. I came to see Mrs. Weddington. She's not here, so I thought I'd look around. Is that your pony?"

"His name's Eddie," the child said. She still kept the pony between her and Angie, but she didn't seem as frightened. "Daddy calls him Lord Dilworth."

Angie wondered if Daddy was the young man she'd met up at the house.

"My name is Angie Kilpatrick," Angie said. "What's yours?"

"Christine Winthrop," the child said shyly.

Harper Weddington's granddaughter. She wondered why the child's mother had let her run off alone. She'd probably gotten busy and hadn't noticed when her daughter slipped away. Maybe kids could go off on their own in the country.

That had never happened to Angie. She had been surrounded by so many servants she'd often felt suffocated. Going to college had been a kind of culture shock.

"Do you want me to help you?" Angie asked. "On second thought, maybe you'd better wait for one of your parents."

"I can ride by myself," Christine said.

"I'm sure you can," Angie replied. She patted

the pony and ran her hands over his limbs. The pony stood perfectly still during her inspection. A well-schooled animal, and a good one despite his showy looks. Someone here knew their horseflesh. "But it's not safe to ride without someone to watch you. I don't think your mother would like that."

"I don't have a mother," Christine said. "She died."

Angie heard fear and loneliness in the child's voice, and she felt an immediate sympathy. She knew all about fear, pain and loneliness. She'd lost her own mother as a teenager. It still had the power to hurt.

"Let's make a deal. I'll help you saddle up if you promise to stay in front of the barn till your father comes."

"I can go to the riding ring if I want," Christine said, somewhat defiantly, Angie thought. "I'm not a baby."

"Of course not," Angie said, trying to decide what was safe to talk about with this high-strung child. "But you're still a little girl."

"I'm seven and a quarter," Christine announced. "I'm going to ride in the Anderson County Championship. Would you like to watch me?"

Angie was certain she wouldn't be anywhere near Weddington Farms on the day of the championship. "I'll have to check my schedule."

"That's what all big people say. It means you won't come."

"I can't promise until I know when it is," Angie

said, clutching at straws. "But if I'm anywhere near Collins, I promise I'll be at that meet."

With a hotheaded father like Dillon, it was no surprise to Angie that the child put little stock in the promises of adults.

"Do you like horses?"

"I love them."

She had started riding at three. She'd turned to her horses when her father left home. They had accepted her tears in silence, her failures without condemnation.

"Hand me that saddle." Angie positioned the saddle on the cloth and tightened the cinch. "I'll give you a leg up. But promise you'll stay close."

Christine nodded in agreement.

Angie linked her fingers. "Up you go."

Christine put her foot in Angie's hands, and Angie boosted her into the saddle. The child gathered the reins and Angie took the bridle to lead Eddie to the ring.

Just as they stepped out of the barn, she felt the reins tighten. She looked up at Christine, but the child was staring straight ahead, her expression hard to read. Angie turned her head. Dillon stood before her as though emerging from an explosion of sunlight.

He looked like a god. Pagan, of course. He seemed to exude raw energy. His blue eyes were brilliant with ill-concealed emotion. He seemed too still, unnaturally so, like the quiet before an explosion.

Angie realized she was staring. She wasn't acting the least bit like a woman in control.

"What are you doing?" he asked.

His tone was brusque. No, it was rude.

"You said I could look around."

"What are you doing *here?*" he demanded as if he thought she were going to steal something.

"I helped Christine saddle up."

"So I noticed." His anger flared in his eyes, but he kept a tight control on his voice.

"She promised she wouldn't leave the barn area until you got here."

His gaze didn't become any friendlier. Men usually appreciated what they saw when they looked at Angie. This man didn't seem to see anything to his liking.

He walked over to Christine. "Get down a minute." Ignoring the child's protests, he lifted her off the pony and removed the saddle.

"Did I use the wrong saddle?" Angie asked, as confused as Christine was upset. "It's the one Christine handed me."

"I have to make sure you put it on correctly. I won't have my daughter hurt or the horse injured because you don't know what you're doing."

Under Angie's shocked and stunned gaze, he proceeded to resaddle the pony. His actions were so completely unexpected she hardly knew whether to laugh or hit him.

"Did I saddle him properly?" she asked, her tone barbed, when he had helped Christine into the saddle again. No one, not even her stepfather, doublechecked her work.

"I didn't find anything wrong."

"Can I go?" Christine asked impatiently. She seemed totally unaware of the tension between the adults.

"You can go to the ring, but don't try any jumps. Work on your gaits. I'll be there in a minute."

Together they watched Christine canter her pony toward the riding ring. Angie turned back to Dillon, but he spoke first.

"I don't know who you are or why you're here, but keep your hands off my daughter."

His attack shocked and angered her, but she controlled her temper. She was in the wrong. She shouldn't have interfered, but she'd just been trying to help.

"I'm sorry, but I meant no harm. She couldn't saddle her pony by herself."

"She's not supposed to." His gaze was still unforgiving.

"Did you reach your mother?" she asked in an effort to get back to the purpose of her visit and to get herself on firmer ground.

"No."

Angie was disappointed. She didn't want to talk with him. "Do you think it'll take her long to get here?"

"I couldn't say."

Was he being intentionally unhelpful? "Try."

"I really don't know. She sometimes gets tied up at the mill for hours."

Angie looked at her watch. One thirty-seven. She didn't want to have to come back tomorrow. She wanted to give the place a quick once-over and get back on the road. She could be in her Charlotte office by the end of the workday.

Dillon's expression stiffened. "You could talk to me."

Angie decided that wasn't a good idea. He didn't seem to be the least bit cooperative.

"I'll wait."

"Why?" he asked, bristling. "My mother doesn't keep anything from me."

Considering he didn't know about the farm being for sale, Angie could hardly take that statement at face value.

"Nevertheless, I'd rather wait." They stood glaring at each other heatedly.

"What would a woman like you want a place like this for?"

Angie decided to ignore the first part of his question. "Old Southern mansion, magnolias, green fields as far as the eye can see. Who wouldn't want a place like this?"

"All this grandeur comes with a bit of decay," he replied, bitterness in his voice. "That's expected, you know. Folks don't feel like they've found a piece of the real South unless the paint is peeling and the floorboards are rotted through."

A blue Toyota drove up. A woman got out and headed in the direction Christine had gone. Dillon seemed to recall who he was talking to, that he was divulging too much to a stranger. He stopped talking abruptly.

"Is that Mrs. Weddington?"

Dillon shook his head. "Christine's riding teacher."

Angie didn't know why she didn't just go away and forget she'd ever met Dillon Winthrop. He wasn't the kind of man she normally found attractive. Until now, she'd divided her attention between up-and-coming young executives and successful horsemen, all well groomed, wealthy and perfectly at home against a sophisticated background. She imagined Dillon would feel very much out of place at a cocktail party or an opening night.

His face looked familiar. Maybe like some action movie star, one she wouldn't recognize because she didn't go in for that type of film. As she watched his expression harden, she decided he wouldn't consider the comparison flattering.

"I can't waste time chitchatting," Dillon said. "I've got a horse to check on."

"I can wait by myself." In fact, if he was the only available company, she'd prefer it.

"Determined, aren't you?"

He didn't seem reluctant to be rude. "Aren't most women?"

He continued to scowl. "I bet you're a Yankee. Or from California."

The statement was so unexpected Angie couldn't help but laugh. "Would that make any difference?"

"I bet you're not married, either."

This conversation was getting too bizarre. She couldn't possibly take him seriously. "My, you Southern boys do get to the heart of things in a hurry. What makes you say that?"

"Most women around here don't talk like you."

"Why? Do you beat them? Or do you still subscribe to the barefoot-and-pregnant theory?"

He didn't smile. Clearly the man had no sense of humor.

He studied her a moment, his head tilted to one side as if he didn't know how to classify her. She liked that. Despite the mansion, the horses and a pedigree that probably reached back a hundred years before the Civil War, she'd bet he was one of the good old boys who thought of women as "honeys" and "babes" and "fillies" who couldn't survive without a man's help. She couldn't wait to buy this farm out from under him and show him how wrong he was.

But damn he was a hunk. Angie felt something flutter inside. It just might be possible to ignore a little chauvinism when it was attached to a body like that. For a little while at least.

Not that his face was exactly ugly. His dark brown hair was thick and wavy, plus he had a tanned complexion and brilliant blue eyes. Christine must take after her mother. Her blond hair and sharp, almost pointed features owed nothing to this man.

"Did you come down here to cause trouble?" he asked, his hostility undisguised now.

"Could I?" Now she was being provocative. She wasn't sure why. Neither was she certain what kind of reaction she hoped to provoke. "Don't answer that. I'm interested in farms, and yours seems to be the biggest one around."

His gaze took in her boots, hose and form-fitting suit. "You're not properly dressed for a tour."

"Did you expect me to show up in jeans and a plaid shirt?" she asked. "I thought Southern women were expected to go visiting in high heels and big hats."

"I wouldn't know. My mother was something of a rebel."

Angie decided she was tired of fencing. She was

also disturbed by the physical attraction that persisted despite his hostile attitude.

"I've decided not to wait," she said. "I'll be staying at the motel. Have your mother call me when she's free."

"You can save yourself the trouble. The farm's not for sale."

"I think I'll wait until I hear that from your mother."

She left him looking furious. Apparently he wasn't used to having his wishes ignored. She wondered how her stepfather had avoided this compulsion Southern men had to dominate. She also wondered why she didn't just throw in the towel and move on to the next place she was considering buying.

She got into the car and backed out. Dillon Winthrop was still standing where she'd left him, looking as enticing as ever. She hoped he wouldn't be around tomorrow. He was definitely a threat to her concentration.

CHAPTER NINE

DILLON WAS STILL standing in front of the barn when his mother came hurrying toward him. Some of the tension drained from his body when he saw her anger. Maybe this foul-up wasn't her fault.

"A woman came by to look at the place," he said as soon as she was within hearing distance. "She said she'd talked to Burton Rust about buying it."

Dillon saw embarrassment mingled with anger in his mother's expression. His tension returned. Angie's being here might have been a mistake, but her belief that the farm was for sale wasn't. He saw it in Harper's eyes. A sick feeling welled up from the pit of his stomach.

"Dammit, Mom, why didn't you tell me you were trying to sell this place?"

"Now, Dillon..."

He ignored her placating tone. "You let Burton Rust send some woman in here and make me look like a fool for not knowing a thing about it. I may not own the place, but I've got a stake in it." A moral right, but no legal claim. It made Dillon crazy to have his hands tied like that.

"Dillon, I never authorized Burton to look for a buyer. I asked him to find out what the place would bring. That's all."

It didn't matter what she'd intended. She'd talked

to the bank without telling him. That made Dillon feel more on the outside than ever. His daughter didn't like him, and his mother wanted to sell the farm without consulting him. So much for his plans.

"Well, are you going to sell or not?"

Harper hedged. "I haven't made up my mind, but I've got to consider my options."

"And one of them is selling the farm?"

"It always has been."

Dillon knew that. And he knew why. Because WedTech was her baby. And WedTech was in trouble.

WedTech had become Harper's life after Dillon left for college. She had worked at her father's side for years, fighting with him over the issue of upgrading. But Sam Weddington was a stubborn man who believed that what had worked once would always work. When he died, Harper had nursed WedTech through tough times, borrowing to make changes a little at a time. But now the equipment was so outdated that the only way to keep the mill competitive was to rebuild from the ground up.

"Did you show her around?" Harper asked.

"She said she'd rather talk to you. I'm sure she felt there was no point in talking to a man who's little better than your farm manager."

"Dillon, that's ridiculous. You know this place is as much yours and Christine's as it is mine."

"Then why is Burton Rust acting like it belongs to *him*?"

Harper rubbed her forehead and walked to the paddock fence. She leaned against it, her shoulders sagging. Times like this, when the financial pressure got to her, she almost looked her age. "I guess you could say Burton owns more of this place than we do."

"What the hell does that mean?"

"I borrowed against the farm. I was certain I could pay it back. It never occurred to me Burton might foreclose."

"Foreclose!"

"After all the help Sam gave him to get his bank started... Anyway, he called last week. Said the loan was due." She glanced at him, her violet eyes bleak. "When I said I couldn't pay him yet, he said he'd have to put out some feelers to see what kind of money the farm would bring in. Otherwise he would have no choice but to consider foreclosure. I had no idea anything would happen so quickly."

So the farm *was* for sale. It didn't matter how or why, just that it was. Dillon was going to lose the only thing that had ever given him a real sense of belonging.

Since childhood, Dillon had felt the ache of being fatherless. Then, as a young man, he'd learned the truth. There had been no Kenneth Winthrop, no tragic automobile accident. His mother had made up the story, the man, the name. Ever since, Dillon had felt rootless, unattached. Only the land gave him a sense of belonging.

He loved this farm. He used to ride it with his grandfather and listen eagerly to the stories of the generations of Weddingtons who had farmed the land before him. "We go all the way back to the Revolution," his grandfather used to say. "There have been Weddingtons on this land for nine generations. You're the tenth."

Dillon had always counted on that. Even when he

was in college. Even when he took that job in California to be near Christine. He'd counted on it especially when he got custody of his daughter. He'd never wanted her to grow up as a latchkey kid living in an apartment in Redondo Beach.

Now his dream was falling apart. It made him so angry he wanted to fight somebody, anybody.

Harper put a hand on his arm. "Please don't worry, Dillon. I'll work it out. I'll ask for another extension."

"That's not the point, Mom," Dillon said. "The mill is the problem, and it's not going to get any better. You ought to get rid of it. You don't need to work so hard."

"And do what? Crochet?"

"You could help me run this place. You handle the selling, I handle the growing. It's more than enough to keep you busy."

"I don't like the farm. I never have."

He knew that. She'd never shared his love for the acres of fields and forest, but it was her home, dammit! She ought to feel something for it.

"Do you want to see this place turned into a housing development with a golf course in the middle?"

"Of course not."

"Then sell WedTech and put the money into the farm."

"I won't sell the mill. The people in this town are my friends. I grew up with them. They've depended on us all their lives. They'd have nowhere to turn."

"What about Christine and me? We'll have nowhere to turn when you sell the farm and the mill goes bust."

"It won't go bust. I'd have the money I need to retool."

"I don't give a damn about the mill!" Dillon thundered. His mother couldn't understand. She never did when it came to that mill. "I'm concerned about us!"

"*I* care about you, too."

"No, you don't. You don't even think of us most of the time. You're willing to sacrifice your family for a damned town that could take care of itself."

"I'd never do that. You and Christine are the most important people in the world to me. We'll find a nice place, a smaller place that will be easier to manage. We'll all be happier. You'll see."

"I can manage just fine where we are. You're the one who can't manage."

Dillon was sorry if he'd hurt his mother's feelings, but she was doing a pretty good job on his right now. He never used to question her love, but her loyalty to the people of Collins was making her blind to what she was doing to him and Christine.

Harper could never understand why the farm was so important to him, especially when he hadn't lived here in ten years. And he couldn't explain to her the only reason he'd endured ten years away was because he'd known it was here. He'd defied his grandfather and gotten a degree in agriculture instead of textiles because he always intended to come back to the farm.

It was his only heritage. He wanted to pass it on to his daughter. If he could teach her to love the land the way he did, maybe she could learn to love him, too.

"That Kilpatrick woman said she'd be back in the

morning," he said. "Call her and cancel the appointment."

"No," Harper said after a moment's thought. "I don't like what Burton did, but I need to know how much the farm will bring."

"Then put the mill on the market. Find out how much *it* would bring."

"No. I'll never sell WedTech."

"Dammit, Mom, are you going to keep ignoring me until you lose everything?"

Harper shook her head. "I see Mrs. Owens heading this way. Christine's lesson must be over."

She was cutting him off. She always did that when they argued about the mill.

"Go help her unsaddle her pony," Harper said. "And see if you can mend a few fences while you're at it."

"How the hell am I supposed to do that when you just pulled the props out from under both of us?"

Harper refused to return to their argument. "Keep trying. It's the only way you'll ever be the father you want to be."

"Maybe the father I want to be isn't what she wants."

"It's what she needs."

His mother wouldn't talk to him anymore, but Dillon hadn't given up yet. He'd fight until the ink dried on the page. Some way, somehow, he'd prevent her from selling the farm.

DILLON WATCHED enviously as his mother got more out of Christine in one minute than he had in an entire afternoon.

"Did you have a good day, Christine?" Harper asked as they sat down at the dining table.

"No," Christine said.

Harper looked at the little girl with concern in her eyes as Floretha dished up vegetables for Christine's plate. "What happened?"

"The teacher kept fussing at me. She said I had to speak up, that nobody could hear me. Then when I went out to play, they wouldn't let me go first. They said Emily got to go first because I went first yesterday.

Dillon had asked his daughter the same question. All he'd gotten was a disgruntled "Okay." He knew Evelyn and her parents had poisoned Christine's mind against him. Even now, from three thousand miles away, the Stringfellows tried to keep their hold on Christine by sending her presents far beyond what he could afford to give her.

At first they had bombarded her with gifts every week—dolls, a TV, video games, clothes, jewelry—jewelry for a seven-year-old!—until he'd told them they could send gifts only for Christmas and her birthday. But that hadn't been a success. It had taken an entire UPS truck to deliver her birthday gifts. At least a dozen presents were still locked away in the attic.

"Dumb Eddie didn't want to jump," Christine was saying. "Mrs. Owens wanted me to try again, but I told her I was tired." She made a face. "Grandpa Stringfellow would buy me a horse that could jump that stupid old fence."

Dillon felt the bile rise in his throat as it always did when Christine compared him to her grandparents.

Harper turned her attention to Dillon. "Did you have a good day?"

No, he'd had a miserable day.

It had started by his discovery that his favorite horse was lame. Next, his tractor wouldn't start. It was practically held together by chewing gum and baling wire because Harper had used their money to pay somebody's orthodontist bill. Then Christine had come home in one of her moods. The final straw had been that city-bred blonde telling him Weddington Farms was for sale.

"We need to talk about a new tractor," he said. He knew his mother didn't have the money for a new one. But it wouldn't hurt to remind her there were other things in the world besides that mill and the unending needs of the people of Collins.

"Are we going to move?" Christine asked unexpectedly.

Dillon noticed she'd stopped eating.

"Whatever made you ask that?" Harper glanced at her son.

"Mrs. Owens heard it at the bank."

Dillon's curses were vivid and plentiful. Floretha raised her eyebrows in his direction.

"The farm's not for sale," Dillon snapped.

"Mrs. Owens said it was."

"Mrs. Owens is wrong. It isn't for sale, and it never will be."

Christine looked at her grandmother. The stricken look on Harper's face refuted every word Dillon had said.

"Where will I live?" Christine asked. "Can I take my dolls with me? Mrs. Stuart doesn't want to move again."

"I told you the farm wasn't for sale," Dillon repeated.

"Can I live with Grandpa Stringfellow?" Christine asked.

"No!" Dillon hadn't meant to shout, but the frustrations of the day had finally gotten the better of him.

Christine burst into tears. She jumped up from her seat next to her father, ran around the table and buried her face in her grandmother's lap.

"I don't want to move again," she sobbed. "I might get lost."

One of her favorite dolls had gotten lost in the move from California, and Christine had never forgotten it.

"Hush," Harper cooed, trying to calm the frightened child. "Nobody will ever lose you."

The feeling in the bottom of Dillon's stomach got colder and heavier. His daughter had run to his mother for comfort. She wanted to live on the other side of the country from him. Would he ever figure out how to set things right?

"No matter what happens, you'll always stay with your daddy and me," Harper assured her. "Nobody will lose you."

Christine stopped crying. But when Harper suggested she finish her dinner, she said, "I'm not hungry. May I go to my room?"

"Are you sure? You haven't eaten much."

"I don't want anything else," Christine said.

"Then you may go. I'll be up to tuck you in later." Harper watched, her expression worried, as the child left the table and trudged toward the stairs.

"I don't like it when she doesn't eat. She's too thin now."

"That's nothing to what she'll be when she finds out you *do* want to sell the farm," Dillon said. "She probably won't eat anything at all."

"We don't *know* that we'll have to sell. Besides, the last thing she needs is to be worrying about us leaving her."

"Nobody's leaving her."

"I know that and so do you, but she doesn't. The most important person in her life did leave her. She hasn't gotten over that."

"She doesn't seem to be trying very hard. She hates everything I do. She hates *me*."

"No, she doesn't. She's just afraid of you."

"Why?"

"Her mother's dead, she's separated from her grandparents and she's living with two people she hardly knows. All she has to hang on to is her dolls, and now she thinks they'll be out of a home soon."

"What am I supposed to do?"

"She needs to feel loved."

"I do love her. I show her every day."

"Not in ways she can understand," Harper said. "You're always barking at her. You don't mean to, but you do. It scares her."

Floretha rose to clear the table. "You listen to Miss Harper," she said. "That child wants to love you, but she's afraid."

"As far as I can tell, she never tries." He was tired of taking all the blame. He'd done everything he could think of to change Christine's dislike for him.

"Dillon, it isn't up to her to try. She's only a child.

She doesn't understand. You have to keep on showing her you love her whether she responds or not.''

"Will she ever respond?"

"When she stops being afraid.''

"How do I make that happen?''

"By being here every time she needs you. Her
mother's death was a terrible shock. So was leaving
her grandparents. It will take her a long time to feel
safe again.''

Dillon's curses earned another frown from Floretha. It seemed the harder he tried, the further behind
he got. He had to learn to be patient. Christine might
learn to trust him—and hopefully love him—if he
gave her time.

But not if she had to be uprooted again.

"Which brings us back to this Kilpatrick woman,''
he said.

Harper shook her head. "I'm tired and you're out
of sorts. We'll see Miss Kilpatrick tomorrow, then
talk to Burton and decide what to do. Now, you never
did tell me about your day.''

Dillon didn't want to. He didn't want his mother
to hear the resentment in his voice, suspect the anger
in his heart. All his life she had hidden things from
him—important things—and now she had done it
again.

He couldn't understand why she was ready to put
the mill and the damned town ahead of her own flesh
and blood. After the lies she'd raised him on, surely
she owed him more than that.

HARPER DROPPED SEVEN kisses on Christine's solemn little face, just as she did every night at bed-
time—one on each eye, one on her chin, one on each
ear and one on each cheek. One for each year, she

had explained the first night her granddaughter came to stay. The little girl had been reluctant to accept a good-night kiss from a grandmother she barely knew, and Harper had decided to make a game of it, hoping Christine would warm to it.

"And what about when I'm eight?" Christine had asked after the first few times. "Then what happens?"

"Oh, that's a secret," Harper had replied. "You have to wait until you're eight to find out."

"Will you kiss me on my forehead?"

Harper had made a great show of studying the little girl's forehead. "Oh, I don't know. There's such a big frown there. We'll have to wait and see."

Almost every night now, Christine made another guess. Tonight, she hadn't guessed. Tonight, she lay stiffly under the covers, arms folded across her chest, staring at the ceiling, resisting attempts to draw her out. So Harper simply kissed her and tiptoed out of the room.

Sighing, she went back downstairs in search of company. She found Floretha on the screened sunporch off the main parlor, the one where Sam had waited up for his wayward daughter all those long-ago nights.

Those days still haunted Harper. So many things she would change if she could. Except for Dillon. She wouldn't change Dillon. Well, maybe a little. For his own good.

"He's too much like me, isn't he?" she said without preamble. "Willful and stubborn."

Floretha chuckled. Her voice was growing thinner these days, but it was the only thing about her that showed much sign of aging. Floretha had weathered early, but her later years had been kind to her. Harper hoped she'd had something to do with that. The old woman was family as far as she was concerned.

"That he is," Floretha said.

"What can I do about it? How can I make him see where he's going wrong with Christine?"

"You can't, child. He's got to make his own mistakes."

"And break hearts in the process. Like I did."

"Broken hearts are part of the bargain."

Floretha's words, as always, brought Harper a certain calmness. The old woman was the only constant in her life, the one person who had always loved her unconditionally. Floretha had been there when Harper came home armed with a baby and an implausible story about a dead husband. Floretha had been there when Sam ranted and raged, before he finally agreed to go along with the fabrication to keep the scandal to a minimum. Floretha had been there when Harper didn't know how to mother a child, showing her by example how to give love.

And Floretha had been there when her mother died, followed a year later by Sam's death, leaving Harper saddled with an estate that was more of a liability with each passing year.

"Am I wrong to want to sell this place if it means saving WedTech?"

Night sounds—a chorus of crickets, and once or twice a bullfrog—swept across them as Floretha pondered the question. Sometimes, sitting out here like this, miles from the rest of the world, Harper felt they must be the last people on earth. When she thought about moving, she fantasized about a smaller place, where neighbors would drive by and wave, where you could see the lights from someone else's porch twinkling through the night. All her life, Harper had felt separate from everyone in her world. For once, she wanted to feel a part of that world.

"We don't need a place this size," Floretha said. "But there's something about this place that boy of yours needs."

"I know. But why?"

"Who knows why we need the things we need? He wants to belong somewhere."

Floretha's insight into her son clutched at Harper's heart; she knew that feeling. But, stubborn as always, she couldn't bring herself to acknowledge that it was justified in Dillon's case. "He can belong anywhere."

"Not to his way of thinking. He's got a hole in his soul, you know. Feels like an outsider."

And that, Harper knew, was her fault. When she'd thought he was old enough to understand, she had told him the truth about his birth. With all her heart, she'd believed she was doing the right thing, both in protecting him with a fantasy when he was young and in telling him the truth once he was older. But he'd instantly resented the lies he'd been told as a child, and he'd never let go of his resentment.

No, Dillon had never been the same since he'd learned the truth—or what part of the truth she'd been able to tell him. The rest was something even Harper could rarely bring herself to face squarely.

But she still remembered the look in her son's eyes when he'd said, "So what you're telling me is that my...that the man who...that he just took off and left us? That he didn't care enough to stick around?"

"It wasn't like that, Dillon. Please understand..."

Dillon had held up shaking hands to fend off her words. "I don't want to hear any more!" he'd shouted, running from the room.

She'd let him go, to give him time to calm down. She'd tried, later, to talk with him about it, but he'd always cut her off. She'd messed up so many things.

And here she was, thinking she had to do the right thing for everyone. But what in the world made her think she could figure out what was right? She'd never been right yet.

ANGIE SLOWED HER CAR as she approached the entrance to Weddington Farms. She also cut off the air conditioner and opened the windows. She might as well get used to the heat.

Her morning had been full of surprises. By the time she'd finished her preliminary research on Weddington Farms, she had completely reevaluated her position. She had learned of the increase in productivity since Dillon had taken over its management and had been pleasantly surprised. To get a feel for just how desperate Harper Weddington's situation was, Angie had mentioned a ridiculously low price to Burton Rust. When he said he'd confer with Harper, she had difficulty not showing her surprise. Harper must be under enormous pressure.

Those two facts put a whole new complexion on the situation.

Plus, Collins was in the heart of South Carolina's horse country. Many stables trained here year-round. Others wintered close by. Not only would there be plenty of potential borders, there would be a ready market for the oats, hay and straw the farm produced. And plenty of room to lay out additional jumping courses—even a hurdle and steeplechase course. And if she got ambitious enough to compete with Camden and Aiken for the thoroughbred market, she had plenty of space for a training track.

Angie restrained her growing excitement. She kept telling herself it was best to start small. But all the possibilities she'd ever dreamed about lay before her, within her grasp. It was impossible to restrain her imagination.

She turned into the farm entrance. She'd make changes, of course. She liked the stone columns and iron sign that marked the entrance, but she didn't like the dirt road and mud holes. And the house was half hidden by trees, some of which were just beginning to turn. If she straightened the lane and cut down a half-dozen magnolias, the effect would be stunning.

Picturesque pastures stretching to a band of pine trees in the distance lined each side of the lane. She would paint the miles of board fence that enclosed them a pristine white. All except the last pasture were grown up with hay. According to the bank, two cuttings had been made this summer. They were expecting to make a final one before the first frost. That was good. So was the fact that the fields of oats provided grain for feed as well as straw for bedding. Weddington Farms grew far more than it needed.

The last field contained horses. Angie's pulse quickened at the sight of their glistening coats and rippling muscles. If she loved anything in this world with an unconditional passion, it was horses. There was no animal in the world so beautiful, so graceful, so powerful, yet so gentle and loving. A cat could give you warmth, a dog companionship, but a horse was your partner.

Angie hadn't spent so much time in the boardroom that she had forgotten the excitement of jumping, of helping the horse gather himself, feeling his muscles tense, of leaning into the jump with him. Nor the sheer exhilaration of a hard gallop. Her horses had helped her through the terrible years as she gradually learned to accept that her father wanted nothing to do with her. They had helped her through the dark period after her mother's death.

Seven mares quietly grazed in the pasture, each with a foal. All were chestnuts, ranging in color from blond to golden to red. Each was of excellent size and conformation and radiated good health and contentment. The foal nearest the fence turned to gaze at the passing car. Two others stopped in their play. One nursed, one hid behind its mother, and two dozed in the shadows of their mothers. The mares greedily cropped the grass as if knowing winter would soon put an end to it.

Angie was strongly tempted to stop the car and climb the fence. Her fingers itched to rub a soft muzzle, pat a muscled shoulder, cuddle a foal. She was stopped by the certainty that Dillon Winthrop wouldn't welcome her in his pastures.

But she meant to go over every acre today, and she'd come dressed for it. She wore a pearl-colored tailored shirt, white jeans, and cream leather boots that had been made for her by a very chic firm in London. She smiled at the big hat resting on the seat next to her. She'd bought it this morning at a local shop especially for the occasion. It was a wide-brimmed straw hat trailing yards of crepe.

She hoped Dillon would notice it. She intended for him to notice the rest of her, too. She refused to be attracted to a man who looked right through her.

And she refused to consider why that should even matter to her.

CHAPTER TEN

ANGIE WAS PREPARED not to like Harper Weddington. After all, the woman had stood her up, kept the truth about trying to sell their home from her own son, and—maybe most important—had raised a son who bristled at every turn.

What could there be to like?

She was surprised to see Harper in jeans and a faded denim shirt. She didn't look old enough to be Dillon's mother, much less the grandmother of the little girl who sat waiting with her on the porch.

"I must apologize for not being here yesterday," Harper said when Angie introduced herself. "I'm afraid Burton Rust and I had a breakdown in communication."

Okay, she'd said the words, but Harper's smile didn't reach her eyes. Maybe she was no more happy about this sale than her son. Or maybe she was naturally reserved. Angie decided to withhold judgment.

"Is Dillon going with us?"

"No."

Angie felt a twinge of relief as well as disappointment. "That's too bad. I bought this hat just for him."

Harper looked puzzled.

"He seemed to think I was overdressed yesterday. I said I thought Southern ladies always visited in big hats. I didn't want to disappoint him, so I bought it this morning.''

For a moment, amusement sparkled in Harper's eyes. ''What did he say?''

''He said he wasn't sure what most Southern ladies did, that you were something of a rebel.''

''No, I wasn't your typical mother.'' Harper's appraising gaze traveled over Angie from top to bottom. ''Did you choose the rest of your outfit for him, also?''

''No, for me.'' She was sure Harper didn't believe her. ''I don't feel half as comfortable in a suit as I do in jeans.'' It was also part of being in control. She knew how men reacted to her, and she meant to take advantage of it.

''I hope you don't mind taking the truck. There's not a car made that can get over all the ruts on this place.''

''I'd rather ride,'' Angie said, ''if you can trust me with one of your horses.''

Harper looked surprised at Angie's request.

''Can I go, too?'' Christine looked up at Angie.

''I don't mind,'' Angie said, ''but it's not up to me.'' She wasn't getting into *that* trouble again.

Christine immediately started begging Harper. ''Angie can saddle my pony. She helped me yesterday.''

''I didn't know you two had met.''

''Dillon got held up. Christine didn't want to wait.''

Harper looked at them both. ''And she let you help?''

Was it her imagination, or did Harper's gaze become even more cool? ''Sure. We got along fine.''

"Eddie likes her," Christine said.

"And I like Eddie. He's a beautiful pony."

Harper seemed to hesitate. Angie figured she didn't know what to think of her prospective buyer. Angie liked that. It gave her the upper hand.

Harper reached her decision. "We'll need Dillon's help," she said. "Shep has already turned the horses out." She called Dillon on a portable phone and arranged to meet him at the barn.

Christine raced ahead. Angie and Harper followed more slowly.

"Is it always this lovely here?" Angie asked as they walked down the tree-shaded lane.

"No. In the dog days of summer, it can get so hot and humid you don't feel like moving a muscle for days."

"It's like that in Pittsburgh, too," Angie said.

"Is that your home?"

"Yes, though I've been living in Charlotte recently."

They talked easily, but Angie got the feeling Harper was reserving her opinion, as well.

The barn was cool and quiet. Angie loved the smells. She doubted the aromas would ever replace perfume, but they represented pleasure and comfortable companionship.

They had Eddie saddled and waiting by the time Dillon brought the horses in from the pasture.

He looked even better than yesterday, but not any happier. He looked as if he could chew nails and enjoy it. She wondered if he managed the farm because he liked it or because they couldn't afford to pay someone else to do it.

He looked as if he did manual labor, as well. He

was wearing jeans, and the sleeves of his damp shirt had been rolled up to reveal his biceps. Angie decided there was something very appealing about well-developed muscles.

But she was still certain he was a good old boy. She couldn't imagine him in a three-piece suit, white shirt and tie, wearing Gucci shoes and sitting behind a desk in an office. Or even in an elegant restaurant. He worked in the open and probably preferred to eat at barbecue pits and fish camps.

On the other hand, she'd always liked barbecue and had been curious about fish camps for years. She wondered if he'd take her to one....

Dillon gave Angie's outfit a thorough going over. The sight of her hat caused a momentary lifting of his frown.

"Do I pass muster?" she asked, batting her eyelashes and pretending to be coy.

"I hope you didn't go all over Collins looking like that."

"Couldn't have," Harper said to Dillon. "I haven't heard the ambulances carrying any heart attack patients to the county hospital."

"Don't the local girls wear jeans?" Angie asked, unsure if Harper was ribbing or criticizing.

"Yes, but not like you do."

Angie was pleased she had succeeded in getting Dillon to notice her, but she had the feeling she'd overdone it.

"When are you going to saddle up?" Christine asked impatiently. "You're talking and talking."

"You're right," Angie said, suddenly uncomfortable under Dillon's intense scrutiny. "But adults are like that."

"I don't see why."

"Neither do I. Now, where are the extra saddles?"

"I'll show you," Christine said. She grabbed Angie's hand and pulled her toward the barn.

"Come on," Harper said to Dillon. "I don't think Christine can stand to wait much longer."

Dillon led the horses into the barn. "They haven't been ridden in a while," he told his mother. "You sure you'll be all right?"

"I think I can manage," Harper said, smiling wryly at her son.

"You don't ride as much as you used to, that's all," Dillon said.

"I still remember how."

Angie could see the affection between Harper and Dillon. Harper's eyes glowed when she looked at her son; Dillon smiled despite his sour mood. He turned to Angie. "You been on a horse much?"

"Enough to know how to saddle one," she retorted. "You help your mother. I'll take care of myself."

"Okay," Dillon said, but Angie noticed he kept an eye on her the whole time. They led all three horses outside. Dillon boosted Christine into the saddle. Harper's mount was restless, but Dillon held on to the bridle until the animal calmed down.

"I guess I'm the only one left," Angie said.

"You sure about this?" Dillon asked.

"Positive."

"Okay. Here goes."

He boosted Angie into the saddle. Her horse was younger and had a stronger objection to having a saddle strapped to his back. He reared before Dillon could grab for the bridle. He tried to bolt when he came down, but Angie kept the reins so tight she practically pulled his head down on his chest. He shied and danced about in circles, but she quickly got him under control.

"You've ridden a lot," Dillon observed dryly.

"All my life," Angie replied with a challenging smile. "I plan to open an equestrian center." She turned to Harper. "Are you ready to go?"

Christine was out of the yard and cantering down a lane before Harper could reply.

As they rode from the yard, Harper asked, "You didn't tell him you knew horses, did you?"

"No."

"He doesn't like being made to look foolish."

That sounded like a criticism, but Angie didn't care. After yesterday, he deserved it. "What man does?"

"None I ever knew."

Some emotion flickered across Harper's face. It was gone too quickly for Angie to identify, but she had the feeling she had disturbed the memory of something that had once been very important to Harper.

"If I'd known that's who wanted the horses, I'd have brought them up myself."

Dillon turned to see his foreman, Shep, studying Angie's retreating form with undisguised admiration. Because they'd been best friends since first grade—when they were the only two fatherless boys in the class—Shep seemed to have the notion he could say anything at all to Dillon and get away with it.

"You'd better keep your distance. That female would have you for lunch."

Dillon was irritated at himself, his mother, daughter and Angie Kilpatrick. He wasn't sure what had come over him to start acting as though he liked that blond-haired farm stealer, but he was irked she'd captured his attention. He didn't have time for a flirtation. Certainly not with that female shark.

Shep chuckled. "But what a way to die. Did you see that body? I could—"

"You'd better put the brakes on your imagination before your radiator boils over," Dillon warned. "That filly is way beyond your means."

"I don't notice you closing your eyes," Shep countered.

Dillon hadn't needed to look. Just touching Angie when he'd helped her mount had made his body ache with hunger. "I doubt her outfit can be bought south of New York. The price tag would make your eyes roll back in your head."

"I don't care if she's fishing or just trawling," Shep replied. "She sure baits a hook real good. She looks damned fine in the saddle to boot."

Dillon had noticed that, too. He was irked that she knew so much about horses. He cringed when he remembered resaddling Christine's pony.

"Put a lid on it," Dillon advised his friend. "She wants to buy this place. The first thing she'd do would be to get rid of both of us." The idea of her waltzing in waving her checkbook, as if buying and selling people's lives wasn't worth the snap of her fingers, set his teeth on edge.

"You're sour on the world, man," Shep said. "Besides, she doesn't seem like such a barracuda. She gets along with Christine. It's nice to see a smile on the kid's face."

That's right, rub it in. That woman threatened more than his security and self-control; she even threatened his shaky place in his daughter's affections.

"The woman is a menace," Dillon said. "She's got to go."

"I LIKE THIS PLACE," Angie said to Harper. "I'd like to make you an offer."

They had finished their tour of the farm and were watching Christine take Eddie through his paces. The time together had convinced Angie that Harper Weddington was likable. After being in the sun for nearly an hour, it was wonderful to relax in the shade of the huge oaks that surrounded the riding ring. Their horses waited patiently to be unsaddled.

"It's really not on the market yet." Harper sounded uneasy. "I just asked Burton to find out what it would bring so I could consider my options."

"I don't want to rush you. I can wait a day or two if I can stand the motel that long." It was awful, right next to the highway. Semis had whizzed by all night, keeping her awake.

"Why don't you stay with us?" Harper asked.

The invitation surprised Angie. She was pleased that Harper had thawed, but she didn't know quite how to take this sudden invitation. "I couldn't impose on you like that."

"It wouldn't be an imposition. I should have asked you last night. My mother would have had your bags in the guest room before dinner."

Angie wouldn't normally have considered such an offer, but she hadn't finished with Dillon Winthrop, as childish as that seemed. He needed a little more humbling for treating her as he had.

Besides, she loved being astride a horse, the wind in her face, the sun warming her body. The physical activity sharpened her senses, heightened her enjoyment of everything around her. Each time she got back in the saddle, she wondered how she ever managed to spend weeks at a time closed up in an office.

Christine completed the course. Angie and Harper applauded. "At least think about it before you say no," Harper said as Christine rode toward them.

But Angie was thinking about Dillon. She was more strongly attracted to him than she liked to admit. She'd proved it by buying that hat. A few days of being exposed to his sweaty muscles and hot emotions at close range, and she might forget all her common sense. It wouldn't do for her to fall for him. Then he'd have the upper hand.

"I still can't get the double jumps," Christine complained when she'd brought her pony to a stop by the fence.

"You come at them from an angle," Angie said. "You've got to make a wider circle and go at them straight on. When you come at them from the side, Eddie doesn't see them until it's too late."

"Would you show me?" Christine asked.

Remembering Dillon's earlier reaction to her helping his daughter, she said, "I'm not sure your father would like that."

"Please," begged Christine.

"Go ahead," Harper said. "Dillon won't mind."

Angie wasn't sure Harper was right, but she itched for an excuse to enter the ring. "I don't promise anything," she said, leading her horse into the paddock. "It's been months since I've jumped anything but a dead battery."

"IT SEEMS SHE'S an accomplished horsewoman," Dillon said as he leaned against the fence next to his mother.

"She's showing Christine how to take that oxer. She's a better teacher than Mrs. Owens. Christine has jumped it twice already."

"It seems there's no end to her talents."

They watched in silence for a few minutes, Dillon's irritation mounting.

"I've invited her to stay with us while she's here," Harper said.

Dillon whipped around. "Why?"

"She can't stay at the motel. It has roaches."

"And what other reasons did you have?"

Harper didn't meet his gaze. "I want you to have time to learn more about what she wants to do with the place."

"That won't change how I feel."

"It might if you knew it was in good hands." She looked up at Dillon. "How about a compromise? There's a wonderful little farm only a few miles from here. The house isn't so big and there's only three hundred acres, but this place will work you into an early grave."

"It's not the number of acres or the house, Mom. This is where my family has lived for over two hundred years. I wouldn't want to leave even if I knew it would work me to death. Considering what you've done for that mill, you ought to understand."

"But none of that was for me. It was…" Harper shook her head. "It doesn't matter. We're in a mess.

The only important thing is to figure a way out."
She turned her gaze back to Angie.

"What did she say when you asked her to stay?"

"She didn't. I think she's afraid of you."

Dillon made a sound between a snort and a hoot.
"That woman's not afraid of anybody."

"She knows you don't like her. You growl at her
every time you get within ten feet."

"I don't growl and I don't dislike her, just what
she wants to do."

"Then try not to look like she's a dentist and
you're having a root canal."

Dillon's gaze shifted to where Angie and Christine
were studying a jump together. He hadn't seen Christine so animated, so open and natural, since her
mother's death.

That's all he needed, a rich Yankee buying his
farm out from under him and stealing his daughter's
affections. No, that wasn't quite true. Christine had
no affection for him to be stolen.

Hell! He didn't give a damn about Angie's ideas
for the farm, but he was tired of fighting with the
only two females he loved.

"Let her stay. I don't care. But I don't promise
not to growl."

ANGIE WAS ALREADY warm from the exercise when
she rode up to the fence, but she felt the color in her
cheeks heighten further when she saw that she was
alone with Dillon. She patted her horse's neck.
"Where's Harper?"

"Gone back to the mill."

Angie felt uneasy without the buffer of Harper's
presence. It was one thing to *plan* to go head-to-head

with Dillon. It was quite another to do it. "Christine's a quick learner. I hope you plan to keep on with her lessons."

"She's been pestering me to let her stop," Dillon said.

"That's not what she said to me. Have you thought about getting her a bigger horse?"

"No."

"Do. And maybe even a new teacher. There are some top-notch trainers in the Camden area. With the right kind of coaching she could be championship caliber."

"Looks like you could be championship caliber yourself."

He made it sound like a fault.

"I was never that good," Angie said as she dismounted. "Besides, I spent too much time doing other things. Now I don't ride regularly enough. I'll be sore tomorrow."

"Then you can ride again tomorrow. Mom says she's invited you to stay while you look things over."

She shouldn't even be considering the idea. She'd seen all she needed to see for her equestrian center, but her mind was full of the new possibilities. She needed time to think them through before she made a decision. Staying here a day or two would give her the chance to do that. Besides, if she had any questions about the property or the area, she could ask Dillon.

"Don't let my temper drive you away," he said. "I've been impossible to live with for years."

The admission sounded grudging. She wondered if he really believed it.

They watched Christine in silence. It finally became clear to Angie that if she didn't start the conversation, he wouldn't say anything else until Christine finished.

"Your mother is a dynamo."

"I wish she'd start worrying about herself as much as she does other people."

"Does that somehow refer to me?" Angie asked, completely at sea.

"No, the people of Collins. That's why she's knocking herself out over that mill. That's why this place is in hock—so she won't have to lay people off. I can't make her realize that even if she sacrifices everything she has for this town, they still won't thank her."

"So she's endangering something important to you, and you think she'll get nothing for it in the end."

"Something like that."

"And you're angry."

"Wouldn't you be?"

"I suppose so. What will you and Christine do?"

He stared at his daughter as she schooled Eddie the way Angie had taught her. "We'll stay with Mom. We're the only family she's got." He cursed under his breath. "I thought when we came back home, everything would work out. Christine would have Mom, I'd have the farm and Mom would have a family again. But the mill has ruined everything. The best thing for us would be for the whole damned thing to burn down."

"How about the town?"

"Look, I've got to go. I shouldn't have said so much, but if you buy this place, you'll be in the middle of it. You might as well know what you're getting into.''

''I can't see how what happens in Collins would affect me.''

''In a small town, everything affects everything else. You'll see.''

Angie's gaze followed Dillon as he led the horses to the barn. He seemed a man weighed down by difficulties centering around the two people he loved most in the world. No wonder he was irritable. She didn't imagine she'd be any different if their positions were reversed.

Maybe she wouldn't try to get even. He had enough problems. But it was nice to know he was vulnerable, that he had feelings. She didn't even try to figure out why she cared.

CHAPTER ELEVEN

DILLON WALKED OUT to the front porch. Night was one of his favorite times.

A thousand tiny pinpoints of light pierced the sky, setting every tree and building into clear relief. Heat radiating from the warm earth softened the chill in the autumn evening. The breeze had died. Everything was still. Even the frogs and crickets seemed to be sleeping. But it was a comforting stillness, the kind he'd always enjoyed as a boy, the kind he'd missed when he was away.

All his life this had been the only place he felt truly at home.

He walked down the steps and picked up a piece of dead pine tree limb, systematically breaking it into tiny pieces. Now his peace was threatened from every angle, and Angie Kilpatrick was trying to take away the land that had always given him his sense of belonging.

Worst of all, he was attracted to her in spite of himself. Wealthy, beautiful and supremely self-confident, she reminded him too much of his ex-wife.

He had met Evelyn in college. The attraction was immediate, physical and beyond their ability to resist. They had become lovers immediately, certain their love could never be used up. The first crack appeared when Evelyn discovered she was pregnant. Morning sickness caused an open rift. By the time she was six months pregnant, she was furious at him for ruining her life. The only reason she didn't throw him out was that her parents wanted her to do just that. They were married two weeks before Christine was born. A month later, Evelyn moved in with her parents and started divorce proceedings.

When Christine was six years old, Evelyn died in a car accident with one of her lovers. Her will named her parents as Christine's guardians. Their granddaughter was the Stringfellows' only link with Evelyn, and they desperately wanted to keep her. They refused to hand her over to Dillon until the court awarded him custody.

Then Angie Kilpatrick had walked in, upsetting things even further.

He threw down the last bit of broken twig, climbed the steps and settled into a chair. But Angie was a guest, and for his mother's sake, he'd decided to put aside his animosity. It had been surprisingly easy. She was an enchanting woman and he'd almost grown to like her. No, that wasn't exactly the truth. He lusted after her. He'd like nothing better than to spend the night wrapped in her arms.

Angie had come down to dinner tonight wearing a white dress made out of some filmy material that clung to her body like plastic wrap to a sliced tomato. The scent of her perfume nearly drove him crazy.

Dillon had escaped before Floretha put dessert on the table. Christine's constant demands for attention had made it easy. He was surprised when Angie came out and sank into a rocking chair opposite him.

"Did you finally choke Christine or did you just run away?" he asked.

Angie laughed softly. "Your mother sent her off to get dressed for bed. I promised to tell her good-night."

"You're being awfully kind to a child you never saw before yesterday."

"I've enjoyed her company. Most of the time, people don't want to hear me talk about horses. My mother never cared for them, and my stepfather doesn't understand anything that can't be reduced to a column of figures. It's wonderful to have someone hang on every word I utter as though I were an expert. But I imagine you know just as much as I do."

"It doesn't make any difference if I do. I'm her father. Not nearly so interesting."

Dillon felt uncomfortable discussing his inadequacies as a father with a virtual stranger, but Angie seemed like a different person tonight, one for whom he was developing a dangerous attraction. He needed to remind himself why she was here. He changed the subject.

"Why do you want to open an equestrian center? After running corporations, what would you find to keep you interested?"

"Do you enjoy your work?"

Just like a woman not to give a straight answer. "Is this a game? I ask you a question, then you get to question me?"

"If you like. But I'm the guest. I get to go first. Or, if you don't buy that, how about ladies first."

"You're as bad as Christine. When you want your way, you mean to have it." He was irritated at himself. He was letting her smiling good humor cause him to lower his guard.

"You're stalling."

"You business types are all alike. You ask a question and you expect an answer in thirty seconds, all neatly arranged by paragraphs in order of preference."

"It's a failing we Yankees have. I'm waiting."

He didn't doubt that her good looks and charm—which she could turn on when she liked—contributed a lot to her business success. And that dress would give her an unfair advantage in any gathering of males. Dillon forced himself to ignore the stirring in his groin.

"I like being my own boss," he said. "I like making a decision without having half a dozen people tinker with it."

"You sound like the last untamed man. Is that why you got a degree in farm management instead of textiles?"

Warning signals sounded immediately. "How did you know that?"

"Everybody in Collins knows."

He probably shouldn't be annoyed, but he felt as if she'd been spying on him. "I always liked working out-of-doors. I managed one of the few farms left in Southern California."

"Why aren't you there now?"

"I was living in a one-bedroom apartment, and I didn't want Christine to grow up there. I wanted her to have space for horses, a chance to feel part of something permanent."

"Why here? This is your mother's place."

Dillon got to his feet. That still grated. He hoped Angie couldn't see it in his eyes. "This is home."

She didn't pursue that. "What else do you like about it?" she asked.

"It's hard to say. It's dirty, sweaty, hard work. And it's outside no matter what the weather."

"But that isn't what speaks to you, is it?"

He didn't want to keep talking to her. He didn't want her intelligent understanding to force him to change his antagonism toward her. But her interest felt so genuine, her perception was so quick, he couldn't stop himself.

"No. It's the land itself. I guess you have to grow up on a farm to understand that. Sometimes I think you belong to it more than it belongs to you." He felt something settle down within himself and realized that simply talking about this land calmed him. "My grandfather told me the name of every Weddington who ever owned this farm. He never let me forget I was next in line."

"I can see why you don't want your mother to sell."

No, she might think she did, but not even Dillon had fully understood how important this place was to him until Angie had come bouncing down his driveway. He sank down on the porch railing, his arm around one of the massive columns, his back to the fields and moonlight.

"Now it's my turn to ask why you want to give up all that power and position for a few horses."

"I guess you would say I'm not giving it up so much as leaving the day-to-day work to someone else."

"It's like having your cake and eating it, too."

"That would be one way to put it."

He didn't want to see it that way. He wanted her

to tell him she was different from Evelyn, that she could live without money and position. Her face was beautiful and pale in the moonlight, like the flawless porcelain of Christine's dolls. It would be so easy to think of her as a desirable woman and forget her threat to his happiness. "How do you see it?" he asked.

"I may own the company, but I'm not necessarily the best one to run it, especially if my real interest is somewhere else."

"So you can afford to be a dilettante."

She flinched. "I intend to make the center work," she said, a distinct edge to her voice. "If I didn't think I could, I'd stay in banking. I'm head of overseas investments. I'm very good at it."

"Are you going to look at other places?"

"Yes."

Hope lifted his spirits. "So you're not definite about buying Weddington Farms?"

"No. If I do, I'll need to change some of my plans."

Dillon felt a weight slide from his shoulders. He had a chance. If he knew what she wanted, maybe he could steer her somewhere else. "Tell me about your center."

"It's pretty much what you'd expect," Angie began. "It would be a place where professionals and Olympic hopefuls could train for jumping and dressage all year round."

Dillon's interest grew as Angie went into specifics about the number and kinds of barns, the training facilities, living quarters for the people who would care for and train the horses. This wasn't some spurof-the-moment whim of a bored, rich woman or of some dreamer with no head for business.

"I have detailed plans back in my office," Angie confessed. "My stepfather would have a fit if he knew how many of my appointments during the past year have been with architects and farm managers."

"Won't you be cutting yourself off from your friends if you come down here?" he asked. Maybe he could scare her off with fears of loneliness.

"I'll make new friends."

"How about the men in your life? Are they likely to follow you here?"

She turned toward him, a teasing smile on her lips. "Are you discreetly asking if I have a love life? Or are you just as discreetly implying that I'm not attractive enough to make men want to follow me into the wilds of South Carolina?"

"Neither. It's none of my business." He got up and walked down the steps. Now that some of the pressure was off, he could feel his attraction for her growing dangerously fast. He had to get away from her.

"Are you going to run off and leave me? I've always heard Southern men are gallant."

Instinct told him to run. But years of training—and hot desire—caused him to turn around slowly. "Would you like to join me?"

"Even a Yankee can tell that's a reluctant invitation."

"Not really. I was just thinking about something every good old Southern boy does when he gets a chance."

She came down the steps to join him, a teasing smile on her lips. "And what might that be?"

Dillon had to turn away to keep from responding to her olive branch. This woman was dangerous. He was a fool to keep flirting with temptation. But his resistance was only halfhearted. "Come with me and you'll see."

They began to walk toward a lane that ran in the opposite direction from the barns.

"I'd bet my life you've never had anything to do with 'good old boys,'" he said. "You may not spend your free time at the ballet or the opera, but you sure don't spend it going to wrestling matches or stock car races."

"Actually, I prefer movies, walking outdoors and almost anything to do with horses."

"Movies? What kind?"

"Promise you won't laugh."

"I'll try not to."

"Faint heart."

"Okay, I promise."

"I like the kind where the woman is in danger and the hero risks his life to save her. Silly, isn't it?"

Hell, that's exactly what he liked, though he'd never admit it. "No."

"Sure it is. What successful professional woman needs rescuing?"

She didn't sound like a high-powered executive. To Dillon, she sounded very womanly and very approachable. "One who hasn't been rescued often enough. Don't you have any red-blooded American boys in Pittsburgh or Charlotte?"

"Sure, but rescuing a woman like me is a tall order. My stepfather runs the company, and I'm his second in command and the biggest stockholder."

He had forgotten her money. The dose of reality

was like a face full of cold water. "Somebody should've tried."

They were walking between fields of drying corn. A light breeze moved over the dry, rustling fronds like a wave over the beach.

"Actually quite a few have, but they seem to have at least one eye on my money. Poor little rich girl. Tragic, isn't it, and nobody understands."

He understood more than she could guess. Money had come between him and Evelyn. Once the magic disappeared, she could see only the enormous difference in their wealth. She couldn't imagine anyone could love her for herself alone.

He had a sudden desire to reach out, pull Angie to him and give her a hug. Only he couldn't do that. He'd been angry with her practically from the moment she set foot on the farm. Such an abrupt about-face would make her question his motives.

They stopped in the middle of the lane. The house lights glowed in the distance. The fields around them were cloaked in shades of purple velvet.

"Have you ever walked barefoot in the grass at night?" he asked.

"No, I don't think I have," she replied, apparently startled at his question.

"You can start now. It's warm and the grass is soft."

"Are you serious?"

"Sure, it's what good old Southern boys do," he said, already wondering why he'd suggested such a stupid thing to a city woman. "I used to do it all the time when I was a kid. You aren't wearing panty hose, are you?"

She laughed. "You Southern men are the most

incongruous combination of rigid propriety and easy-going informality. No man in Pittsburgh would dare ask that.''

"Well, are you?" He'd already dug his hole. No point in not diving in now.

Besides, there was invitation in her eyes, no sign of the barracuda, just a lovely woman who had heated his blood to a boil. Something about her made him feel reckless. He hadn't felt like this since he'd met Evelyn.

"No, I'm not wearing panty hose."

"Then all you have to do is take off your shoes."

She looked at him as if he were crazy.

"Ladies first," he reminded her.

She laughed. "I assume it's against the rules for men to go barefoot in the presence of a shod lady."

"I'd be struck off the dinner party circuit for at least a year."

Laughing as if she thought they were both a little crazy, Angie removed her shoes. "Now it's your turn."

Dillon kicked his foot in the air and his shoe flew off. The other came off just as easily. He bent over, pulled off his socks and picked up his shoes. He felt like giving a hop and a skip. Putting his toes in the dirt lifted his spirits no matter how down he'd been feeling.

"I get the impression you do this a lot," Angie said.

"Nearly every night when it's warm. Here—" he held out his hand toward her "—let me show you something."

Angie hesitated only briefly before she put her hand in his. "I feel like a little girl again."

"Good. Being a grown-up is hard work. I believe in giving myself time off for good behavior."

Angie laughed. "I can't wait to try that philosophy on my stepfather."

"He'll never understand if he stays in the city."

They were swinging hands as they walked. Dillon felt almost carefree.

"Where are we going?" Angie asked.

"Afraid of the dark?"

"It's not dark out here. I thought it would be."

"Can't be, not with a moon and all those stars shining as hard as they can."

They came to a small pasture between cornfields. An open shed had been built in a stand of pines along one edge of the field. Dillon gave a sharp whistle. A horse that had been grazing in the shadows raised its head. Dillon whistled again, and the horse started toward him at a fast walk. Almost immediately something moved in the shadows.

"A foal!" Angie exclaimed.

It quickly got to its feet and followed its mother.

"She's less than two weeks old," Dillon said.

"She's beautiful," Angie cooed. "Is she Christine's?"

"They're both mine," he said, fondling the mare as she thrust her head between the boards of the fence. "My grandfather gave her to me on my eighth birthday. She's twenty-one. This will be her last foal." He fed her a cube of sugar. The foal came to the fence, curious about what her mother was eating. Angie stuck her hand through the fence and petted her. Startled at the smell of a stranger, the foal scampered behind her mother, then immediately peeped out from behind her haunches.

Angie leaned against the fence, her arms folded under he chin. "She's darling. What are you going to do with her?"

"Keep her."

Dillon leaned against the fence next to Angie. Without thinking, he put his arm around her shoulder. It seemed the natural thing to do, what he wanted to do. With moonlight shining on her hair and starlight in her eyes, bare feet in the dirt, this Angie had little to do with the sleek, efficient woman who'd come to take his land. There was an enticing softness about her now.

Angie turned to look at him. "So you really do like horses."

"I've kept all seven of Duchess's daughters. You probably noticed them on the way in."

"I would never have guessed this when we first met."

"We got off on the wrong foot."

Angie made no move to escape from the arm he'd placed around her shoulder. Common sense told him not to move ahead until he'd tested the ground; experience told him this woman was not going to take anything on faith. Inclination told him not to wait. She was attractive. He was drawn to her. She liked him at least well enough not to draw back. Maybe she wanted this as much as he did. All he knew for certain was that his loins ached with wanting to make love to her.

So he kissed her.

Her lips were soft and slightly parted. And warm. They moved invitingly under his. His arm tightened around her, pulling her toward him as he deepened their kiss. She yielded, allowing her body to be drawn against him. He could feel the pressure of her breasts against his chest, the curve of her leg as it moved against his, her abdomen as it brushed his stiffening body.

A shudder of desire ran through him. She opened her mouth to welcome his seeking tongue, their bodies pressing together with more intimacy. The intensity of their kiss increased until Dillon felt he had to break off or melt from the heat.

But something unexpected happened when he looked into Angie's eyes. He saw mirrored there his own surprise at the nature and intensity of the feeling that had exploded between them. They both knew it was something more than sexual desire, more than the buildup of animal lust between two healthy young people.

He wanted to speak first, to say something to diffuse the tension, but he couldn't think of a word that didn't sound foolish and out of place. Angie saved him.

"I promised Christine I'd tell her good-night." She ran her hand over her hair in a nervous gesture. She touched her lips briefly, tentatively, then self-consciously let her hand drop to her side. "I imagine she's been wondering what happened to me."

He didn't move. She looked at him questioningly.

"Maybe you shouldn't go."

"Why?"

"I don't want her to get too attached to you."

Damn, she looked hurt.

"It's just that she seems to like you so much, and you'll be gone in a day or two. She already knows too much about losing people."

"Then you go. You're the person she really wants."

"She's never wanted me."

"She won't learn to want you if you keep avoiding her."

When he didn't move, she took his hand and tugged. He hesitated. "She won't want to see me."

"Sure she will. She just doesn't know how to show it. I imagine you're very demanding and critical. Most men are."

With a shrug of resignation, he fell in beside her. "Maybe she'll like me better if we go together," he said. "A spoonful of sugar to help the medicine go down."

CHAPTER TWELVE

WHEN DILLON AND ANGIE reached Christine's room, the child was sitting in her bed, a doll on either side, talking to Harper.

"Mrs. Stuart says Angie likes Daddy more than me," Christine was saying.

"Maybe she's afraid you'll start to like Angie more than you like her," Harper said. "She probably doesn't realize people can like more than one person at the same time."

Christine looked doubtful.

"Don't you love Mrs. Stuart and me?"

Christine nodded, and Dillon's heart beat a little faster. This was the first time Christine had admitted she loved anyone besides her mother and grandparents.

"Well, I love you and your daddy. We can love lots of people at the same time."

"Mrs. Stuart doesn't love anybody but me."

At Angie's urging, Dillon slipped into the room after her.

"Angie!" Christine's eyes lit up when she saw Angie. Dillon would have traded the whole farm if she'd only look at him that way.

"Sorry to be so late," Angie said, "but your daddy took me to see the foal."

Dillon tried to hang back, but Angie pulled him forward.

"Mrs. Stuart said you'd forgotten me," Christine said.

Angie took Harper's place next to Christine. She signaled Dillon to sit on the other side. He didn't expect anything to come of it, but he did it anyway. He couldn't pass up a chance to be near Christine.

"I wouldn't forget you," Angie said. "Your father and I hurried back. Why didn't you tell me about the foal? She's beautiful."

"Mrs. Stuart says she's not as pretty as Eddie."

"I think it's time for Mrs. Stuart to go to sleep." Angie took the doll, gave her a kiss and tucked her under the covers. "I like Mrs. Stuart, but I like talking to you better." Angie lowered her voice to a confidential whisper. "Daddies don't understand dolls like your grandmother and I do. I think you'd better talk to him yourself."

Christine looked warily at her father. "What does he want to say?"

"He wants to kiss you good-night and tell you he loves you."

Dillon wanted to tell her more than that. He wanted to tell her he thought she was beautiful, to tell her how good it made him feel to see her smile, how his heart ached to have her smile at him.

"Good night," was all he managed. It seemed a paltry thing to say, but he knew if he said only half of what he felt, he'd scare her again. He placed a nervous kiss on his daughter's forehead. "I love you."

"Now you have to kiss him good-night and tell him you love him," Angie coaxed.

Christine looked at her doll.

"Mrs. Stuart would want you to."

Christine looked as though Mrs. Stuart wouldn't want any such thing, but Angie's confidence made her uncertain.

"Good night," Christine mumbled. "I love you."

It was an almost inaudible whisper, but Dillon heard it. His heart swelled with happiness.

"Now put your arms around his neck and give him a big hug and kiss," Angie said. "When I was a little girl, I couldn't go to sleep until my father hugged and kissed me."

The child did as she was instructed, and Dillon was almost afraid to reciprocate. What if she drew back from him? But his need was greater than his fear. He let his arms enfold her tiny body and pulled her tenderly against his chest. It was an awkward embrace at first, but it grew warmer the longer it lasted. It was obvious when they separated that his daughter was as surprised as he by their feelings.

Christine stared at her father. There was no anger or fear in her gaze. Only loneliness. Dillon hugged her again, more fiercely this time. When he released her, his eyes were moist.

Angie kissed Christine on the forehead, gave her a hug and stood up.

"Now everybody's kissed and hugged you good-night," Harper said as she tucked Christine into bed. "Time to turn out the light."

"Mrs. Stuart wants to know if Angie will be here in the morning," Christine asked. She included Dillon in her glance.

Angie smiled. "You can tell Mrs. Stuart we'll all most definitely be here in the morning."

"Now close your eyes and go to sleep," Harper said. "You have to get lots of rest if you want Angie to help you with your jumps tomorrow."

When they were out in the hall, Harper turned to Angie and said, "You seem to know as much about children as you do about horses."

"I just did what my mother and stepfather did," Angie confessed. "It always worked for me."

"That's the first time she and her father have ever kissed good-night."

"That's awful," Angie said, turning to Dillon.

"She didn't want me to kiss her," Dillon replied gruffly. It irritated him to have to explain his failures to Angie.

"There are times when you don't ask, you just do," Angie said. "I think you already know something about that."

Dillon felt his desire for Angie surge to the surface. He wondered if she had any idea just how much he wanted to do.

Angie smiled. "Now I'm going to bed before you both discover I haven't the foggiest notion what I'm talking about."

ANGIE CLOSED THE DOOR behind her and leaned against it. She didn't know whether she was trying to lock herself in or keep out the swirling currents of emotion she had encountered since coming to Weddington Farms. She'd been caught up in them, and now she didn't know what to do about it.

She'd been surprised by Dillon's friendliness after dinner and pleased he'd invited her to see the foal. She had assumed he was trying to make amends for being so unfriendly earlier. She hadn't been averse to sharing a kiss with an attractive man. But what may have started as an act of animal magnetism had ended up as something quite different.

At least for her. Her feelings for Dillon and Christine had changed from casual curiosity to something emotional. She felt a connection with them that hadn't been there before. She also had some sense of how her intended purchase of Weddington Farms might affect their lives.

But she didn't know whether she was sorry Dillon was losing his farm, sorry for Christine because she had lost her mother or sorry for both of them because they were missing so much love and wanted it so much. There was always the possibility she was interested in Dillon for herself, but she held back from accepting that. It raised too many questions she wasn't sure she could answer.

He could be pretending to like her to keep his farm. She knew a dozen men who could fake any emotion if enough money was at stake. She didn't think Dillon was like that, though. His emotions were too near the surface. At the same time, she wasn't sure she wanted to become enmeshed in his problematic relationship with his daughter. What did she know about helping other people build a family relationship? If it weren't for her stepfather, she wouldn't have any family at all.

The smartest thing for her to do was put it all out of her mind, go to bed and get a good night's sleep. Things might look different in the morning. And if they didn't, at least her head ought to be clear enough for her to deal with them. All this Southern hospitality and warm nights and bare toes in the grass had disoriented her. Nothing like this had ever happened in Pittsburgh.

HARPER STUDIED the expression on her son's face as he watched Angie Kilpatrick go to her room. She wasn't sure she liked the idea of his being so fascinated by this woman. She was even less certain about her granddaughter's instant attachment.

"That was unexpected." Harper started downstairs.

Dillon followed. "Yes."

"I can't handle you or Christine that well, and Angie's only known you one day." Did that mean the woman was well versed in manipulating others, she wondered, but didn't say.

"She didn't *handle* me," Dillon protested.

"Maybe not." They paused at the bottom of the stairs. Harper almost smiled at the streak of muleheadedness that showed in her son's square jaw and the stiff line of his mouth. She loved that face. She hoped to see it happy again soon. And she worried that a woman like Angie Kilpatrick wasn't the one to bring that about. "Coffee?"

"Yours or Floretha's?"

Harper laughed. "Floretha made it before she went to bed."

"Coffee it is."

Harper switched on the kitchen light as they invaded Floretha's domain. The room was exactly as it had been when Harper was growing up—the big, round table with spindly-legged chairs occupying the center, copper pots and iron skillets hanging from the ceiling, a clay planter of fresh herbs in the window over the sink, every surface gleaming from Floretha's efforts.

Harper poured two cups of coffee while Dillon rummaged through the refrigerator for a late-night snack. He found the last of the blackberry cobbler Floretha had served for dessert and joined Harper at the table.

"Do you like her?" he asked.

Harper wasn't surprised his thoughts were still on Angie. "Yes."

She supposed he heard the hedging in her voice. "But what?"

Harper sipped her coffee and tried to work out the right reply. How did she tell her son that she under-stood rich young women far too well? That she knew how easy it was for them to become so self-centered they never thought of anyone else? Who knew what Angie Kilpatrick's motives were in being so nice to Dillon and Christine?

She only wished she'd thought to ask that question of herself before she'd invited the woman to stay with them.

Never mind. She would be gone soon.

"I just think you should be careful of her. That's all."

Dillon gave her a sharp look and paused with a spoonful of cobbler halfway to his lips. "Why?"

Harper shook her head and smiled. "I'm sure she's very nice, Dillon. Maybe she just reminds me too much of myself when I was young."

Dillon smiled. "That doesn't sound too bad to me."

If he only knew.

"Just be careful, son."

"Believe me, Mom, I've made all the mistakes with women I intend to make."

Harper wasn't reassured.

"YOU MEANING TO RIDE with me today?" Shep asked when Dillon climbed into the cab of the flatbed truck they used to transport hay and straw.

"I've got a little business to conduct with Mr. Bowman."

Shep chuckled. "You mean you aren't going to let him have this hay until you get your money."

"In cash," Dillon said.

"Did that woman make you an offer for the farm?" Shep asked after they'd pulled onto the main road.

"It's Mom's place," Dillon answered, his tone discouraging any more questions. "She wouldn't make any offers to me."

Shep was impervious to hints. They came from different ends of the social scale, and Shep was as short, wiry and blond as Dillon was tall, muscled and dark, but their friendship recognized no differences.

"What are you going to do if she sells?" Shep asked.

Dillon didn't want to think about the Angie who'd come to wreck his home. He much preferred the sweet-lipped, warm-bodied woman who wriggled her toes in the grass and kissed him with a heat equal to his own. That Angie had touched something inside him he thought Evelyn had killed.

He preferred to think about the woman who'd convinced his daughter to hug him. He hadn't been prepared for the force of his feelings when he'd held Christine in his arms. Nothing like that had happened before. Any contact between them had been tentative and uncomfortable.

But that had changed in the few seconds it took Christine to hug him and for him to hug her back. She was his daughter, his flesh and blood, and he loved her more than he ever thought possible. He had to find a way to convince her that he loved her, to let her know he wanted her to love him.

To do that, he needed a home, one he could call his own, one no one could sell out from under him. But that wasn't all. Christine's response to Angie had showed him something he'd tried to ignore. Christine needed a mother.

But that was another question altogether, one Dillon didn't feel ready to face just yet.

"If she sells, I won't stay here," Dillon said. "I know a couple of places in Virginia looking for a good manager right now." He couldn't watch his mother waste his heritage on that mill. Neither could he watch his land be taken over by strangers, fields cut up, barns pulled down.

"Your ma won't sell if it'll make you leave."

"I don't know." Shep didn't understand how his mother felt about the mill. Hell, for that matter, neither did he. "We both have a lot to think about."

"Like the buyer?" Shep said, giving him a dig in the ribs.

Yeah, like Angie. That was something else he hadn't figured out. He had headed down the lane with a pretty woman who excited his lust. He'd come back with a woman who'd somehow captured his heart.

What the hell was he going to do about that! What did he want to do about her? He didn't know. Well, that wasn't exactly true. On one hand, he knew exactly what he wanted. His body had been screaming the message loud and clear from the moment he took her in his arms.

But that wasn't the part that bothered him. What he'd felt last night was different from the passion-filled nights he'd indulged in since his divorce, different from what he had felt for Evelyn. He felt a strong physical desire for Angie, enough to last for months, maybe even longer.

But it was the other element that confused him because he couldn't put a name to it. It couldn't be love. He knew little about her except that she was rich, had a stepfather, and wanted to buy his mother's farm. Hardly enough on which to base a permanent relationship.

Yet that's exactly what he was thinking. She wasn't the kind of woman you could roll in the hay one night and forget the next. And if he'd been foolish enough to think so, her handling of Christine would have convinced him otherwise. And therein lay the dilemma. She'd burst into his life in three areas—his home, his livelihood and his family. Each confused rather than clarified the other.

He was probably reading too much into things. Too much moonlight, too much emotion. Things would probably look very different in a day or two. Besides, Angie might decide not to buy the farm. He didn't want her to buy it, but he didn't want her to leave, either. He was startled to realize he liked her right where she was.

"What do you think of the lady?" Shep asked as he blasted his horn at a truck disputing his right to the center of the road. "She sure looks grade A, number one to me."

"None of your business," Dillon said. "And next time don't try to take the side off the truck or you'll have the hay scattered over half the county. We'll play hell getting any cash out of old man Bowman then."

Shep laughed and didn't slow down one bit.

ANGIE HAD NEVER KNOWN what it was like to be part of a busy household. Even when she was a child, her home had been filled with quiet and solitude. And she'd lived alone since college. So she was immediately knocked off center the next morning by the flurry of activity engendered by eating breakfast as a family and all the preparations for getting Christine and Harper on their way to school and work.

She'd envisioned enjoying a cup of coffee and the morning paper surrounded by the quiet of the countryside. Instead, Christine had latched on to her and enlisted her help getting dressed. The girl had discarded three outfits before settling on shorts and a T-shirt with a surfer on the front. Then she needed help with her ponytail as Floretha called to them from downstairs.

Breakfast was not exactly calming, either. Floretha hovered while nagging Harper and Christine to eat slowly. The abundance of hearty Southern cooking almost enabled Angie to forget her disappointment that Dillon had eaten more than an hour earlier.

Then it was over, and Angie finished her coffee while Floretha cleaned up. Floretha declined Angie's help.

"I've been cleaning up around here for almost fifty years. I wouldn't know what to do if I didn't keep on."

"After that long, I'd think you'd want to retire," Angie said, forgetting for a moment that the housekeeping arrangements at Weddington Farms were none of her business.

"I could have. My daughter wants me to go live with her. She's got a nice job in Kansas City." The old woman topped off Angie's cup of coffee. "I was considering it when Dillon and Christine came home. That child is my third generation of Weddingtons. I couldn't leave." She laughed heartily. "Did you know Harper tried to hire a housekeeper to help me? I don't need somebody else getting in my way. Besides, if I left here for Kansas City, I'd be sitting around that apartment all day waiting for my girl to come home. This way I have family all day long and get paid for it besides. But Dillon better find himself a wife to take over one day. I can't keep doing this forever."

Angie left Floretha to her work and went out in search of Dillon.

"He took a load of hay and straw to the other side of Camden," one of the men told her. "They ain't paid us for the last load. Dillon said he didn't aim to leave the place until old man Bowman coughed up his lungs or the money."

So Angie saddled a horse and spent the morning riding the lanes, estimating the cost of putting in training facilities, determining how many of the present buildings could be adapted to her needs and making projections about future expansion. She was trying to decide whether a drainage ditch could be incorporated into a steeplechase course when Dillon rode up.

"See everything you wanted to see?" he asked. The hard edge had returned to his voice. Last night she'd been his companion, but this morning she was a threat once more.

"Pretty much," she answered.

His clean jeans and shirt clung to every curve of his well-muscled body. He rode a powerful chestnut gelding she hadn't seen before.

"Did you get your money?"

He looked puzzled.

"From the man you were going to throttle until he coughed it up?"

His smile took some of the stiffness out of his expression. She wished he'd smile more often. He was a very handsome man.

"Yes. He'd just unloaded a van with nine horses from a big stable up north. They had to pay or bed them down on clay. I went straight to his bank and cashed the check."

Angie couldn't hide her surprise. "You mean you carried that much cash all the way back from Camden?"

"Sure. In my hip pocket. That way I know I've got it."

Angie was so used to dealing with checks and credit transfers she'd almost forgotten what money looked like. Cash to her was a line of numbers on a computer screen. For reasons she couldn't quite explain, Dillon's exchange of money for hay made everything seem much more vivid, the value of that money to the farm easier to understand.

She should have realized earlier that Dillon was the kind of man who would want the real thing. For him, getting his hands dirty and his muscles sore made the farm something worth working for.

With the exception of her horses, Angie had always worked at a distance from anything so real. But Dillon was real, and he was right next to her.

Angie felt a strange quiver in her abdomen. She was suddenly exquisitely aware of his physical presence. She couldn't imagine what she'd found so attractive about three-piece suits and blow-dried hair. As far as she was concerned, a little bit of dirt and sweat did more for a man than anything that came with a Dry-Clean-Only label.

"How much land were you looking to buy?"

"Not this much," she said, jerking her thoughts away from the powerful thigh that nearly brushed against her own. "I'd probably leave all but a few hundred acres under cultivation until I needed it." She could tell by his narrowed gaze she had caught his attention.

"What about the house?"

"I'd need that. I need some kind of headquarters, something to give the place character, a place for me to live and where I can put up important guests."

Angie was having difficulty keeping her business and romantic interests separate. That was a new experience for her. She'd never considered the possibility of combining them but Dillon was destroying her preconceived notions as quickly and thoroughly as he was destroying her composure.

He was also making her wish she could keep him on the farm, though whether for his benefit or hers, she wasn't entirely sure. The more she found herself thinking this farm was ideal for what she wanted, the more she felt guilty for taking it away from Dillon. She didn't see why fulfilling her dream should deprive Dillon of his. That would destroy some of her pleasure in her own success.

An idea occurred to her that was so brilliant in its simplicity she didn't know why she hadn't thought of it before. "Would you consider being my farm manager? I'll have my hands full trying to run the business end of things."

Dillon gaped at her in surprise. "Your farm manager?"

Angie couldn't understand why the idea should be such a shock to Dillon. The more she thought about it, the more she liked it.

"There's far more land here than I can use," Angie explained quickly, hoping he would give her a chance to show him the advantages before he rejected the notion completely. "It makes sense to keep anything not required for training horses under cultivation. There'll be plenty of acreage left over for cash crops and your horses."

She could see his skin pale under his tan. His eyes grew hard. He leaned forward in the saddle, staring at her as if she was a murderer.

"No!"

The word sounded more like a cannon shot than an answer to her question.

"Why not? I know it wouldn't be the same, but you'd still be working with the land."

"You don't understand," Dillon nearly shouted at her. "To you, this place is a big house that needs work. To me, it's memories, where I grew up, where

I fell down and skinned my knees, where I hid when I was hurt.

"It's the same with the land. You see it as so many training rings, obstacle courses, potential tracks and fields to grow your hay and oats. To me it's where I come from, where I belong.

"All people like you care about is the bottom line, profit or loss. You can't offer me a piece of this place, expect me to love it and tend it, then tear off another piece when you're ready. It's like watching something I love die a little at a time."

"I'm sorry. I didn't understand."

"No, you didn't, and people like you shouldn't even try. You should stay in your cities where you don't need memories or feelings about land and houses and trees."

Angie was so angry she started to shake. It made her even more angry that she felt like crying. If she didn't get away from Dillon, she was going to burst into tears.

"I didn't make that offer to hurt you. It may have been ill-advised, but it was well-intentioned." She gathered up the reins. "It's true that I don't love any land or house the way you love this place, but I like to think I'm capable of such feelings."

She backed her horse up. "You needn't worry that I'll force myself on you a moment longer. Give me an hour and I'll be out of your house."

She turned toward the barns and dug her heels into the horse's side.

"Wait!"

But she couldn't. How could she have fooled herself into thinking Dillon had any special feeling for her? At least now she had the answer to her question about whether he might pretend to like her as a way of holding on to his farm. He didn't like her at all, and not even his farm was inducement enough to make him pretend he did.

CHAPTER THIRTEEN

DILLON'S EMOTIONS were at war with themselves. He couldn't believe Angie would make such an offer. How could the woman who was so sensitive to Christine be so blind to his needs? She might as well have asked him if he wanted to watch while she cut his heart out.

At the same time, he knew she had tried to do something to ease his pain. She just didn't understand that nothing could do that, not if he lost his farm. But she had tried. He had to catch her and tell her he appreciated that.

Angie had no intention of letting him catch up, however. As he drew closer, she urged her mount into a gallop. When he narrowed the gap, she pressed the horse into a full-out drive. She was looking over her shoulder when her horse stepped into a rut, unbalancing her. Before she could right herself, the horse veered and jumped a mud hole.

Dillon realized to his horror that Angie was falling out of the saddle.

He watched helplessly as she tumbled end over end into a hay field. He was out of the saddle before his mount could come to a stop. He hurtled through the tall grasses to where she lay. His heart nearly stopped beating when he realized she wasn't moving. He would never forgive himself if she was hurt.

He knelt beside her. She lay on her side, and none of her limbs were at an awkward angle, but falling into a hay field didn't provide much cushion. He could see the rapid rise and fall of her chest. At least she was alive. He put his arm under her to lift her up.

"Don't move me," she said without opening her eyes. "I deserve to be left in a hay field. It seems a suitable punishment for such a shocking display of ineptitude."

He breathed a sigh of relief. Worry for Angie had overcome his anger. He saw only the woman he had hurt, and he was ashamed of himself. "I'm sorry. I never could control my tongue when I'm angry."

"Forget it. I shouldn't have made such an offer. It was insensitive."

She looked so helpless lying there, so vulnerable. He didn't know how he could have gotten so furious at her.

"Are you hurt?" he asked.

"Only my pride."

"Lie still," he said. He lifted each arm and then each leg to make certain nothing was broken. "How about your ribs? Does it hurt when I touch them?"

"No, but it tickles," Angie said. "Unless you want me knocking all your hay down, you'd better leave my ribs alone."

Dillon was so relieved nothing was broken his mood turned buoyant. He was so relieved he kissed her.

Angie looked shocked but not displeased. "You're certainly a man of swiftly changing moods. Just a moment ago I would have sworn you were ready to kill me. Now you're kissing me."

"I don't see any conflict there."

"That's what I don't understand. Most people would have to clear out one emotion before they could deal with the other. You can juggle several at once."

He'd been juggling conflicting emotions from the moment he met her. Only now the emotions had changed. He settled into the hay next to her. "Haven't you ever been angry with someone you found attractive?"

"Yes, but I can't recall kissing them at the same time I wanted to wring their necks."

"You've missed a lot."

"So it seems." She smiled a smile that was like the sun coming out after a rainstorm. "Kiss me again."

He smiled back. "Why?"

"I've never been kissed lying in the middle of a hay field. The novelty hasn't worn off yet."

Dillon found that an easy request to fulfill. She looked adorable half buried in hay. A green stain on each knee. Hair out of place. Her shirt torn at the elbow and a couple of scratches on her arm.

She lay back on the hay, invitation in her eyes. Dillon leaned over and kissed her gently on the lips.

"I'm not that fragile," she said. "If a tumble from a horse didn't break me, I don't think another kiss will."

Dillon lay down next to her, pulled her to him and kissed her hard on the mouth. He couldn't believe how good it felt to hold her in his arms. She felt slender and fragile, warm and soft. But she kissed him back with all the energy and hunger of a strong, self-confident woman.

He kissed her again, letting his tongue invade her eager mouth. He'd never kissed anyone lying in the middle of a hay field with the sun warming his limbs, the crushed green stalks cushioning his head. It was a deliciously decadent experience. Maybe that accounted for the unanticipated feeling that he could never get enough of this woman, that there was something different about her.

There was nothing coy about Angie's pleasure in his embrace. She responded to him eagerly. It seemed so natural, so easy. She made him feel better about himself than he had in years.

Angie's sudden laugh broke the spell. "I can't believe I'm lying in the middle of a hay field kissing a man I hardly know. If my stepfather could see me now, he'd have me locked up."

"Is there some other place you'd rather kiss me?"

She laughed again, and something tight and hard inside him seemed to unravel.

"That isn't the point. I'm a serious, organized, systematic, rational business executive. I don't do anything without thinking it through several times. I don't even buy underwear on impulse. Yet here I am—"

"I'm here, too."

"I know, but you're as changeable as spring weather." Her expression turned solemn. "What's happening?"

"I don't know. Are you frightened?"

"A little."

"Me, too." That was a lie. He was petrified. "Do you want to go?"

She shook her head. "What do you want to be happening?"

"I'm not sure I can put it into words." He'd always boxed his feelings up, locked them away, tried to ignore them.

"Try anyway."

He was afraid to try. Suppose he got it wrong? "Ever since I can remember, I've felt misplaced, like I should have been put somewhere else. Now I feel as if I just might be in the right place after all."

"Because of me?"

"Yes."

"How?"

"I don't know. I don't understand it yet."

"But you're sure it's because of me?"

"Yes."

Her smile was warmer than the sun, sweeter than the breeze. "That's enough. I can wait for the rest."

She pulled him down to her, into a passionate embrace. He could stay here forever, holding her close, kissing her soft lips, loving the feel of her body against his own. But mere mortals are seldom allowed to linger in paradise. His enjoyment was interrupted by the sound of an engine. He sat up quickly. "Someone's coming."

Angie sighed. "That's the trouble with having a lot of people working for you. There's always somebody peeping around the corner."

Dillon stood up and waved at the truck. "It's Shep."

Angie got to her feet. She was stiff, a little slow to move out of the field, but she was clearly uninjured.

Shep stopped the farm pickup. "Nearly gave me a heart attack when those horses came trotting down the lane," he said as he slid from the seat. "You two all right?"

"He didn't fall. I did," Angie said. "But not hard enough to do any more than hurt my pride."

"Let me help you in," Dillon said, leading Angie around to the passenger side.

"Ouch," she said as she hoisted herself into the truck. "Walking's a lot easier than climbing."

"What you need is some liniment rubbed all over you," Shep said, his eyes dancing with mischief.

"I'd smell like a horse," Angie replied with a laugh. "I think I'll try a hot bath first."

"Suit yourself," Shep said, "but liniment does it every time. It'll be no trouble to bring a bottle to your room."

"I'm casting my vote for the bath," Dillon said, glaring at his friend. "I have to eat at the same table with her."

Dillon and Shep climbed in on either side of Angie, and they bounced their way to the barn. They rolled up to the house just as Harper's car came up the drive.

Christine stomped out of the car the instant it stopped. She slammed the door with a fierce shove. Harper looked troubled as she got out. Christine stormed toward the porch.

"Christine, couldn't you at least speak to Angie and your father?" Harper asked.

Christine whirled on them as she reached the top of the front steps and cried out, "No! I hate Collins! I hate this stupid farm! And I want to go live with Grandma and Grandpa Stringfellow!" Then she turned and ran into the house.

"Young lady—" Dillon started, alarm making his voice stern.

Harper's hand on his arm stopped him. "Give her a few minutes to calm down."

"Mom, she can't be allowed to act like that."

"I know, but you're in the wrong mood to correct her."

"Then you do it."

"I tried all the way home from school."

"Well, somebody has to talk to her, and there's nobody left but Shep."

"Not this cowboy," Shep said, backing toward the truck. "I vote for Angie. I can tell you now, she'd sure turn my mood around in a hurry."

Angie? Dillon bristled at the idea. It would be an admission of his failure. But if Angie could get through to Christine as she had the night before, it would be worth it. "Would you?" he asked.

"I don't really know much about children," Angie said, clearly hesitant. "And I don't want to intrude."

"You won't. Please." That was one of the hardest words Dillon had ever said.

"What happened?" he asked Harper as Angie started toward the house.

"I don't know. She wouldn't tell me."

He looked toward his daughter's bedroom window. "Maybe I ought to go up. This isn't Angie's problem."

"You're upset. She won't talk to you when you're like this."

"I have a right to be upset. And Christine needs to learn that she can't talk to people like that. Mom—"

"I agree, son, but you've got to go about teaching

her those things in a different way. She's a wounded child, and you're not helping when you're harsh with her.''

''But Angie can help,'' Shep said. He'd never been slow to point out Dillon's mistakes with his daughter. ''I watched her with Christine the other day, riding. She seems to work miracles with her.''

''She's too much like Evelyn,'' Dillon said, his back up now. ''Rich, beautiful and used to getting her way.''

''I like her,'' Shep said. ''You could do worse, you know.''

Dillon's demon of anger pushed him hard. ''And what do you think she'd say if she found out I was a bastard as well as a lousy father?''

Harper's face turned white.

''Lots of women these days have babies without getting married,'' Shep said. ''Maybe Angie wouldn't care, not if she was sweet on you.''

Dillon felt heat rise in his face. He'd sworn never to mention that in his mother's presence. If he didn't get a grip on his temper, she'd be as angry with him as Christine was.

CHRISTINE SAT on her bed, Mrs. Stuart clutched in her arms. She didn't glance up when Angie entered the room. Angie sat down next to her.

''Things didn't go well at school today, did they?''

Christine hid her face in the folds of Mrs. Stuart's dress.

''That bad?''

Still no answer.

''When things used to go badly for me, I'd saddle my pony and ride until my daddy got home. Then

I'd throw myself into his arms and he would hold me until everything was better.''

Christine gripped her doll more tightly.

"What happened?" Angie asked.

Angie remembered how tough it had been when her own mother died. She'd been older than Christine, too. For nearly a year her stepfather had taken her with him everywhere. He'd never told her he didn't have time. By the time she'd recovered, Angie had come to depend on him more than she'd depended on her mother.

"Daphne Louise hates me," Christine said.

"Why?"

"She's always telling me how important her granddaddy is, that people like him a whole lot better than they like Grandma Harper 'cause he owns the bank. She says she's always bringing expensive presents to school to show everybody. She says that proves her grandparents are richer than mine. But Daddy won't let me take my presents to school. He says it's rude to show off. He says it hurts people's feelings.''

"He's right."

Christine's grip on Mrs. Stuart didn't slacken. "Then why does Daphne Louise do it?"

"Not everyone has such good manners as you. What else did Daphne Louise do?"

"She said my daddy doesn't have a daddy. She says when Grandma loses all her money, we're going to have to go away.''

Angie was amazed at the cruel things children said to each other. She wrapped her arms around Christine, doll and all. She knew Christine didn't really

understand the slur against her father. It was having
to leave Weddington Farms that frightened her.

But the ugly little rumor wasn't the kind of thing
a child would make up; Daphne Louise must have
heard that tale from someone else. Angie wondered
if Dillon had heard it, too, and how far something
like that would go toward making a man gruff and
alienated.

"People say awful things just to be mean. They
used to say things about my father, too. It used to
make me cry."

"You cried?" Christine asked in surprise.

"Oh, yes. Then I learned not to believe anything
until I talked to my father." Angie figured she didn't
need to explain that she was talking about her stepfather, that her real father had deserted her when she
was just a child.

Christine was silent.

"You see, nobody else loved me like he did. I
knew as long as he was near me, I was safe. If you
have a question, ask your daddy. But I can tell you
he won't leave you. He loves you very much. Now
I think you ought to go downstairs, give your father
a hug and tell him you're sorry."

"Why?"

"Because you hurt his feelings when you said you
didn't want to live with him. Just like Daphne Louise
hurt you. You don't want to do that, do you?"

Angie could tell this was a new concept for Christine.

"Do all grown-ups get hurt?" she asked.

"Yes. Sometimes a whole lot worse than when
they were little."

This appeared to be more than Christine could believe.

"Now, go down and give him a hug and tell him you love him. He cares for you very much."

Christine was reluctant, but once she started to move, she didn't hang back. She marched downstairs and did as Angie had told her. The words sounded as if she'd learned them by rote, but she said them. Angie just hoped she'd soon be able to believe them.

DILLON HADN'T EXPECTED to see Christine again until dinner. She often sulked for hours. He was stunned when she came downstairs, announced she loved him and told him to bend down so she could hug him. His reaction was immediate. He picked her up and hugged her tight.

Christine wiggled to get down long before he was ready to let her go. "I've got to go change," she said. "It's time for Angie to help me with my jumps."

Christine ran back to the house, but she looked over her shoulder before she went inside. Dillon wanted to believe it was a warmer look than she'd ever given him before.

Dillon looked to where Angie stood on the steps. He didn't know what to do about this woman. With one hand she was trying to take away his home. With the other she was trying to give his daughter back. He feared she was too much like Evelyn, but he felt himself wanting her more each day, *needing* her more each day.

She smiled at him, a crooked, sweet, half-apologetic smile. That's pretty much how he felt inside.

What the hell was he going to do!

CHRISTINE STARED into space, Mrs. Stuart in her arms, the riding outfit on the bed momentarily forgotten.

She could still feel her daddy's arms around her. It hadn't been a duty hug. She could tell. Her mommy used to give duty hugs when she was in a hurry to go out with one of her men friends. Grandma Stringfellow did, too, when she was all dressed up to go to the club. Daddy had squeezed her tight, and he hadn't let her go for the longest time.

"Mommy said Daddy was mean, that he didn't want me," Christine said to Mrs. Stuart. "Grandma said he would never ever let me see her again. But Angie says he loves me very much and won't ever leave me. What do you think?"

Mrs. Stuart looked at her out of glassy eyes.

"He does not like Angie more than he likes me. He likes both of us. Grandma Harper says so."

Christine marched over to a chair, sat Mrs. Stuart down so hard her glass eyes bounced.

"You shouldn't say mean things. If we have to move away, Daddy and Grandma Harper *will* take me with them. They will never leave me. Angie said so."

HARPER PICKED AT the chicken salad on her plate, even though it was the best thing on the menu at Deana's Diner, formerly the old dressmaker's shop on Broad Street. From across the table, Dessie reached for her plate and held it up to sniff the chicken salad.

"Doesn't smell spoiled to me," she said.

Giving her co-worker a strained smile, Harper put

her fork down and gave up the pretense. "Don't tell Floretha. She'll make me eat double portions tonight."

"You can't let this mess get to you," Dessie said. "You'll make the best decision you can, but that doesn't guarantee everybody's gonna be happy."

"But my *son?* Shouldn't I at least be trying to make my own son happy? Instead of trying to rescue the whole damned town first?"

"Let that boy work on his own happiness."

Bless Dessie's heart, she never minced words and she wasn't soft on anybody. That's what made her so invaluable at work, and as a friend.

"I'm afraid he's falling for this woman who's thinking about buying the farm," Harper said.

"Yeah? Dillon and a city slicker. Now there's a pair."

"It's more than that. Oh, Dessie, she's so much like me."

"Funny, some folks I know might think that would make her a pretty good catch."

She gave her friend a wry smile. "Not if you remember how I was when I was young. So determined to have everything my way, the rest of the world be damned. Oh, lord, Dessie, she's just so darned... rich."

Dessie chuckled. "And we know what trouble those rich women can be."

Despite herself, Harper laughed. "All the ones I ever knew, anyway."

"What is it you're really afraid of, Harper?"

"That she's toying with him to get what she wants." She lifted the paper napkin from her lap and began to twist it. "I think she knows I'll have trouble selling unless Dillon comes around. Dess, what if she's using him?''

''Harper, he's twenty-eight and I fully expect he knows his way around women.''

She wasn't convinced.

''There's more, isn't there?'' Dessie said.

Harper swallowed the lump in her throat. Where in heaven were all these emotions coming from, all of a sudden? ''He...he asked what Shep thought she'd have to say when she finds out he's...a bastard.''

Dessie dropped her fork onto her plate. ''Oh, for... Does he really think folks today give a damn whether his mother and father were married or not?''

''Apparently, or he wouldn't have brought it up.'' Harper stared into Dessie's concerned eyes and thought of something Floretha had said to her many years ago. ''And that's my fault. If I'd told him a long time ago, if I hadn't lied to him when he was young and tried to sugarcoat it, maybe he wouldn't feel this way. Maybe he wouldn't be having so much trouble with Christine. Maybe—''

''Maybe the national debt wouldn't be in the trillions, is that it, Harper? Sometimes you talk like a plain fool, woman. Shoot fire, most of us make plenty of mistakes when we're young. How long you gonna beat yourself up for yours, for Pete's sake!''

In her head, Harper knew that Dessie made good sense. But her heart had yet to be convinced. ''It's not that I'm trying to play the martyr. It's just...''

''Just what? You screwed up. You had a baby. How many other women in this world—in this *town*—do you think have done the same damn thing? And they don't find it necessary to shut themselves up in a smelly old textile mill for the rest of their lives.''

"This is old territory, Dessie. Besides, I haven't exactly been a hermit.''

Dessie grunted skeptically. Harper had gone out with men a few times after coming home. Most of them had been men Sam had approved and encouraged. Men who, in those days, were more interested in the Weddington wealth than in Harper and her son.

But behind her dissatisfaction with the men who had shown an interest in marrying the Weddington heir—gossip, reputation and all—was one bitter truth: the man Harper wanted, the man Harper still loved, she had driven away with her lies.

CHAPTER FOURTEEN

DILLON IGNORED the protests of Burton Rust's executive assistant and flung open the door to the banker's office. Burton might think he had Harper over a barrel, but Dillon had a surprise for him.

Burton looked up, surprise on his narrow, pinched face. Harper glanced over her shoulder, her expression bordering on hopeless. Angie looked unperturbed and unapproachable in one of her power suits.

"He won't extend the loan, will he?" Dillon asked.

Harper shook her head.

Dillon had never really expected Burton to give Harper more time to pay off the debt, and he was glad he hadn't sat by and done nothing.

"Come on, Mom," he said. "Let's get out of here."

"Now, listen, young man—"

"I talked to Bill Mott at the bank over in Clover," Dillon said in response to his mother's questioning gaze. "He says he'll give you the money to pay off this bloodsucker." He turned to Burton. "You remember the Motts, don't you?"

Rust smiled condescendingly. "Old Wendell Mott? He swept up at the mill back when Sam ran things, didn't he?"

"Right, but that job put Bill through college. Now

he's a banker and he said he'd be happy to help Mom.''

"Why, nobody from Collins has taken their business to Clover within living memory," Burton said, fairly sputtering. "Your grandfather would turn over in his grave.''

"If he knew what you were trying to do to my mother, he'd rise out of it and beat the hell out of you." Dillon slapped his hands on the desk and leaned so far across it Burton Rust started to back up. "Unless I get around to it first.''

Burton blanched. "That still doesn't solve the problem of the mill.''

"That won't be your concern. Come on, Mom, let's go." He turned to Angie, wanting to ask her to come with him, wishing she would decide to without his asking.

Her gaze was steady, but a faint smile curved her lips and her eyes were bright with interest. She gave her head a tiny shake.

After much pleading from Christine and another apology from Dillon, Angie had agreed to stay on at the house. She'd been a little reserved since then, but he'd never seen her conduct business. She was positively emotionless. To a man of his volatile temper, that was as frightening as it was incomprehensible.

He hesitated, then followed Harper out of the office. And there, in full view of three secretaries and one frowning executive assistant, his mother kissed his cheek.

"Still trying to rescue your mother from dragons.''

"That one, at least." He tucked her hand into the crook of his arm and walked out, wishing he weren't thinking about the woman still sitting in Burton's office.

"I appreciate what you've done, Dillon, and I'll speak to Mr. Mott right away," Harper said. "But Burton is right, you know. It still doesn't solve the problem of the mill."

"I know. Mom, there's one other thing."

"What?"

"It'll help if you can decide what to do without worrying about me." He unlocked her car door to keep from looking her in the eye. He didn't want to see her expression. Even more, he didn't want her to see his. "I've been on the phone to a couple of places in Virginia. They're looking for a farm manager with my experience."

The worst was over. He'd said it, committed himself.

"When did you decide this?"

"I can't wait around and let Burton Rust or anyone else decide what's going to happen to my life. Christine needs a place where she can feel safe. So do I."

Harper sank into the car seat. "Maybe I could..."

"Mom, you're never going to sell that mill. It can't stay open unless you replace all the equipment, and you're not going to get the money without selling the farm. That's not going to change, not now, not five years from now. I don't want to go, but anything is better than watching that damned mill swallow the farm one mouthful at a time."

"I'M SORRY FOR the interruption of our meeting, Miss Kilpatrick," Burton Rust said to Angie after the door closed behind Harper and Dillon. His complex-

ion was still ruddy with outrage. "Dillon Winthrop
has been an embarrassment to this community since
the day he arrived."

"I'm familiar with Mr. Winthrop's moods." And
not the least bit put off by this one. Neither did she
mind Dillon's suddenly taking the ball right out of
the banker's court. She liked to see a man defend his
turf. She stood. "I'd better be going."

"No need. Harper will be back."

"I don't know what Dillon or his mother will finally decide about the sale of Weddington Farms, but
I doubt they'll ever do business with you again. I
know I won't." She hoped her tone was as freezing
as it sounded.

Burton's reaction showed his astonishment at her
remark.

"The next time you or a member of your family
decide to say anything about Dillon's paternity, I
suggest you wait until your granddaughter is out of
the room. Those remarks were used to taunt Dillon's
daughter on the school grounds."

Burton turned fiery red.

"Good day, Mr. Rust."

G. E. Trent had long since run out of patience
waiting to hear from Angie. When he finally heard
his stepdaughter's voice, he was already grouchy.

"I expected to hear from you before now." He
knew he'd been sharper than he'd intended from the
moment of silence on the other end.

"Bad day?"

He sighed. "Sorry. How's it going?"

"Well, not exactly as I expected, to tell the truth."

"Trouble?"

"No, just a lot of possibilities to consider."

He was surprised at how hard his heart was thumping. He didn't want to hear about possibilities. He just wanted to hear that it was over and done with. "Such as?"

"Mrs. Weddington has far more land than I need, at least for my original plan. I was wondering if it would be a good idea to consider expanding into thoroughbreds."

Mrs. Weddington. The words stirred something painful and bitter in him. She wasn't a "Mrs." at all, of course. What a farce. He tried to imagine what she looked like after all these years. It was all he could do not to ask. "Buy the place now. You can go into that later."

"Dad, they've got three thousand acres. I can't use a quarter of that, even with thoroughbreds. But Mrs. Weddington's son is a farmer. I'm hoping to talk him into a partnership."

Her words blew a hole in his gut. "What?"

"They can pay off the debt and he can run the farm."

"You want to be partners with the Weddingtons?"

"Why not? I'll have the land and buildings I need, room to expand, and all the oats and hay grown right here on the farm. It's perfect."

Why not, indeed. He tried to think of a way to explain why not to his logical, business-minded stepdaughter. How to explain to her that this wasn't about making a profit? That this was about righting old wrongs, healing old hurts.

"Forget it, Angie. Buy the place outright. If you want to keep the farm running, we'll hire you a manager."

"But I like Dillon. And you would, too, Dad. He's—"

"I wouldn't like him," he snapped. Angie liked the boy. Damn, what a mess! "And if you think he likes you, think again. He's used to money, remember. And he doesn't have any now. How does that add up to you?"

Her silence said he had stung her, and he hated himself. He knew where she was vulnerable. And under these circumstances, he wasn't above playing on that fear.

"Look, maybe I'd better forget this," she said, her voice tight. "There are plenty of other places."

"Buy the farm. If you don't want it, buy it in my name."

"Whatever for?"

"Never mind what for. Just buy it and get out of there."

When they hung up, he realized his hands were trembling. He'd dug himself quite a hole. He couldn't even explain to himself what he'd hoped to gain from putting Harper Weddington and her family out of their home. He'd sent Angie down there and now she was entangled with the Weddingtons. With the son. He wondered if the son had red hair. Or violet eyes, like his mother. Sometimes the wondering almost drove him crazy.

Mostly, though, he didn't wonder about the son, just the mother. Maybe it was time to find out.

ANGIE WASN'T SURE how she'd found herself in Dillon's car, headed for a horse show in Charleston, with Christine between them. It was Saturday. She'd made a new offer to the bank in Clover, and nothing more remained for her to do in Collins.

But here she was, still hanging around Weddington Farms.

Still hanging around Dillon.

Angie didn't look at Dillon. She wasn't sure she could trust herself to be with him all day without doing something she hadn't planned on. If the kiss in the moonlight had been unexpected, the few minutes in the hay field had stunned her. It was clear Dillon liked her. Despite the issue of the farm, he still wanted her company. She wanted his, as well.

She gave up all thoughts of staying in control. For once she was going to let things happen. The prospect scared her, yet it excited her, too.

She didn't know quite what to expect from herself. She'd never had such a strong physical response to any man. But her feelings for Dillon extended far beyond the physical. Her thoughts had begun to center around a relationship that extended into the future.

Could she be falling in love with him?

The idea was preposterous. She'd known him such a short time! She was too levelheaded, too businesslike, too experienced to let that happen to her!

He was attractive, she liked him, she enjoyed being with him, but that wasn't love.

Yet what about her need to be close to him? Something had to account for all the excuses she'd given herself for staying on.

Maybe it was his vulnerability. She liked knowing a man was strong, but it was also important to know things mattered to him, that he could suffer a feeling of loss.

Angie admitted she also had a soft spot for Christine. Like her father, the little girl was afraid her world would fall apart again. They struggled to reach out to each other, neither understanding the other's need. Dillon loving, Christine needing to be loved, neither believing the other could accept or give what the other wanted so desperately.

Angie didn't know what she could do to make things any different, but she wanted to try. Was that love?

"Stop!" Christine shrieked as she pointed to a fast-food restaurant. "I want a hamburger."

"Floretha packed our lunch," her father said. "We'll eat as soon as we get to the fairgrounds."

"I don't want Floretha's lunch," Christine said. "I want a hamburger. Daphne Louise has them all the time. Please! I promise I won't complain about the horse show even if it's boring."

Dillon laughed at his daughter. "That's some promise." He looked over at Angie. "What about you?"

"I'd love a hamburger," Angie said.

"And french fries and ketchup?" Christine asked.

"Of course," her father said. "What's a hamburger without fries and lots of ketchup?"

Dillon pulled off the road and into the parking lot. "Hurry," Christine pleaded as she jumped out of the car and pulled her father toward the entrance. She grabbed for Angie's hand and pulled just as hard. "Come on," she said.

Angie looked into Dillon's eyes. She'd never seen him so full of laughter. He seemed to be saying that as long as the three of them were together, nothing else mattered.

For a moment Angie could almost believe it. She wanted to. She wanted to be part of this man's life. Dillon put his arm around her waist and pulled her along with him, just as if she belonged at his side.

"If I'd known about hamburgers, I could have bribed her into liking me a long time ago."

But Angie could tell he believed his daughter was starting to love him. She could also tell by the way he held her, the way he kept looking at her, that he included her in that feeling.

And Angie *felt* included. She felt as if she belonged.

Love, family and hamburgers. It was the American way.

"THIS ISN'T ANY prettier than your house," Angie said.

"It's a lot older." Dillon liked the feeling of satisfaction that spread all through him.

They'd stopped at the Ezra Walker Plantation on the way home from Charleston. Dillon said he wanted to show Angie something of South Carolina's history. What he really wanted to do was postpone going home. He wanted to prolong the day.

Christine dashed from one room to the next, looking out windows, behind furniture, into closets and around corners when the guide would let her. It was like being in a huge dollhouse. She constantly called to Dillon to come see something else she had discovered. He'd never felt closer to her than he felt now.

He knew a large part of his contentment came from Angie.

"Daddy, Daddy," Christine called. "She said we can go up into the attic."

"Why don't you go ahead. Angie and I want to look at the pictures."

"Okay," Christine called over her shoulder as she scrambled up the steep, narrow stairway.

"Has she worn you out?" he asked Angie.

"Just the reverse. I've been itching to get on a horse all day."

"If you had two or three of your own like her, you'd probably feel different."

Their eyes met. There seemed to be a new warmth between them. He'd never thought of more children. Now he did. Angie's children.

They wandered along the picture gallery, commenting on likes and dislikes. Angie was the perfect companion. She was the calm, steadying influence that balanced his temper and Christine's impetuosity. She knew just what to do, when to react, when to ignore him. It was as though she'd known him her whole life.

They kissed in front of a landscape. They held hands as they looked at a Louis Seize vase. They kissed again while the guide chattered on about carved paneling and heart-of-pine floors.

"What are you doing that for?" Christine asked. She had caught them ignoring a mahogany drum table.

"I like Angie," Dillon said.

"But why are you kissing her?"

"I kiss you because I like you, don't I?"

"Oh." That seemed to answer Christine's question, and she was ready to go.

Dillon wished he could answer his own questions

as easily. How was he going to separate the Angie at his side from the Angie who wanted to buy his farm? He couldn't. They were one and the same. He didn't know how he was going to deal with that.

THE IRONY OF DRIVING down the curving lane toward Weddington Farms in a shining silver Rolls-Royce escaped G. E. Trent. He was already focused on what waited at the end of the lane, already playing out a scene he had rehearsed in his head a million times these past twenty-nine years.

What he would say to her. Her tears. Her excuses. His disdain.

He knew already, of course, that it would never be the way he had imagined it. And that was what made his heart thump as wildly as it had when he'd been barely twenty. He'd had no idea then what he was walking into; he had no more idea now.

On first sighting, the house looked the same. Sprawling elegantly on a slight rise, white and shuttered, finished off with tidy sunrooms on either end, shaded by towering magnolias.

But as he drew closer he realized how different things were. The decades had taken their toll on the house, as they had on him. The paint was peeling in places, the shutters needed reattaching at this corner or that, and one of the columns appeared to be rotting at the top. His first reaction was regret, until he reminded himself that this deterioration was exactly what he'd hoped for. It was what made it possible for him to arrive like this with every certainty he would drive away the winner.

No matter how much he told himself that, however, he didn't feel it in his gut. There he felt every inch the ragtag interloper he'd been a lifetime ago.

He parked near one of the magnolias and got out slowly, still taking in the scene before him—the overgrown garden, the subtle signs of decay. He'd never imagined the sight of the place would fill him up so, would take him back so easily to who he'd been and how he'd felt. He wandered toward the back for a look at the barns and paddocks, in no real hurry now to see her. Seeing the place was enough.

He knew immediately that it was her, boot hooked over the lowest rung of the paddock fence. He knew from the shape of her hips in that denim skirt, though they were fuller now. He knew the toss of her head, with its short, dark curls. And he knew the flirty motion with which she reached across the fence and pulled down the brim of the hat on the young man in the paddock. And he knew her laugh, that lilting trill he had chased across bars and ballrooms, always hoping it would be hers and always disappointed.

Yes, it was Harper, still flirting with the farmhands.

"Some things never change," he said, loud enough for her to hear.

She stepped off the fence, turning so slowly that he knew she had recognized his voice. He watched her face for her reaction and discovered that some things had changed. Harper Weddington had learned to mask her feelings.

"Well, Trent," she said so coolly he couldn't begin to guess whether her unconcern was genuine or not, "I always knew you'd be back. I just never thought it would take you twenty-nine years."

CHAPTER FIFTEEN

Collins, South Carolina, 1968

SHE KNEW he would come back. He simply had to.

Day after day, she huddled in the window seat in her bedroom and stared down at the winding lane, hoping—praying—to catch a glimpse of his rusty old Chevy. Night after night, she listened for the uneven rumble of its engine.

With each day, with each night, her anxiety grew. What was she going to do?

Summer passed. She managed to hide the truth, although everyone wondered what had come over Harper.

"You're not yourself," Leandra said.

"You're up to something," Sam said.

"You are too weird for words," Annie Kate said.

Only Floretha knew the truth, and she finally convinced Harper to tell her parents. Three days before she was to leave for college, an oversize sweatshirt covering the jeans that would no longer zip, Harper put on her don't-give-a-damn mask and dropped the bomb during Sunday dinner.

"Congratulations," she said so casually she was proud of herself. Inside, everything churned around in such a fury she felt certain none of her insides were in the right place.

Sam looked across the table at Leandra, who barely looked up from the chicken cordon bleu. "For what?"

Harper smirked. "You're going to be grandparents. In about three months."

Leandra actually dropped her fork. Sam turned so red in the face Harper thought he might actually explode.

What he did was move so fast to get her into a home for unwed mothers in Atlanta that Harper barely had time to say goodbye to Annie Kate. She promised to write and explain what was going on, but she never had the nerve. For the next few months, she sat in the big, dingy old house and watched scared-looking girls come and go. She listened to the girls talk about the life growing inside them and how much they loved their babies and hated to let them go. Harper felt nothing but despair. Although she'd felt the same way at first, now that reality had set in, she hated this baby because she hated its father.

Because it had driven away the man she loved.

When she got out of here, she thought, she would find him. She would make him understand how scared she'd been and how sorry she was.

The baby didn't come early in November, when she'd expected it. It didn't come by Thanksgiving, either. Her baby was a Christmas baby.

"Do you want to hold him, just once?" whispered the nurse, who wasn't supposed to offer that option to the girls from the home.

"No," Harper said, no longer sullen and angry, just weary and feeling battered.

"Well, he's a perfect little doll, never mind his being a preemie."

Something sparked in Harper's chest. "A what?"

"Premature. Probably four weeks early, the doc said."

Harper sat straight up in the bed, her weariness suddenly gone. She counted from March in her head and confirmed the date Red's baby should have been born. "He's not early. He's late. He should have been born six weeks ago."

The nurse laughed merrily and patted Harper's hand. "Oh, no, darling. Not this one. I know late from early, and this one's definitely early."

"You're sure?"

"Sure as my mother's Irish."

Oh, God. If it was true... "I want to see him."

"That's my girl. You'll be glad you did. You'll see."

Impatient and on edge, Harper waited for the nurse to sneak the baby into her room. Suddenly afraid, she took the tiny bundle in her arms. It was warm, it squirmed and it seemed very little heavier than one of the kittens back home.

"It's so tiny," she whispered.

"That's what I'm telling you, darling."

With trembling fingers, Harper nudged the blue blanket away from his face. Sandy fuzz covered his pink head, and unfocused blue eyes stared back at her. A delicate notch dimpled his tiny chin. Harper's heart filled with anguish, then joy. For she knew the truth.

This was Trent's baby.

HARPER TOOK HER BABY and ran away in the middle of the night.

"You need a name," she whispered to her new-born son as they rode the Greyhound bus to its next stop. Where hadn't mattered. She only knew she had to get out of Atlanta, where Sam would surely look for her. "And you need a father."

The tiny fellow didn't pay her much attention. He kept dozing off. She started trying out names on him.

"Ethan," she said, and he grimaced. "Flint." A yawn. "Jeremy."

When she said, "Dillon," he finally opened his eyes and looked at her. "You like that one? Okay, Dillon it is. And next, I'll find your father. I promise."

She tried. She had her savings—all the money from graduation and birthday gifts that she had saved to finance her getaway after high school—and she did everything she could that next year to find Trent. Terrified of being alone and completely responsible for this fragile creature, Harper knew she had to find his father. He would know what to do. He had loved her once, and when he saw this little baby who looked more like him every week that passed, what could he do but love them both?

But she had little to go on. He had vanished, it seemed. Even his mother didn't know where he'd gone.

A year later, broke and defeated, Harper and her son got on another bus. When the bus stopped in Collins, she walked the rest of the way to Weddington Farms.

Sam and Leandra were less than thrilled with her story of the young husband who had died a tragic death. Sam was outraged.

"You don't think anybody's really going to swal-

low this crock of horse manure, do you?'' he'd bel-
lowed.

"They won't dare say otherwise to our faces,"
Leandra had replied.

Stymied, Sam had walked over and looked at the
sleeping child curled up beside his daughter on the
sofa. Gazing from his daughter to his grandson and
back again, his expression changed from fury to
something approaching hope.

"Always did want a son," he said at last. "If he
doesn't have too much white trash in him, maybe
things'll turn out."

Things had turned out. Dillon had been the light
of all their lives, serving eventually to begin the healing between father and daughter.

Collins, South Carolina, 1997

NOW, HARPER REALIZED, things were unraveling.

Now, after all those years of wondering where to
look for this man who had fathered her child, Harper
wasn't at all glad to be staring him in the face again.

"You don't look pleased to see me," he said, his
voice tinged with a bitterness she noted right away.

"I might have been," she said evenly, "if you
hadn't waited quite so long."

She wondered if he knew. She wondered what had
brought him back after such a long time. She wondered how he could still despise her. Unwelcome
emotion welled up in her chest.

"I want to know what's going on here," he said.

Shep swung his legs over the fence and landed
beside Harper. Trent glared at him. "This must be
your son."

Shep tensed, waiting only for a signal that his help was needed to fend off this silver-haired man in the European-cut suit and Italian leather shoes. Harper put a hand on Shep's arm. "It's all right."

"You sure?" Shep asked. "Dillon'll have my hide if—"

"I'm positive," she said. "I need to talk to him alone, Shep."

Trent looked as ready for a scrap as he had looked the day he ran out on her. And she had no intention of allowing that to happen in front of her son's best friend. She waited for Shep's reluctant retreat.

Then she leveled her toughest gaze on the man she had once wanted to see so desperately and said, "I don't have time for this."

She walked toward the house, heart racing. He was at her side before she reached the back door, taking her by the arm and whirling her around to face him.

"Where is Angie?"

Angie. He knew Angie. With every bit of control she possessed, Harper tried to hide the way her heart constricted painfully in her chest. "Oh, is she a friend of yours?"

"She's my stepdaughter."

Harper barely caught her gasp before it escaped. Oh, no. Poor Dillon. Poor Christine. Poor Angie, even, for Harper couldn't believe the girl knew anything about Harper's connection with Trent.

"Get off my land."

She stalked into the house, aware that he followed her, aware that they were now alone. Of all days for Floretha to be away. She glanced at the kitchen clock. Barely lunchtime. She couldn't count on anyone to rescue her. Her thoughts appalled her. The only person she'd ever thought of as a rescuer was bearing down on her, an unwelcome presence in her house.

"You needn't blame me for all this," he called out, coming through the dining room as she reached the curving stairs. "You were the one looking for someone to trap. I just happened to be there when you threw the bait out."

What he said was both fair and unfair, she thought, true and untrue. And no more than she'd said to herself a million times since.

She stood two steps up, looking down at him, and knew there was only one thing she wanted to say to him. The words swelled in her chest, but she knew she had to get them out.

"You're right." She couldn't keep the emotion from thickening her words, but at this point it hardly mattered. "I was a spoiled, selfish child. And I tried to use you because I was afraid. But I loved you. Only you."

He looked ready to protest, so she let the final words in her little speech tumble out. "And I always have."

Barely registering his stunned expression, she dashed up the stairs and sought out her room through a blur of tears. She dropped onto the bed, muffling her sobs in her pillows. Surely he would leave now. Surely this was the last thing he wanted to hear.

But God help her, it was true. She had loved him all these years, had held the hope alive in some bright corner of her heart. The hope that he would come back like some returning warrior and beg forgiveness for abandoning her. And here he was, her knight in Gucci loafers, looking a bit weathered around the eyes even if those eyes were still startlingly clear, the silvery curls suited him and his European suit clung to a body that was still trim.

But the years hadn't healed him. She saw it in his eyes and heard it in his voice, and that was what hurt the most. That they'd sat alone in their different parts of the world, hurting over foolishness perpetrated by a spoiled child.

And now that he was back, it was only a matter of time before he learned the most horrible truth of all. That he had a son he had never seen.

Through her sobs, she heard it then, a thump on her bedroom door, stunning her to stillness. She raised her head and looked back at the door, her hurting heart once again racing.

"Harper!"

Harper felt paralyzed. She couldn't let him see her like this.

"Harper! I'm warning you! Answer me or I'll—"

"Go away!"

The house fell silent and she imagined his soft shoes retreating on the worn carpet. She lay back on her bed, tears trickling down the sides of her face.

The next sound was her bedroom door slamming against the wall. She cried out, sat up and saw Trent standing there, glaring at her for all the world like an avenging hero. The moment was so perfect, so dreamlike, Harper almost laughed through her tears.

But before she could respond, he was above her, pinning her shoulders to the bed, his tortured face close to hers. "Don't say that. Don't ever say that again."

"But it's true," she whispered. "I'm not sure I

knew it myself until now, but it's the truest thing I've ever said.''

"Harper—'' The expression on his face grew pained and he closed his eyes tightly. She studied him as he fought whatever emotions warred for control of him. The lines on his face, some deep, some the merest tracing, seemed unreal to her. In her mind, Trent had never aged, had remained forever young and cocky. His silvery curls looked soft to the touch, and the line of his jaw looked as stubbornly sharp as it always had. His thigh, she realized, was resting against hers and his fingers were bruising her shoulders.

"Harper," he said again, and this time the fight had gone out of his voice. "Why?''

A faint smile stole across her lips as she heard the beginnings of forgiveness in his voice. "I was a silly fool, Trent. A silly, seventeen-year-old fool.''

"Oh, God.''

With no warning, he covered her lips with his harshly, demanding some satisfaction for the years and the betrayal and the pain. She understood everything she felt in his crushing kiss, for she felt it, too, and answered it with her lips. He had never kissed her this way then, when he'd thought her young and inexperienced, but it was the right kiss for now. The right kiss for a man and woman who had caused each other such bitterness, such anguish. Deep and hard and searing, it completed the cleansing that had begun with her words of confession.

Almost imperceptibly, the kiss softened. Trent's tense body also softened, lowered itself to hers. His weight warmed her. She slipped a hand beneath his jacket and felt the cool, soft cotton of his shirt, pressed her palm to it to absorb the heat and the giving firmness of his flesh.

No dream, she thought. *This is real.*

Fresh tears spilled from her eyes. She kept touching him, relishing the swell of his back and shoulders. She raised her hips slightly to press the pulse of his erection against her belly.

"We can't," he said, loosening his grip on her shoulders. But his words begged her to tell him otherwise.

Harper doubted that a moment of foolishness at forty-six could heal the wounds caused by a moment of foolishness at seventeen. But she didn't care. She had this, even if all turned to ashes in the very next instant.

"We must," she replied.

He looked into her eyes, a searching look she wasn't sure how to answer. Then he lowered his hand to her knee, drew it under her skirt, along her thigh, stalking her heat as he had the first time he'd touched her.

She moaned softly, heard the rustle of his zipper. With little adjustment, he was inside her, a deep, hard thrust to match the kisses they had shared. She cried out and began to meet his thrusts with a fierceness of her own. She clutched his shoulders, drew her legs around him, felt the fury in their every move.

Swiftly, their emotions peaked. She felt him swell within her, felt her own electric moment pulsing through her. She cried out and so did he, a sound ripped from his throat as if against his will.

He fell against her and she wrapped her arms around him. She reminded herself this wouldn't last. Reality would intrude all too soon, robbing her of this reminder of how it felt to be close to someone else, so close you weren't sure where you left off and he began. This brief connection would have to do her for the next thirty years, she supposed.

But it will be okay, she told herself. *I will be okay.*

When he rolled back, he touched her cheek tenderly, the way he used to do. The empty bleakness in his eyes had disappeared, replaced by that sense of wonder she had often seen there, after.

"You're crying," he whispered.

She shook her head, although her damp eyes made a lie of the gesture.

"This isn't..." He brushed an errant curl off her forehead. "I didn't intend to be such...such an animal."

She felt the tremble in her tentative smile. "It's how you felt."

He studied her for a long time, perhaps as unsure about what would happen next as she felt. "And how did you feel?"

"Like it's all unreal. Just another one of my..."

He waited, and when she didn't go on, he said, "Say it."

"Just another one of my dreams."

He nodded. "We have to talk."

And now, the end of the dream. "Yes."

Awkwardly they slid off opposite sides of her bed and straightened their clothes.

He paced the room, looking at things as if her personal belongings might offer some explanation for what had just happened. Harper's heart leaped when he stopped at her dresser and picked up the framed photo of Dillon and Christine.

"This is the boy," he said.

"Yes." *Please,* she prayed, *let him put it down. Give me a chance to explain first.*

"Hardly a boy, I suppose," he said, and set the photo back in its spot between her mother's Tiffany lamp and the silver music box Dillon had given her for her thirtieth birthday.

She let out the breath she'd been holding. "No."

"That's his daughter?"

"Yes. Christine."

"So you're a grandmother."

And you're a grandfather. "Let's go down, Trent. There's a lot we need to…"

He picked up the photo again. She knew the minute recognition dawned from the way his back and shoulders tensed. He turned to her, the color drained from his face. She closed her eyes, sagged against the chest of drawers.

"My God," he said. "Oh, my God."

"Trent, let me explain."

He laughed, an ugly sound that chilled her. There was no anger in his face, but the coldness that had come into his eyes immobilized her. He looked at her, then back at the photo. Still clutching the photo, he turned and walked out of the room. By the time Harper managed to get her legs moving, he was down the stairs.

"Trent, wait," she called.

He didn't even slow down. He walked out the way he'd come. She was still standing at the top of the stairs when she heard his car roaring back down the lane toward the highway.

CHAPTER SIXTEEN

THE CAR HAD barely stopped in the driveway when Christine tumbled out into the dusky twilight, eager to tell her grandmother about the day's events.

"I never thought she'd be so excited about a horse show," Dillon said to Angie.

"She did seem to have a good time," Angie agreed.

Dillon smiled as he watched his daughter run up the steps. "The best since she came to live with me."

The day had been the happiest Dillon had spent in a long time. Christine had chattered almost nonstop. But more importantly, she had chattered to *him*. She'd ignored him for so long he felt overwhelmed by her sudden attention.

"I enjoyed it, too," Angie said. "Thanks for letting me go along."

Reluctant to let go of the day's magic, Dillon wasn't ready to go into the house. He turned toward a barely discernable path among the azaleas. "Do you mind walking for a few minutes? Christine won't stop talking for half an hour."

"I'd love to if you're sure the azaleas won't swallow us up."

He knew the house and grounds needed attention, but he hadn't noticed until now how badly overgrown everything had become. He hadn't noticed a lot of things until Angie arrived. It was as though he had been sleepwalking through life, postponing everything that mattered.

His life had no focus, no purpose. He'd come home with his daughter to find one. But he realized, now that his plans were blowing up in his face, that purpose wasn't something he could find on the outside.

And what was the answer? He wanted his land, his daughter, a family, a feeling of belonging, the satisfaction of good clean physical exhaustion at the end of the day. He was a farmer, a country boy, and he'd never be anything else.

They walked together down the path dotted with patches of weeds between the stepping stones.

"Summer and fall nights are always beautiful here, but I like spring the best. I always was a sucker for the promise of a new season."

"Did you always want to farm?"

"Always. Nothing is more essential to life than the earth under our feet."

"That's an unusual attitude for a man these days."

"No more unusual than a woman leaving a successful career in banking to open an equestrian center." They had wandered into a forest of azaleas. "Actually, I want pretty much the same things as most people."

"And what would they be?" She smiled softly. "I don't think you're at all like most people."

She was going to make him put it into words.

"I want a better relationship with Christine. I'm short-tempered and I don't know much about children, but I want her to come to me when she needs comforting. I want to see her smile and laugh with happiness when I come home."

They had reached the small gazebo in the middle of the yard. It looked forlorn, abandoned, its paint nearly gone.

"That all?" Angie asked.

"I want someone to share my life," he said. He watched her face. It was easy to see in the moonlight, but he couldn't see any change in her expression. "Someone who'll love me, Christine, the life I've chosen. Someone who can bear with my temper."

He sighed as he squared his shoulders and shrugged off some of the tension brought on by his confession.

"Now it's your turn."

Angie smiled. It was such an easy, natural smile.

"I want my horses and enough land to enjoy them," Angie said. "I also want a family. I want stability, a feeling of belonging. I've never lived anywhere for long. And I lost both my parents. Maybe that's why I've clung to my horses. They wouldn't leave me, even if they do dump me on my backside from time to time."

"Doesn't sound like we're very different," Dillon said.

"That's what I figured," Angie said.

Then she was smarter than he was.

"Do you trust the slats?" Angie said, speaking of the bench in the arbor.

"We'd better not."

He knew it was his turn to speak. He wanted to, but the words wouldn't come. Everything seemed to well up and jam in his throat. He compromised by taking her hand.

She let him.

It seemed right. He could see himself still walking in the shadows of the oak and magnolia trees years from now, holding Angie's hand, searching for words to explain his feelings. He wanted to walk with her, to share his days, to share his nights, to share himself as no one had ever let him share.

With her he didn't feel the sense of loneliness that had been his companion so much of his life. Is this what a man felt when he fell truly in love? Could it be as simple as the desire to walk hand in hand through a garden, hearts forever linked?

Giving in to impulse, he pulled her into his arms and kissed her gently.

"What was that for?" she asked a trifle breathlessly, when she emerged from his embrace. "Before you answer, let me warn you that it had better not be thanks for keeping you company all day."

He held her close. "It is, but only a little bit."

"It had better be very little."

"What would you want it to be?"

"That's one question you have to answer. You'd better think carefully before you do."

He chuckled softly. "I don't have to think about what I feel. I just have to try to understand it well enough to put it into words."

"So far, so good," she said, leaning against him as they started to walk again.

"I like you."

"That's a relief. It's nice to know you don't go about kissing women you dislike."

"I'm thinking about a partnership," he said, welcoming the lighthearted feeling she injected into the evening.

Angie stopped dead in her tracks and turned to face him. "If you're going to start talking business—"

He kissed her. It might not be the most effective way to silence her, but it was the most enjoyable.

"I see you're not."

"No," he whispered without letting their lips completely lose contact. "But about that partnership..." He didn't finish his thought. It didn't seem necessary at the moment. Angie was kissing him back, and he found that more to his liking than talking.

"About this partnership," she murmured a little while later when her head was resting against his shoulder.

The screen door to the house slammed. "Daddy!" It was Christine. "Angie! Floretha says it's supper time!"

"You'd think with three thousand acres, a man would have a little privacy," Dillon grumbled. But he wasn't entirely unhappy. Christine had called his name first. "We'll have to continue this later. Don't forget where we left off."

"Not a chance," Angie assured him.

TRENT WALKED THE STREETS of Collins, feeling once again like an exile, an outsider.

His suit lay in a heap on the floor of his room in the motel outside Camden, which was how far he'd driven before his fury ran out. Then, with the freeway back to Charlotte just a few miles off, he had realized that running away wasn't the answer. Not this time.

Trouble was, he didn't know the answer.

He'd sat on the foot of the king-size bed trying to

focus on the motel TV, where baseball aired on the sports network. His mind wouldn't stick to the game. He was restless. He was making himself crazy, staring at the framed photo he'd carried out of the house at Weddington Farms.

He'd changed into jeans and a faded sport shirt and headed out for a drive. Just to clear his head. He'd ended up in Collins, parked along Broad Street.

So he walked.

He paused in front of the fire hydrant, remembering the first time he'd laid eyes on Harper. He noted the new sign and the new name for the textile company she now ran and tried to reconcile his memories of the reckless hoyden she had been with the idea of her as a businesswoman. He walked until he found the mill cottage he'd lived in those few short weeks and was pleased to see how nicely all the houses on the street had been renovated.

He couldn't find the spot in the woods where he and Harper had first made love. The land had been cleared and houses built during the boom in the seventies.

"Whatcha lookin' for, mister?"

Trent turned toward a freckle-faced boy, maybe eight or ten, sitting on his bike at the end of the cul-de-sac.

Good question, Trent thought. "Nothing, really. I used to hang out here, that's all."

The boy looked skeptical. Trent supposed it was hard for this kid to imagine a silver-haired old geezer like Trent ever being young enough to hang out.

"Are you homeless? Mom says homeless people don't have cars and that's why they walk around all the time."

Homeless? "I suppose you could say I am."

The boy's eyes grew wide, and in a flash he pedaled away, no doubt having been warned about strangers. Trent smiled and kept walking, between two houses and into the woods beyond.

Was he homeless? He hadn't thought so, but he supposed he'd really been nothing but an interloper for thirty years now. Living in somebody else's house, living off somebody else's money, loving somebody else's daughter. None of it was his. None of it made him belong.

The one thing he'd belonged to, he'd walked out on.

He hadn't expected to be so moved by the sight of Harper. She was older, of course, but no less beautiful than she'd been as a girl. More so, actually, because the willful petulance had left her eyes and no longer molded her lips into a pretty pout. The years had added grace and softness. Or maybe it was simply life, and the pain it always brought, that had made the difference in her.

But it wasn't her beauty that had caught him by the throat. What had shaken him was the realization that he had built his life on self-deception, a foundation Harper had snatched from beneath his feet.

When Trent left Collins, angry and wounded, he'd told himself he hated Harper, as he hated all rich people. His anger had driven his marriage to Angie's mother, a marriage that had turned out better than he had any right to expect. He had never felt great passion for his wife, but he grew to love her tender ways. And he dearly loved his stepdaughter, who became the focal point of his life.

Although Trent had been a good and faithful husband for many years, he had never been content. Over the years, whenever he thought of Harper, the only emotion he allowed himself was a glimpse of his old anger. The purchase of Weddington Farms, the site of his worst humiliation, was to have been the death blow to whatever anger and hurt remained. With that gesture, he'd told himself, it would be over.

But when she told him she'd loved him all these years, Trent had realized the truth about himself. He couldn't have nursed this grudge for so long if he hadn't still loved her, too.

For a few moments, that had seemed to make things so simple. For a few moments, he had been inside her, been a part of her, and his heart had soared with the certainty that love could overcome three decades of bitterness.

Then he'd seen the picture and had known the truth. He had a son. And she had kept that from him.

But why? None of this made sense. He'd heard her himself, the day they'd planned to elope, crying on Floretha's shoulder about the baby she was carrying. The baby she'd tried to foist off on him. The baby she'd said was Red Jannik's.

Why?

An ache began in the center of Trent's being, and spread like a mushroom cloud of longing and poison. His son. A boy he'd never seen growing up. A man he couldn't hope to reach at this late date. The need to drive back to Weddington Farms, to see this young man with his own eyes, to hear his voice—the need was so powerful it hurt clear to the ends of his fingers.

Harper had robbed him of so much.

How could he forgive her? How could he forget?

DILLON AND ANGIE hadn't been able to resume their interrupted conversation. Neighbors had dropped by after dinner Saturday night. By the time they left, Angie and Christine had already gone to bed.

But the biggest reason was Harper. She had been acting downright peculiar ever since they got back from Charleston. She would sit in silence for long periods of time, seemingly unaware when people spoke to her. When she did talk, she left half her sentences unfinished. She was in a fog and showed no signs of coming out.

Floretha, who had also been gone for the day, didn't know what was wrong. Dillon thought he'd solved the mystery when Shep told him a man had stopped by Saturday afternoon. Dillon wondered if it was Bill Mott with bad news, but Harper assured him she had talked to the Clover banker by phone and things looked promising.

What with worrying about his mother and a small emergency at the farm, it was Sunday afternoon before Dillon found himself alone with Angie again.

Actually, they weren't alone. They were leaning against the fence watching Christine ride Eddie around the jumping ring. Dillon had had to practically restrain Angie from saddling up and joining his daughter. It made him wonder if Angie could ever love him more than she loved her horses.

Because he was convinced she *did* love him. She had to know he'd been on the verge of asking her to marry him last night. She'd seemed as disappointed as he when they'd had to go inside. As long as he didn't think about the farm, he had no question in his own mind that his feelings were strong and clear.

He was about to broach the subject again when he

noticed a silver Rolls-Royce coming down the lane toward the barn.

"Who could that be?" he muttered.

Christine rode up to the fence. "Did you see me?" she asked. "I didn't miss a jump."

"We saw," Dillon said, turning back to his daughter. "Why don't you ask Angie if it's time to raise the jumps?"

"Not yet," Angie said. "Give it a few more days and—"

"That looks like Grandpa Stringfellow's car!" Christine exclaimed, pointing toward the approaching vehicle.

Dillon felt a chill of dread destroy the warmth of the afternoon. If the Stringfellows had come all the way from California, it could only mean trouble. He was relieved when a man he didn't recognize stepped out of the car.

"Dad!" Angie called.

Angie sprinted away, and Dillon found himself feeling jealous. He thought of Angie's affection as belonging solely to him and Christine. It was clear that her love for her stepfather was even greater than anything that had yet had time to develop between them.

"Is that Angie's daddy?" Christine asked.

"It seems so," Dillon replied.

"He looks like you."

Dillon paid no attention to Christine's comment. He was too caught up in the way he had overreacted to the situation.

"Is he going to take Angie away?" Christine asked.

"I don't know," Dillon replied. They were coming this way, Angie holding on to the man's arm. "I guess we'll know soon."

As soon as Trent laid eyes on the strapping young man with his hair and his eyes and his chin—maybe even the same chip on his shoulder—he knew he'd made a mistake.

Angie slipped her arm around his waist and returned his squeeze. "Why didn't you let me know you were coming?"

She was leading him to the gate, where the young man and a little girl on a horse waited. Trent's resolve faltered.

He stopped. "Come with me, Angie. We need to talk."

Angie slipped from beneath his arm and looked at him, puzzled. "Can't it wait? I want you to meet Harper and her family."

Trent stared into the smiling face of the young woman who had trusted him with her happiness for so long and knew an added anguish. How could he ever explain his willingness to use her in his petty little scheme?

"Later, Angie. We can do that later. First—"

"Angie!" An impatient child's voice interrupted them.

Angie laughed. "I was just telling Christine how well she's riding. You're the one who'll have to wait." Then she took him by the hand and dragged him with her.

What had he done?

"Dad, this is Christine Winthrop, soon to be one of the premiere horsewomen in these parts."

Trent looked into the tiny, heart-shaped face of the

little girl sitting on the fence. She smiled proudly at Angie's words, revealing one missing tooth and a dimple that was destined to be a heartbreaker. This child was his own flesh and blood. Feelings he'd never expected overwhelmed him. He ached with the longing to put his arms out and have her fling herself into them, the way Angie had at that age. He had to swallow hard to ease the lump in his throat.

Christine. His granddaughter.

He put his hand out to shake hers, and she hesitated only a minute before leaning across the fence and taking it shyly and quickly.

"I can't tell you how pleased I am to meet a soon-to-be premiere horsewoman. If anyone would know, it's Angie."

"She's teaching me to jump. I didn't fall once. Wanna see?"

"I expect he wants to talk to Angie, Christine. Why don't you take Eddie back to the barn?"

Christine didn't move, but the stern voice commanded Trent's attention. He looked into the eyes of his son.

The young man radiated power, from the work-roughened fists on his hips to his sun-bronzed face and the hard glare in his eyes. He looked sure of himself, and protective of everything within his reach. Christine, Weddington Farms and, yes, even Angie.

Trent wondered how much he knew.

"And this is Dillon Winthrop. Dillon, my step-father, G. E. Trent. I can't get over this wonderful surprise!"

After glancing at Angie, Dillon also thrust out his hand. "Welcome to Weddington Farms."

Some part of Trent wanted to laugh at the brusque-ness of the welcome. The young man had obviously also inherited his manner from his father. Drawing a deep breath, Trent accepted the handshake. It was, as he would have guessed, firm. A challenge, man to man.

Angie is mine now, the handshake seemed to say. *What do you have to say about that?*

Oh, what a mess to straighten out. He thought for the moment the only thing to do was walk away from it, trust that he and Harper could keep this secret another thirty years.

"Thanks," he said, surprised he could find his voice. "Thanks for...taking care of Angie."

"Mr. G. E., why do you look like my daddy?"

The words shot through Trent, leaving him feeling naked and unprotected. He expected to look around and see horror in the eyes of his stepdaughter, his son. But Angie merely laughed.

"Don't be silly, Christine," Dillon said. "It's just that we're about the same size, that's all."

"Why don't we go in," Angie said. "I want you to meet Harper."

"We've met," Trent said without thinking.

"When?" Angie sounded astonished.

"You know my mother?" Dillon sounded not the least bit pleased by the revelation.

"Yes," Trent said, knowing he'd made a mistake and not knowing how to get out of it. "A long time ago."

"You never told me that."

"Well, I—"

"Grandma says I have a dimple in my chin just like Daddy," Christine interrupted with the obstinacy of a child who won't let go of an idea until her curiosity is satisfied. "She says that makes me Daddy's little girl. You have one, too. Does that make Daddy your little boy?"

Trent looked from Christine to Angie to Dillon. He saw the naive certainty in the little girl's eyes. He saw the confusion sweep into Angie's eyes as she studied his face, then Dillon's. And he saw the challenge in his son's eyes deepen to mistrust.

"Christine, take Eddie back to the barn."

"I only asked. Grandma says it's not rude if you ask politely."

"Now!"

Trent's heart pounded painfully. His palms were sweaty, his throat dry. He had to get out of here. He cast about for the words that would dispel Angie's doubt, Dillon's anger. But as his gaze locked with Dillon's, he knew his son could read the truth Trent didn't know how to hide.

"Dad, I don't understand," Angie whispered.

"I want you to tell me what the hell's going on here," Dillon said, taking a step forward.

Trent expected a flying fist to follow at any moment. "I think you'd better talk to..." He held a hand out to Angie. "Angie, come with me?"

"But Dad..." She didn't move. Her voice trembled with uncertainty.

Everything was closing in. Trent didn't know what to do, what to say. He'd never intended this to happen. All he'd wanted—needed—was to see his son.

"I'd better go," he said.

He backed away, watching his son's stunned reaction as Angie took her stepfather's hand.

DILLON GAPED AT THE MAN as though he were a raving maniac. But even as his brain told him there must be some reason why Mr. G. E. Trent didn't simply tell Christine she was wrong, his brain registered the similarities Christine and Angie had already seen. It was almost like looking into the mirror and seeing an older version of himself.

"It can't be true."

Dillon heard himself speak the words, but they seemed to come from someone else. He was locked into immobility, staring at a suspicion so shocking his brain wouldn't accept it. It was as though everything in his life shifted. Everything was out of place, out of focus, out of the realm of possibility.

The full implication of Christine's words sank into Dillon's benumbed brain, and hot rage exploded all through him. He uttered a blistering oath and headed for the house.

ANGIE COULDN'T TAKE her eyes off her stepfather's face.

"Dillon isn't your son, is he?" Angie asked as she walked alongside Trent toward his car. "You aren't related. He just happens to look like you."

Trent stopped and faced his stepdaughter. "I'm sorry, Angie. Dillon is my son."

Angie didn't want to believe the words.

"How?" It was a stupid question, but it was the only word that came to mind. "That would mean... You'd have to... I didn't know you'd ever been to Collins."

"I talked to Harper yesterday. She told me then."

"You mean you didn't know?"

"It's a long story."

"I don't care. I want to hear it."

Trent gestured toward his car. "Can we go, Angie? We can talk while I drive."

She shook her head. "No. I... Just tell me."

He sighed. "I worked here. We were kids. We weren't supposed to fall in love, but we did. We had a misunderstanding. I left town."

"You never came back?"

"No."

"And you didn't know about Dillon?"

"No."

Things began to fall into place in Angie's mind. Her father's interest in the farm, his insistence that she buy it. She felt a stab of pain followed by a flash of anger. Was Harper the reason Trent had never wholeheartedly loved her mother? She had always felt guilty for receiving so much more affection from her stepfather. And all the time it was because there had been someone else. Harper Weddington.

"Did Mother know?"

"There was nothing to tell. At least, that's what I thought."

Angie could hardly believe it. She certainly couldn't understand it. "Why did you marry my mother?"

"For all the wrong reasons. You know that," Trent said. "But I came to love her. And I always loved you. From the very beginning."

He reached out and caressed her cheek. Angie fought the impulse to pull away.

"You were scared of your own shadow after your mom died. But whenever I was around, you seemed to feel the whole world was right again." He looked tired and defeated in a way she'd never seen before.

"I latched on to you just as desperately. I wanted to be everything you wanted me to be."

"I thought you were," Angie said. "Now I don't know."

DILLON FACED HIS MOTHER, who was sitting on the side porch, quietly talking to Floretha, as if she'd been waiting for him. For the second time in his life, he felt as if he were seeing a stranger. "I just met Angie's stepfather."

Floretha looked from mother to son. "I think I have potatoes to peel."

"There's no need." Harper sounded tired. "You'll hear it all sooner or later."

"Later suits me just fine," Floretha said.

"Who else knows?" Dillon demanded as Floretha departed.

"No one."

He'd always wondered about his father, but he'd never wanted to know who the man was. He'd never wanted to meet him. His anger had been too deep.

It still was.

"Why did he show up now?" Dillon asked.

"He came yesterday, looking for Angie," Harper said. Her shoulders sagged and her eyes looked a hundred years old. "When he saw your picture, he was so shocked I...I wasn't sure he would ever come back."

"I wish he hadn't. He hasn't been interested in me before. I can damned well do without him now."

"Be fair to him, Dillon. Trent didn't know."

"He didn't *know*?"

"No. We don't know what he would have done if he had."

"Why didn't you tell him?"

"I tried to explain all this before, but you wouldn't listen. Are you sure you want to hear it now?"

"I don't want to, but I suppose I must."

Not so he could understand Trent better. He wanted as much ammunition as possible to drive him out of their lives forever.

Then his mother told him a story that sounded like something out of a bad movie. A story about a seventeen-year-old girl and the boy who worked for her father. About a scheme to trick that boy into marrying her.

"Actually, it didn't take much tricking. He wanted to marry me."

"I'll just bet he did. Marrying the boss's daughter came with a lot of perks."

"But I didn't think Trent was your father."

"You mean there was someone else?"

A shadow crossed her face, but she didn't respond. "I knew it was wrong not to tell him, but I was in love and desperate to get away. When Trent found out I was trying to foist what I thought was another man's baby on him, he left town in a rage. Who could blame him? Then, when I realized Trent really was your father... I spent a year looking for him. He was gone."

He had had a father who might have wanted him, who might have loved him. "So you made up Kenneth Winthrop." He tried to hide the bitterness in his voice.

Harper nodded. "Some people didn't believe me. But after a while, they seemed to forget all about it."

No, they hadn't. Dillon could remember a thousand little looks and whispers that had stung him like pinpricks. As long as Harper had stuck to her story, he'd put it down to jealousy of his grandfather's wealth and position. When his own unplanned fatherhood had prompted her to tell him the truth, he had understood.

Now it all felt freshly painful again.

"What does he want?" Dillon asked. "Is he still after your money?"

Harper's laugh was harsh. "He's got enough money to buy and sell me several times over."

Dillon couldn't see any way out of the net that was closing around him. This man was his father whether he liked it or not. Dillon wouldn't put it past the man to threaten to tell everybody in Collins if they didn't sell him the farm.

Well, he could confess and be damned. Dillon had lived with whispers about being a bastard. He could certainly live with knowledge that his father was a rich banker.

But what about his mother? And Christine?

Equally disturbing, what about Angie?

CHAPTER SEVENTEEN

DILLON LEFT THE HOUSE in a daze. He ran into Angie perched on the edge of the dilapidated gazebo, knees pulled to her chest. Her presence stirred him from numbness to anger, until he realized that she looked as shell-shocked as he felt.

"You didn't know, either, did you?" he asked.

She shook her head. She seemed preoccupied, hardly aware of him.

"Where's your stepfather?"

"He left."

"Damn him! What makes him think he can just walk in here, drop his bomb and waltz out again like it didn't make any difference?"

"So Harper says it's true. He is your father."

Dillon cursed again. "I know you love him, but if he comes around here again, I'll break his neck. You can't think I'm going to welcome him with open arms."

"Nobody's asked you to welcome him," she snapped. "Nobody's asked you to do anything at all."

But Dillon was in no mood to be reasonable. For the first time in his life, he had a name, a face he could hate. He finally had a living breathing human being on whom he could pour out his anger and frustration at all the injustices in his life. And he wasn't about to be denied the pleasure of doing so just because it wasn't fair.

"I don't see why it's such a problem," Angie said. "You've always known you had a father. Count yourself lucky. He's a rich man."

"I don't want his damned money." Dillon glared at her. "Why did he send you here if he didn't know about me?"

"I don't know. I never got around to asking him."

"He came to make sure you bought the farm, didn't he?"

Angie shrugged. "I don't know."

"Why does he want it so much?"

Angie stood up. She folded her arms across her chest as she moved restlessly around the small enclosure. "I don't know that, either."

A fearful idea launched itself at the edge of his conscious thoughts. He fought against acknowledging it, but he couldn't shake its hold. Anger and bitterness were fertile ground for suspicion and doubt. He could see the hurt in Angie's eyes, he could feel her pain. But the ugly suspicion wouldn't let go.

What if Angie's falling in love with him had been a pretense, her offer to make him her farm manager a subterfuge, all to get him to agree to the sale of the farm? What if her sympathy for Christine was false, as well?

"Did you do all of this just so you could get the farm?"

"All of what?" she asked, her voice choked with emotion.

"Me, Christine, everything."

Angie looked as though he had slapped her. "You

think I'd pretend to be in love with you just so I could buy your farm?''

''Like you said, I'm as changeable as the weather. Falling in love in two days isn't something a methodical, rational woman like you would do.''

Angie walked over to him and slapped him, hard. She would have slapped him a second time if he hadn't caught her wrist. ''How could you say you loved me and think such a thing?'' she demanded. ''Were you pretending, too?''

The shock and anguish in her eyes brought him to his senses.

''I didn't mean to say that. I'm not thinking straight. I've always hated my father for leaving me. Now I find he's your stepfather, that he wants to take you and my farm from me! It makes me crazy.'' He clenched his fists so hard every muscle in his body grew rigid. ''I want to smash my hand into his face so bad I don't know what I'm saying!''

''Then I think you'd better figure it out before you say something that can't be forgiven.''

Dillon had the feeling he'd already done that. ''I'm sorry. Angie...''

''I'm going for a drive. I've got to think.'' She started back toward the house.

''When will you be back?''

She turned around. ''How can you ask me such a question after what you said?''

''Because I love you. I don't think I can live without you.''

''Then you'd better start learning.''

HARPER TOOK CELERY and carrots and green peppers out of the refrigerator and put them on the counter, telling herself her stomach wasn't quivering.

She took the knife from its rack, telling herself her hands weren't shaking.

At last, everyone knew the whole truth. She wished she knew how that made her feel. She wished she knew how it would make her son feel once the shock subsided.

She wished she knew how Trent felt.

"What in the name of merciful heaven are you doing with that butcher knife?"

Floretha's voice startled her. The knife clattered to the counter.

"Making—" Her voice broke. She paused and willed herself to composure. "Making a salad."

Floretha took her hand and led her away from the counter. "Heavenly days, child, you put that knife away right this minute. The state you're in, you'll find yourself without a finger. And wouldn't you be in a fix then?"

The gentle hand on her arm, the worried tone of the familiar voice were all it took to break her down. She flung her arms around the fragile old woman and held on for dear life. "Oh, Floretha, what a fix I'm in already."

"There, now, child," Floretha whispered. "It's going to be all right. It's all on the mend now. You can take old Floretha's word for that. You hear me, child?"

And like a child, Harper wept until the only emotions remaining were confusion and exhaustion.

Then she sat in one of the old kitchen chairs that had heard so many of her troubles over the years and spilled her heart one more time while Floretha finished dinner.

"What if he hates me, Floretha?" The anguish on her son's face when he'd confronted her filled her mind again, hurting her the way only a parent can hurt.

"That boy's never going to hate his mama. He might not be too cheerful for a while. And he might have a grudge or two against his father. But he'll always love his mama."

"But now he thinks I'm..." Harper struggled, remembering the contempt in her son's eyes when she'd said there had been someone else before Trent. "When I told him I believed, until he was born, that he was someone else's son, that Trent believed I'd tried to dupe him... Oh, Floretha, the look in his eyes..."

Floretha sighed and shook her head. "You didn't tell him everything, then? You didn't tell him the way it was?"

"I couldn't." The truth was, Harper had been able to tell only one person in her life what had happened between her and Red Jannik. She'd never been able to call it by its name. "How can I tell my son I was..."

Floretha put one gnarled finger under Harper's chin. Harper was forced to look her in the eye. "You were raped, child. The shame isn't yours."

Fresh tears streamed down Harper's cheeks. "But I was wild. You know what I was like. I—"

"You were a child and that bastard raped you." The venom in Floretha's words startled Harper. "I'd kill him if I ever laid eyes on him again. You tell your son the whole truth or I'll tell him myself."

"I will. When the time is right. When he's had time to adjust." Then another thought struck her. "If he doesn't leave first. He left once before. What if he leaves again?"

"He came back before. He'll come back again."

If there was a place to come back to. Harper's head began to throb. "I know *he* hates me."

Floretha gave her a long, solemn look. "Trent?"

Harper nodded and smeared away another tear. "He wouldn't even listen when I tried to explain."

"Well, he's sure stirred up a hornet's nest for somebody who doesn't even know all the facts. I'll say that for him." The old woman shook her head, turned back to the counter and took a loud whack at a cucumber. "Let it go, child. You've done fine without him all these years. You'll do fine without him again."

Harper tried to take solace in the fact that Floretha was always right.

IT WAS PAST MIDNIGHT, but Dillon didn't go inside. He wouldn't be able to sleep. Angie hadn't returned. Where was she?

She didn't have to come back for her clothes. She could buy anything she needed. She probably had a whole apartment full of things in Charlotte. She would never return to Weddington Farms because he was a fool.

He had intended to ask her to marry him. Twice the words had trembled on his lips before Trent had walked up and shattered his world.

He couldn't understand why knowing Trent was his father should have coldcocked him emotionally. If his father had to turn up, Dillon should have been pleased he was someone like Trent. He couldn't really blame Trent for leaving, either. Dillon was honest enough to admit he'd have left Evelyn to rot in hell if he'd thought she was trying to saddle him with another man's child. So why was he so angry and why had he tried to take it out on Angie?

"Is she back yet?" It was Harper.

"No."

Harper handed him a mug of steaming coffee.

"What did you say to her?"

"Something pretty awful."

"Oh, Dillon."

"I know. I was trying to hurt that bastard Trent, but I hurt her instead."

"Dillon, I've told you he didn't know about you."

"I know, dammit! I know!" Dillon cursed as he stumbled down the steps into the yard. Now the bastard was coming between him and his mother. He couldn't let that happen. Harper's love had been the rock that had gotten him through many of life's tough moments.

He looked up at the big house. Welcoming light poured from the windows, and he thought of all the years he'd spent here, of all the years he'd spent hoping to come back. And now Trent's presence threatened to drive them all away again.

"You might as well come inside," Harper said. "If she's upset enough to stay out this late, I don't imagine she'll want to talk to you when she gets back."

"She's not coming back." Dillon turned to face his mother. "I love her, but I drove her away."

"I did that once myself."

Dillon climbed the stairs and gave his mother a hug. "Screwing up seems to run in the family."

"Why don't you go to bed. Maybe tomorrow you can—"

"I can't go to bed without knowing what's happened to Angie. I'm going to look for her."

"Where?"

"Everywhere."

But there weren't many places to look, and he didn't find Angie in any of them. He had to face it. She was gone.

The few hours he managed to sleep after dragging himself back to the house didn't help his mood the next day. He still felt angry and in turmoil. Add to that the guilt he felt over the way he'd treated Angie and he figured the biggest favor he could do the world was steer clear of everyone. He managed to keep to himself until it was time to pick up Christine.

All the way home, he tried to think of the right way to tell her that Angie wouldn't be coming back. But she had thrilling news—she'd been chosen to compete in the riding championship—and he didn't have it in his heart to spoil her excitement.

Christine jumped out of the truck the minute it stopped in front of the house.

"Where are you going so fast?" Dillon asked.

"I've got to tell Angie."

His spirits plummeted even lower. "Christine, wait—"

But she didn't even slow down.

Dillon followed her, dreading the scene that was certain to follow. Sure enough, when he walked into the foyer, Floretha was speaking softly, with her hand on Christine's head. The little girl's schoolbag was on the floor. Pencils, erasers and jelly bears were scattered over the polished floor.

"Miss Angie's gone, sweetheart," Floretha was saying. "She called this morning to ask me to pack up her things."

Christine jerked away from the old woman's comforting touch and dashed up the stairs. Doors slammed overhead and Dillon saw Floretha's reproachful glance sweep in his direction.

"I know," he said. "I screwed up again, didn't I?"

Floretha shook her head. "Come with me, young man. We'll get you a tall glass of Floretha's lemonade to take to that child. Then you talk to that young'un. You hear me?"

But when he got upstairs with the lemonade and plate of cookies Floretha insisted would soothe Christine, he couldn't find her. He wasn't alarmed when he didn't find her right away. She'd hidden before—a dozen times in the first month after she arrived at Weddington Farms. But she hadn't run away in at least a month and Dillon had taken that as a good sign.

Fear began to prickle his scalp when he didn't find her in her room, or in the barn with Eddie. What if she ran off too far? What if she got lost? Or hurt?

Finally, he found her in the empty closet in Angie's room. Relieved, he sat down on the floor by the door. Christine huddled back in the corner, clutching Mrs. Stuart.

"I miss her, too," he said.

"Why did she go?"

"She had things to do."

"Couldn't she do them here?"

"I don't think so."

"I could help her. Floretha and Grandma Harper, too." She clung more fiercely to her doll. "Mrs. Stuart says Angie went away because you were mad at her and that man. She says you don't like him. She says you made him go away."

Mrs. Stuart had him there. Every word was true.

"I wasn't mad at Angie. I was upset at Mr. Trent. I don't want him to be my father. You know, like you didn't me to be your father."

Christine didn't say anything for a minute. "Mrs. Stuart says she doesn't mind you being my daddy. Except when you shout. It means we're going to move again."

Christine had never told him that before, but now he understood. Evelyn was forever discarding lovers and moving on to the next one, all of it no doubt preceded by a shouting match.

"Sometimes people can't help arguing, but it doesn't mean they stop loving each other. And it doesn't mean they're going to leave you."

"Angie left."

"She's gone to be with her stepfather."

"She'd come back if you asked her. If you told her you weren't mad at that man anymore."

Could it really be that simple? Trent's face came into his mind, and Dillon knew it was impossible for him to banish years of anger and bitterness that easily. He looked into his daughter's eyes and knew he couldn't tell her that. "I'll make a deal with you. You come down to dinner and I'll call Angie in a few days."

Christine hesitated.

"Don't you trust me?"

By way of reply, Christine jumped up and threw her arms around his neck.

Dillon felt his eyes tearing up. He had waited so long for Christine to show him even the smallest bit of affection. The intensity of the hug was unexpected and nearly overwhelming.

He had almost willed his tears away when he realized that he owed it all to Angie. And she was gone.

HARPER STARED at the phone message and knew she didn't have the emotional energy for another conversation with Burton Rust. He was offering to extend her loan, with generous terms. He must've received her notice that Bill Mott's bank would now be handling WedTech's payroll.

"He'll just have to get over it," she said, her voice lifeless and weary.

Dessie stood in her open office door, hands on hips. "You gonna tell me what's going on or am I gonna have to start believing the gossips in this town?"

Gossips. Harper couldn't deal with that, either. Gossips. How could they possibly know anything? "Leave it alone, Dessie."

Harper didn't know how to get this mental fog to lift. Things were so complicated, and there seemed to be no answers that didn't destroy somebody. The bank in Clover might get Burton Rust off her back, but the debts weren't going to disappear. Selling the farm would break Dillon's heart. Selling to Angie could cause a rift between Harper and her son that might never be healed. Despite Floretha's optimism,

Harper worried that things would never be the same again.

The other possibility was equally hard to consider. She could sell WedTech. The very idea brought an ache to her heart. WedTech and its workers had been her life—her family—since Dillon had left for college.

Now, it seemed, that could be taken from her, too. And she had little will left to fight.

Maybe selling WedTech was the best solution. A bigger corporation could invest in the mill, pay better wages, offer better benefits. And she could use the money to pay off the mortgage against the farm and gave it to Dillon, debt-free. Would that keep him from drifting, help him find the emotional center he didn't even know he was lacking? What if she left Collins? What if...

What if there was nothing to keep her from going to Trent?

She snatched her thoughts back, unwilling to go to that place in her mind. She realized Dessie still stood in her doorway, staring and shaking her head.

"It's true, isn't it?"

"What's true, Dessie?"

"They say some man came to the farm this weekend, beat you up because of some old Mafia debt of Sam's. That's it, isn't it? That's who this Yankee woman is, isn't it? I saw that kind of thing on a made-for-TV movie once, and that poor woman looked like you. Whipped."

For the first time in days, Harper laughed out loud, drawing an offended look from her office manager. She was still laughing when Angie appeared on the other side of her glass office wall. Harper's laughter died in her throat.

"Dessie, I think I have an appointment," she said.

"An appointment? You didn't tell me—" She saw the younger woman then, took in her expensive suit and gave Harper an I-told-you-so look. "I'll be right outside."

Dessie stepped around Angie without taking her eyes off her, then closed the door on her way out.

Harper gestured to a seat. It seemed to her that Angie thought about it a long time before sitting.

"I think my stepfather is still in love with you," she said as straightforwardly as she said most everything.

Harper wanted to smile but found it impossible. To the young, it must seem that simple. She knew better. Trent might have strong feelings for her, yet she doubted if any of their problems could be overcome by something as fragile and uncertain as love.

But she didn't want to talk about Trent, especially not to his stepdaughter.

"And I think my son is in love with you." She didn't like acknowledging that, either. But the fact that he still had his mind on Angie after all that had happened revealed just how deep his feelings for her must be.

Angie frowned and looked into her lap. Harper noted that the younger woman's hands were twisting, restless—the first real sign of vulnerability she'd ever seen in her. Then she thought about the outpouring of tenderness Angie had always shown for Christine, the instinctive way she'd always understood the little girl's insecurities. What, she wondered now, must that say about Angie's own childhood?

"I thought he might be," Angie said. "Now, I don't know. Whatever he feels isn't strong enough to make him forget his doubts or his anger."

Harper thought about how closely Angie's fears echoed her own. She had no hope to offer the young woman.

"We're both hurt," Angie said, and Harper heard the unspoken reproach. "We both feel betrayed. I guess I always knew Dad didn't love my mother. But I never understood why. Now I think I do."

Harper felt the swell of emotions that had sat so close to the surface since the weekend. She had robbed so many innocent people of what should have been theirs. Love and security. A legacy of selfishness and immaturity, that's what she was passing on to all the people she loved most. And now, to this fine young woman, as well.

"I'm sorry," she said. "If I could do anything to right all the wrongs, I would."

Angie studied her and finally said, "I believe that."

"Thank you."

As if suddenly realizing she had to regain command of herself, Angie lay her hands flat in her lap and drew a deep breath. "None of that is why I'm here. I'm withdrawing my offer for the farm."

Relief began a slow trickle through Harper's tense muscles. Angie was right, of course. This made it all so simple. Harper could sell the mill, give the farm to Dillon. No complications. No loose threads to keep everyone tied up in knots for years to come. Without Angie's money to complicate things, Dillon could figure things out for himself. As far as mother and son were concerned, who knew—

But no, that still left Trent. Trent could leave town now, of course, but he would still be there, in the back of everyone's mind. Doubly so if anything came of this relationship between Dillon and Angie.

Oh, lord, the repercussions would never end.

"You're probably right," she said. "It would make everything simpler."

Angie stood and put out her hand. Harper stood, too, and shook hands. Angie turned to leave, but stopped at the door and looked back.

"He's in Camden," she said. "At The Downs."

CHAPTER EIGHTEEN

TRENT KEPT STARING at his packed bag, wondering why he and Angie had hung around Camden as long as they had. What had they hoped would happen? he wondered. What miracle had they expected to set this mess right?

Of course, he supposed some form of miracle *was* taking place. As much as all these revelations had hurt Angie, as distant as she had been these past few days, he'd seen a change in her last night.

They'd driven into Georgia to look at some property, then returned to Camden. Angie had unfinished business here, he knew. Trent supposed he had, too. He hoped Angie was better at figuring out how to handle hers than he was.

They drove mostly in silence. When either of them spoke, it was about the property. Angie wasn't enthusiastic, although it met all the criteria she'd set up. But that was before Weddington Farms.

Before Dillon Winthrop.

"Do you really love him?" he'd said, at last finding the courage to begin clearing away the debris of his past.

"Does it really matter anymore?"

The resignation in her voice tore at his heart. He tried again. "It seems to me, if this mess between his mother and me proves anything, it shows that running out on what you feel doesn't solve a damn thing."

"I'm not running out," she said tightly. "But Dillon can't separate things in his own mind. He had enough trouble when it was just me and the farm. Now it's you, something that's hurt him all his life. He won't get over that."

A few days ago, Trent would have agreed. Now, having had a few days for the anguish in his heart to quiet down, he was beginning to wonder. "Maybe not. Or maybe if I'd hung around long enough to sort things out twenty-nine years ago, we wouldn't all be in this mess today."

"Is that what you wish had happened?"

He reached over to take her hand. "I could never wish away our relationship. I wouldn't trade you for anything."

"Not even your own son?"

His own son. Even having seen Dillon, Trent couldn't quite take in the reality of that. The truth was impossible to deny, of course, but what did it mean to have a grown son you'd never known?

He supposed at least part of the reason he hadn't been able to check out of The Downs was that he couldn't walk away until he'd figured that out.

"I hope Dillon and I can work something out," he said, not realizing until he'd spoken that he'd even harbored such a hope. "But it could never replace what I feel for you."

If he'd hoped for some kind of reciprocal statement from his stepdaughter, he was disappointed. They rode in silence the rest of the way. When he parked at the hotel in Camden and they got out of the car, Angie met him on the sidewalk between their rooms and flung her arms around his neck. Her cheek was damp against his neck.

"I'm sorry, Dad," she whispered. "I love you."

"And I love you, sweetheart." He squeezed her, felt tears stinging his eyes. "I've done a lot of wrong things, but loving you isn't one of them."

Before she went to her room, she looked at him and said, "You did love Mom, didn't you?"

He nodded. "Yes, I did. She was a good woman. When I married her, I was young and angry and didn't give a damn about anything but myself. But being around your mother, it was impossible not to change for the better." He smiled. "She was that much like you."

"Then why did you marry her? Why were you so angry?"

He dreaded telling her, dreaded what he might see in her eyes when she knew the whole story. But keeping secrets all these years had caused nothing but pain. So he leaned against his car and told her about his mother and the rich man who broke her heart and his foolish dreams of revenge.

He'd had his revenge, too, finally. After marrying Angie's mother, he'd bought out the man who'd hurt his mother, had set her up in the house where she'd been a backdoor mistress for so long. But the victory was hollow. His mother had hated the place, had hated the judgmental looks from everyone in town. She had come to live with him and Angie before she passed away.

"So it was all for nothing?" Angie said.

"That's all hate ever accomplishes, I suppose."

"What about Harper? Is that why you wanted her, too?"

"That's how it started out."

"But you loved Harper. Even all these years later, you still love her, don't you?"

"I didn't know that until I saw her again. All those years, I thought I hated her."

"And I thought you were pretty smart."

Her knowing smile had made it hard to sleep the rest of the night, as if she had given him permission to hope. Trent didn't want to delude himself, but it was damned hard not to think of possibilities. Especially when he remembered the hunger with which Harper had surrendered to him.

And what she'd said right before.

I loved you. Only you. I always have.

He heard Angie leave the motel the next morning and decided to leave himself. He needed to get back to the office. Maybe things would begin to make sense once he got back into his routine.

The knock came as he zipped his suit bag. But when he opened the door, it wasn't his stepdaughter on the other side. It was Harper.

He thought his heart might stop or his knees might give way. He searched his soul for the anger and bitterness he'd felt a few days earlier but discovered it was gone.

"I wanted you to know how sorry I am," she said in a nervous rush. "I made an awful mess of things. I've grieved over it for twenty-nine years. I know that won't help, but—"

She shrugged. He couldn't take in how different she was, and how much the same. He thought, as he watched the morning sun brighten the edges of her crisp, dark curls, that he could study her for hours.

"You're more beautiful now, you know," he said.

"Trent, I don't think—"

"Will you come in? So we can talk?"

She glanced into the room uncertainly. Her eyes landed on the unmade bed.

"I promise," he said. "Nothing... Just talk. Don't you think we need to talk?"

She looked into his eyes. He saw so much distress there. Surely she needed resolution as much as he did. She nodded.

They sat at the little round table by the window. He opened the curtains to reassure her.

"It was so strange," he said, "seeing him."

He saw from her expression that she understood, in some small way, how inadequate those words were. For the first time, the impact of the sacred link between him and this woman struck him full force.

"I'm sorry it didn't go well," she said softly. "Dillon can be hotheaded."

Trent found himself smiling. "He comes by it honestly."

They laughed, and the sound was like a balm to Trent's wounded spirit.

"I can tell you about him if you want," she said. "What kind of man he is. And about Christine. My...our granddaughter."

He wanted to know those things, of course. Why else had he been so weak that he'd had to have a glimpse of his son without even considering the upheaval he might cause? But he supposed he would have to learn those things for himself.

"I want to know what happened," he said. "Back then."

Pain skittered across her face. "Oh, God, Trent. I'm not sure I can go through it." Her voice broke and Trent wasn't sure he wanted to go through it, either. "If you only knew how many times I wanted to tell you. Needed to talk to you. But now…"

ANGIE WOULD HAVE GIVEN anything to leave Collins without seeing Dillon. But she could no more leave without speaking to him than she could refuse to admit she still loved him. So she'd come back to Weddington Farms one last time.

He had hurt her badly. She kept telling herself he had suffered a shock, that he didn't know what he was saying, but the words could not be forgotten. She wasn't sure if she could ever learn to forgive them.

She'd finally found someone who didn't care about her money, and he believed she could pretend to love him just to clinch a business deal! She couldn't even imagine what kind of pain could cause a man to say such a thing about the woman he loved.

Oh, yes, she believed he loved her. He would never have made such an accusation if he hadn't. He would simply have turned his back and walked away. The words were born out of his own terrible pain, but that didn't make them any more bearable.

Because the truth was, these revelations had caused Angie pain, too. She hadn't even known where to begin to start sorting through all the hurt and confusion and anger that rolled about inside her like a boiling cauldron. But after talking to her stepfather, some of the hurt had subsided. Even seeing Harper face-to-face had helped, because she understood the hurt and confusion she'd seen in the other woman's face.

Maybe seeing Dillon would help, too. Maybe he,

too, had calmed down. She thought of what she knew of him, and doubted it.

She didn't have to look for him. He and Christine were walking up the lane together. The minute Christine saw Angie, she dropped her father's hand, ran toward Angie and threw her arms around her neck.

"I knew you'd come back. I knew you would."

Angie hugged Christine, but she looked over her head at Dillon, who had stopped where he was.

"I told you I wouldn't go away without saying goodbye."

Christine struggled out of her embrace. "But you can't go away. I haven't told you about the riding show. I'm going to ride with the big people. You've got to come see me. You promised."

Angie wondered why promises so easily given should be so hard to take back. It was a good thing she and Dillon hadn't made any.

"I don't know if I can," Angie said. "I have to go away with my father."

"No, you promised!" Christine cried. "You did! You did!"

"Christine, I'm sorry, but I told you I would if I could."

"You can't go back on your promise."

"Christine."

But her father's voice didn't calm the child. She balled up her fists and stamped her foot. "You don't want to watch me! You don't like me anymore! I know you don't!" She turned and ran toward the house.

"Let her go," Dillon said. "Floretha will calm her down. Then I'll talk to her."

At least something good had come out of this. Dil-

lon could finally talk to his daughter. Angie stood.
She would never have imagined she could feel worse
than she did when she arrived. "I'm sorry. I wouldn't
have come if I'd known it would upset her so."

"Why did you come?"

"You didn't expect me to leave without coming
back, did you?"

"I don't know. When you left that night, I thought
you never wanted to see me again."

"I had to be alone."

He reached out to touch her. She backed away.
She couldn't let him touch her, hold her, kiss her. It
would hurt too much. He looked distraught, but she
couldn't help him. She could barely help herself.

"I'm sorry for what I said. You know I didn't
mean it."

"I don't know what you meant. What's more, I
don't think you did, either. We both need time to
adjust, to get used to things."

"What are you going to do?"

"Look at farms. That's what I came here to do."

"But I thought—"

"You thought I wanted Weddington Farms at all
costs, but I never did. I told your mother this morning
I'm withdrawing my offer."

He looked surprised. And relieved. You'd think
Weddington Farms was the only farm in the world.
It was pretty wonderful, but she might not have
wanted it so much if she hadn't been attracted to
Dillon.

"Are you going to come back?"

"No. Why should I?"

"I love you."

She hoped the pain didn't show in her eyes.

"Maybe, but everything is all tangled up in your mind...me, the farm, my stepfather. At times you don't know what you feel or what you want. I can't live with that. I have to know you love me in spite of everything else."

"I do."

"Maybe, but you were unsure enough to think I could pretend to love you."

"I told you I was angry."

"I don't mind anger, Dillon. Dad shouts all the time, but he never doubts me. You'll have to be able to do the same."

"How can I get in touch with you?"

"If you want me badly enough, you'll find a way."

Dillon moved more quickly than she anticipated. He grabbed hold of her wrist and pulled her into his arms. He kissed her ruthlessly. His arms nearly crushed the breath out of her.

"This is not the end," he said with fierce urgency.

Angie disentangled herself from his embrace and righted her clothes. "I've got to go." She walked to the car then looked back. "I did want this farm, but I wanted you and Christine even more."

She got in and quickly started the motor. He didn't move when she backed up and pulled into the lane. He still hadn't moved when she rounded the bend. Angie sagged. She was leaving behind nearly everything she wanted. Would she ever get it back?

HARPER DIDN'T WEEP and fall into his arms, although God knew she wanted to. And Trent barely reacted at all, although she registered his flinch when she told him about Red Jannik. On some level, she registered all his reactions as he learned about the home in Atlanta, the awful moment when she had realized the truth and made her decision to keep their baby. Anger. Despair. That aching need to call it all back, to do it all over.

"I was supposed to give him up. Some couple was ready to adopt him. But once I knew," she said, "I couldn't do it. I loved him with all my heart, the same way... Anyway, I decided then that I would find you. That I would explain and show you our baby and everything would be all right."

She couldn't look at him for long; the bleakness on his face was too painful.

"But I couldn't find you. Even the people in your hometown didn't know where you were."

"You went to Whitlaw?"

She nodded. "I tried everything. I honestly believed I could set things right. But you'd vanished."

He told her, then, about years on the road, working odd jobs from Alaska to Miami and everywhere in between.

"I was running from all of it. And it's just occurred to me that I was so eager to believe that you were only using me because...because that's what I'd intended. To use you."

"What do you mean?"

"You were rich and spoiled and at first I hated you as much as I wanted you. I had a plan."

Her mouth was dry. "A plan?"

He looked down, then up, directly into her eyes. "You were going to be my ticket. To money. To power."

"Oh."

"So I could get revenge for my mother."

She vaguely remembered the story he'd told her about the rich man who'd broken his mother's heart. Her own heart constricted in her chest for the two young people they'd been.

"But the plan backfired," he said. "When I fell in love with you."

"God, we were fools."

"I didn't stop being a fool for a long time. I dragged Angie and her mother into my little scheme with me."

"But you love Angie. And she loves you."

"That's a gift I don't deserve. By all rights, she should despise me. But Angie... I never knew how unconditionally children love you."

She longed to touch him. Longed to be held in his arms, as if that could wipe out the empty years, the thousands of tears she had shed. But she was afraid of the passion that had ignited between them a few days earlier, afraid of giving in to it again. Reliving those moments these last few days had made it all harder to bear. She didn't need that.

They talked until dusk softened the room. When they noticed that twilight was descending, Harper stood.

"I should go," she said.

He nodded but kept his distance as she went to the door.

"Goodbye, Trent," she said, wondering if it should feel less painful this time than it had that spring day twenty-nine years ago.

"Goodbye, Harper."

She didn't pause long enough to memorize his face, for she doubted it would leave her. As she drove away, she felt something release inside her, something that had felt tight and scarred for far too long. She could only hope that healing had begun, for both of them.

CHAPTER NINETEEN

DILLON SCANNED the faces in the crowd gathered around the riding ring. He experienced a sharp pang of disappointment when he didn't see Angie.

Things had remained touchy between him and Christine until he'd promised to talk to Angie one more time about coming to Christine's competition. He'd left word at her office in Charlotte—she wasn't in, or hadn't wanted to talk to him, he wasn't sure which—hoping she would show up.

Christine had been on edge all day. She seemed less excited about her first competition than fearful Angie wouldn't come. He knew what worried him most.

Angie. Everything hung in the balance. He'd told her he loved her. But everything was so messed up now, he wasn't sure she believed him. Or maybe she didn't believe love was enough anymore.

"Is she here?" Christine asked. "Do you see her?"

"Not yet."

"But it's almost time to start."

"Not for ten minutes yet."

"That's not much time."

"It's enough."

Dillon hoped he was right. Christine had been more concerned with looking for Angie than she had been about saddling Eddie. If Dillon hadn't been there, the saddle would still be in the van and Eddie unattended.

"I don't see Grandma, either."

"She'll be here."

But Dillon was nervous about that, too. Harper hardly spoke at all these days. He was growing short-tempered from his effort to pretend things weren't terribly wrong.

"There's Angie!"

Christine shrieked so loudly both Eddie and Dillon started. Before Dillon could find Angie in the crowd, Christine was flying through the tangle of people and horseflesh, not once looking where she was going.

When he caught sight of Angie, something turned over inside him. It was immediately and blazingly clear that she was just about everything he'd ever wanted in a woman. It wasn't just the slim figure clad in a cream-colored shirt and khaki slacks. It wasn't just the genuine smile that transformed her face when Christine launched herself at her. It was more the questioning, unsure expression he saw on her face when she noticed him.

She didn't look like a wealthy executive who could buy and sell him a dozen times over. She looked like a woman who wanted love and was afraid she had lost it, a woman who knew her happiness was not entirely within her own control.

So here he stood, holding on to the damned pony because somebody had to, waiting for Christine to bring Angie to him, wondering how the hell to make her believe his love for her was stronger than his anger and bitterness.

Dillon helped his daughter into the saddle while

she chattered away with Angie and waved with nervous excitement when her grandmother appeared. But the focus of Dillon's attention wasn't his daughter, it was the woman beside her. The woman who was encouraging Christine, calming her and bringing a light into the little girl's eyes that hadn't been there for weeks.

He knew exactly how Christine felt.

Apparently happy knowing that all the adults in her world were present and accounted for, Christine took her place in the line and rode into the ring. Dillon and Angie hurried to seats reserved for parents of participants.

"I was afraid you wouldn't get my message," Dillon said, watching Angie rather than his daughter as Christine trotted Eddie around the ring. "How have you been? I was worried when you didn't call."

She looked up at him, her eyes still uncertain. "Dad and I had a lot of things to talk about. I had things to work out in my own mind."

"Did you get everything settled?"

"Some." Angie looked up at him. "Too much depends on other people."

"Would I be one of those people?"

"Yes."

"Would it make any difference if I told you I want you to marry me?"

Angie didn't reply right away. The children had finished putting their mounts through their gaits, and the audience was applauding. Then she spoke in a half whisper. "It might."

"That's what I wanted to tell you the night we got back from Charleston. I'm sorry I let all that other stuff get in the way."

The talking and movement among the spectators began to die down. The children had started the dressage events, a complicated series of steps and maneuvers using leg and hand signals. This required a lot of concentration. The crowd grew silent. Dillon wished Angie would look at him instead of Christine. It wasn't easy asking a woman to marry you when you weren't sure you had her attention.

"Look at me," he whispered.

"I promised Christine I'd watch everything she did so we could talk about it later."

"She doesn't care about anything except the jumps."

"Maybe, but dressage is important. It develops control and communication with the horse."

"But I'm trying to communicate with *you,* not the damned horses," Dillon growled.

"Bad timing."

"Is that all you're going to say?"

"What do you want me to say?"

"You could start by telling me whether you love me."

"Answer him," an elderly woman in front of them said. "You've got me curious now."

Angie turned white. Dillon turned red. It was Mrs. Anthony, his eleventh grade United States history teacher. She must be at least seventy by now.

"Yes, I love you," Angie whispered in Dillon's ear. "Now be quiet and watch Christine."

"What did she say?" Mrs. Anthony asked. "I'm hard of hearing."

Dillon grinned and moved a little closer to Angie. "She said she loves me."

"Good," said the elderly lady. "I think young

people ought to be in love. It gives them something to do.''

Dillon took Angie's hand in his. She pulled back at first, then gave in and leaned against him. He felt almost like a teenager sitting next to his girl, so nervous about what she was going to say he could hardly manage to put intelligent sentences together.

"Things are going to change, Dillon," Angie said. "I love my stepfather and don't intend to choose between people I love."

"You think that's what I'm asking you to do?"

"All of us are too tightly bound together to be able to live with anger and dislike. If you want me, you'll have to accept my stepfather—your father. If I want you, I have to accept what Harper meant to Trent all those years he was married to my mother. There's no other way."

"But that has nothing to do with the way *we* feel," Dillon said. "I love you. I want to marry you."

"I know." Angie turned back to the ring. People were applauding as the dressage events concluded. The jumping events were up next.

"Is that all you're going to say?"

"No, but there are a lot of questions you've got to answer for yourself before I can say anything else."

"Like what?"

"There's still the problem of the farm—what to do if Harper sells, what to do if she doesn't, what you'll do if Harper and Trent decide to resume their friendship."

The idea startled him. "What the hell makes you think that's going to happen?"

She looked at him and shook her head, then ignored his question. "Most important is what kind of relationship you'll have with my stepfather if you and I marry."

"Who says I have to have any kind of relationship with him?"

"He's my stepfather, Dillon. You've got to make up your mind about Trent. Not because of me or him, but for yourself."

"And after I've done all these things?"

"I want to marry you, Dillon. I think I fell in love with you almost immediately. It's a shocking admission for a woman who prides herself on studying every situation thoroughly before making a decision. But I can't marry you as long as you're at war with yourself. You'd soon be at war with me. I couldn't endure that."

"You listen to her," Mrs. Anthony advised Dillon. "She sounds remarkably sensible for someone so young."

Dillon wondered if he might not wake up and find this was all a dream. He almost hoped so. Never in his wildest dreams could he have imagined asking the woman he loved to marry him while watching his daughter jumping her pony and receiving advice and promptings from his high school teacher.

He wondered what Mrs. Anthony must think. And what the town would say when they discovered that Trent was his father, that Kenneth Winthrop had never existed, that they had been forced to swallow a lie because Sam Weddington had been the richest man in town. Tongues would wag for years. If he couldn't stand the whispers and stares, he'd have to leave town.

But he didn't want to move. For better or worse,

Collins was his home. He meant to do everything he could to stay here for the rest of his life. He also meant to do everything he could to make sure Angie married him. He didn't need Mrs. Anthony to tell him she was a smart woman. He knew that. He also knew there was a whole lot he liked about her that had nothing to do with her brain.

Then he saw Trent. He stood on the other side of the ring, alone. Dillon tensed.

"I see you've found him," Angie said, her voice edgy.

"Did you know he was coming?" Dillon asked, unable to keep the animosity out of his voice. He could hardly believe Trent had the nerve to show up.

"Yes."

"Why didn't you tell me? She's my daughter."

"She's his granddaughter, whether you like it or not. Besides, where he goes is none of your business. Or mine. That's one of the things I had to get straight. I had a lot of anger that wasn't doing anybody any good. I'll always regret things didn't happen differently, but I'm not angry anymore."

"Well I'm more than angry," Dillon said, raising his voice to be heard over a burst of applause.

"Then you've got to come to some decisions about my stepfather before you can talk about forming any new relationships."

Then she stood and walked away. He called after her, but she acted as if she didn't hear him. "Angie! What the hell does that mean?"

Mrs. Anthony turned around to face him. "She means she's not going to marry you until you make up your mind she's more important than your anger. You're a smart boy, Dillon Winthrop," she said in the same tone of voice she had used to address him twelve years earlier, "but you still haven't learned not to waste your energy on anger."

Angie had walked to Trent's side. Dillon watched, filled with rage, as she gave her stepfather a hug.

He cursed his temper and the anger that still clung to him like a burr.

HARPER WAS KNEADING dough when Floretha came through from the front of the house. She never had learned to cook, but from time to time she coerced Floretha into giving her another chance. This particular Saturday, weeks after all the turmoil had begun, seemed like the perfect day to pound dough.

Floretha threw a kitchen towel at her.

"The South has more chance of rising again than that dough," she said. "Wipe yourself off, girl. There's a good-looking man coming to the door and I don't want him getting the wrong impression about my child. He might think he's found himself a woman who can cook, and I wouldn't want to be accused of misleading anybody."

Harper's hands grew still. "Who?"

Floretha gave her a look. Harper picked up the towel and began wiping the flour off her hands and wrists.

"You've got some on your face," Floretha said, and Harper shooed her away.

"I don't care," she said. "He can see me just the way I am."

Floretha smiled. "I believe he always did."

Tears sprang to Harper's eyes, something that happened entirely too much lately. She put her arms around the narrow, stooped shoulders and said, "Floretha, what in the world am I going to do?"

The old woman squeezed her back, then looked her squarely in the eye, straightening her hair and brushing the flour off her face as she did so. "You're a wise, grown-up lady now. You'll figure it out."

"But I'm not," she whispered, looking toward the front of the house and the sound of the heavy brass knocker on the door. "I'm not."

"Go," Floretha said. "I'm too old to be running back and forth."

Harper started toward the door slowly, but was almost running by the time she got there. What if he left? Gave up and drove away? She flung the door open and found herself too breathless to greet him.

He was too handsome for words. He had been a good-looking boy, of course, if you could overlook his cynical grin and his tough-guy swagger. But the years had turned a rough-edged country boy into a self-assured, suave gentleman, even in a pair of charcoal jeans and a striped, button-down shirt that had clearly been demoted from dress-up status to weekend wear. The faint lines marking the corners of his eyes and the striking silver of his hair gave him the look of a man who had lived thoroughly and had stories to tell.

Harper's blood rushed, set her to tingling.

"You came back," she said. "I...I called for you, but you'd already checked out."

He nodded. "I had things to take care of in Charlotte. And...things to sort through."

"I understand."

"Anyway, it was such a pretty day, I thought you might want to take a ride. No, wait, that's not it. I wanted you to ride up to Charlotte with me. See where I live. Have some lunch. What do you say?''

She looked down at her own jeans and Dillon's well-worn sweatshirt, with sleeves she'd torn off at the elbows when he outgrew it. "I think I'd better change."

He grabbed her hand. "Don't. I like you that way."

She touched her face, remembered she had no makeup, and felt a pinprick of regret for what the years had done to her.

"You're beautiful," he said. "Come with me."

So she did. They spent the day in Charlotte, where he had a spacious condo in a 1920s converted apartment building a few blocks from downtown. A music festival had taken over the streets of town, and they wandered through the crowds, listening to bluegrass bands and watching street clowns and arguing over which type of music was more authentically American. She saw his office and met his best friends, a married couple who lived in the condo next door. They held hands and they kissed in the middle of the street while a small group of college kids who had more beer in their bloodstream than common sense cheered and hooted.

They went back to his condo after the sun went down and called to let Floretha know Harper wouldn't be home.

And they made slow, easy love that was richer and deeper for all the lost years.

"Thank you for coming with me today," he whispered in the dark, his fingertips brushing the side of her breast.

She moved her head to feel the smoothness of his

chest as it grazed her cheek. She shifted to wrap her leg around one of his and marveled at the way she felt. The way they felt together.

"Thank you for giving me another chance," she murmured. "This *is* another chance, isn't it?"

"I don't want another chance, Harper. I want a sure thing."

And because she didn't know what to say to that, she raised herself to his lips and kissed him with all the sweet hope of a girl coming to her first lover.

They spent Sunday together, too. They went to his church, then took a picnic to Freedom Park and sat on the banks of the lake. By late afternoon, Harper felt as if she had been at his side throughout his life, and the way he looked at her said he felt much the same.

"What's going to happen now?" he said as he turned down the lane toward Weddington Farms at the end of the day.

"What do you want to happen?" she asked, not even afraid of the answer.

"I want us to be together. The way it always should have been."

"But we aren't the only ones we need to think about," she said, knowing she wouldn't resist for long if he persisted. "There's Angie. There's Dillon. There's whatever is going on between the two of them."

"I hope they'll be smarter than we were," he said. "But whatever they decide, you and I have to focus on what's right for us. We've wasted too much time already. I don't want to waste any more, Harper."

"You're right," she agreed, taking the hand he offered. "Neither do I."

As he pulled to a stop in front of the house, the front door opened. Dillon strode down the steps and started toward them.

"Do you want me to talk to him?" Trent asked.

Harper shook her head. "Not now. He's angry, and there's no point in trying to get him to listen when he's like this. Let him simmer down. Then we'll talk to him."

Instead of kissing her goodbye under the stern glare of their son, Trent squeezed her hand. She got out of the car and waved as he drove off. Then she turned to face Dillon's fury.

"What do you think you're doing, going off with that man?" Dillon demanded.

"I'm sorry this is making you miserable," she said, walking past her son toward the house, "but I'm a grown woman."

Dillon turned and followed her. "You can't expect me to accept it."

"I don't."

"Yes, you do. You and everyone else. You know Angie's upset, don't you? Hell, everything's such a damned mess!"

Harper paused at the top of the steps. She closed her eyes, feeling her peace of mind slip away.

"What the hell do you think you're doing, Mom?" His tone was more entreating, less censuring. "You can't erase the past twenty-nine years. You know that, don't you?"

Harper turned and looked at her son. His back sagged, his head hung. His misery touched her and she went to him and put her arm around his waist. She felt him stiffen, then put his arm around her shoulder and hug her to him.

"I love you, Dillon," she whispered. "And I'm sorry for all the mistakes I've made and what those mistakes have done to you. I hope you'll come to believe how deeply I mean that."

He hugged her a little harder.

"But I have to take this second chance life is offering me. And I hope you won't turn your back on yours."

CHAPTER TWENTY

TRENT WAS WHISTLING when his office door burst open. He'd spent two evenings this week with Harper and had the promise of the weekend ahead with her, planning their future. He looked up from the report on his desk as his office door banged into the wall.

It didn't surprise him to see Dillon striding toward him. In fact, it pleased him. It also pleased him that Dillon hadn't felt the need to dress up to confront his father on his own turf—he wore clean jeans and a chambray shirt, with work boots that still had a little mud caked on the toe. Good for him. The hostile expression on the young man's face even gave Trent some satisfaction. His son wasn't one to roll over and play dead. He liked that.

"Welcome to AllStates Financial," he said, standing but not holding out a hand. He doubted Dillon was in the mood for a friendly shake.

"I want you to stay away from my daughter," Dillon began without preamble. "She doesn't need you showing up at her competitions or at the house, bringing her presents, making her think you're going to be around all the time."

Trent decided to counter the aggressive anger in his son's voice with as much calmness as he could summon. "I'd like to be around for her. As much as you'll let me."

"And I want you to stay away from my mother."

"I can understand your feeling that way."

"Don't talk to me like I'm six years old. I don't need placating. Just stay the hell away from my family. I know you had your reasons for leaving, but that doesn't change anything now."

Despite the unpleasantness of Dillon's ultimatums, Trent found his heart swelling with pride in this young man who was so determined to protect his territory. Even against a man as rich and powerful as himself. Dillon showed no fear, just determination. He had to remember to tell Harper what a fine job she'd done bringing up their son.

"I do respect your wishes, Dillon. I'll stay away from Christine if you insist, but I hope you'll change your mind."

"I won't."

"But Harper is another matter. Seeing her is something that's between her and me."

"You broke her heart once. Now you've turned our lives upside down. Isn't that enough for you?"

"I know you're angry. You have every right to be."

"You're damned right I do!"

"But I'm going to do everything I can to change that. You're my son, and I'll be sorry as long as I live that I've missed so much of your life."

"It's too late to change things now," Dillon said, turning to leave.

"It's never too late, Dillon. But you and I aren't the ones who are important here," Trent continued, hoping to stop his son before he reached the door. "Harper is. And Angie."

Dillon turned back at the sound of Angie's name.

Trent walked around his desk. "Please help me make
the best of this. For their sakes."

"For their sakes, maybe the best thing you can do
is stay the hell out of our lives."

"Maybe. But I think we can work this out. Face
up to what's real. And what's real is this—I love
your mother."

Dillon backed up.

Trent took another chance. "And I think you love
Angie. Am I right?"

Trent knew the stubborn set to Dillon's jaw; the
last thing the young man wanted was to admit how
he felt about Angie to the man he felt had betrayed
them all.

"Yes," Dillon said, his tone grudging. "I love her
and I want to marry her. She loves me, too. But she
won't marry me as long as this business has us tied
in knots."

"Then let's do what we can to make it all work,
Dillon. What do you say?"

Dillon stared into Trent's eyes for a long time.
Trent watched the struggle, the tangle of emotions
running across his son's face—fury and fear and uncertainty. He kept looking for some sign that Dillon
would relent, could set aside his pride. But Trent
knew how powerful pride could be.

"I'd like to think it could all work out," Dillon
said stiffly. "But I've never been very good at pretending to feel things I don't."

Trent hoped the answer his son gave before he
stalked out the door was the first sign that Dillon was
ready to make an effort, however small.

EVEN BEFORE HARPER said a word, Dillon supposed
he knew why she'd asked him to join her in the par-

lor. She'd probably heard about his trip to Charlotte and planned to upbraid him. Shep already had, and so had Floretha. Maybe he had been out of line.

But dammit, he had to do something. He was losing everyone he loved to Trent.

Trent was beside her on the couch. Dillon had never seen his mother like this. She had a contented glow, despite the fact that she was also clearly tense at the moment.

Dillon didn't like having Trent present. He didn't know what to say to him. He didn't want to say anything at all. His efforts to drive him away had clearly failed.

"Have a seat," Harper said.

"I'll stand," Dillon said. "Floretha will kill me if I get dirt on the chair covers."

He stood there in the middle of the room, his legs apart, his hands clasped in front of him as if he were expecting a blow and wanted to be ready to ward it off.

His mother's words were a greater blow than he'd ever expected.

"Trent and I are getting married."

"But he's been back less than a month!" Dillon exclaimed, feeling more frustrated than angry. Was he the only one who could see how wrong all this was? "How do you know he won't run out on you again?"

Trent started to speak, but Harper beat him to it. "That's for me to worry about, isn't it?"

Dillon struggled to contain his disappointment. His mother had made it clear from the beginning that everything had been her fault. That always left him with nothing to say.

"This is going to cause some big changes, and I wanted to tell you before anyone else."

Dillon stiffened. He and Christine would have to leave Weddington Farms. Of that he was certain. The farm belonged to his mother. Christine's life would be turned upside down again. And all because a man who'd stayed away twenty-nine years couldn't stay away a little longer.

It hurt that his mother had chosen this man over him. And that's what she'd done. That's what Angie had done.

"Trent and I are going to leave Weddington Farms. You know I've never liked it here. It reminds me too much of all the things that went wrong with my life."

He held his breath, waiting for the next blow to fall.

"I'm going to sign the farm over to you. We've settled up with the bank. You can live here, sell it, do anything you like. It's yours. I should have done this years ago."

Thoughts flew about in Dillon's shocked mind like debris in a whirlwind. He could hardly grasp the idea that Weddington Farms was his. No one was going to force him and Christine to leave. Finally, he would have something he could call his own.

He could feel like a man.

"Where will you go?" He couldn't imagine his mother leaving Collins.

"We're going to buy a place a few miles from here," Trent said. "We're going to modernize the mill."

"We?"

"Trent and I have decided to form a second partnership. He'll provide the money for a third interest in the mill. I'll have one third. The other will belong to you."

Dillon felt as if he were on a roller-coaster ride. In one morning he'd gone from being virtually a hired hand to a man whose future was secure. Yet how could he accept this from Trent?

"We'd like you to work with us."

"Me?" He couldn't imagine how he could.

"Trent insisted I ask you. I know you prefer the farm, but it doesn't have to take all your time."

"I don't know anything about the mill."

"I didn't, either, when I began," Harper told him.

"We're not asking you to spend all your time there," Trent added, "but we'd like it to be a family operation."

"It wouldn't work," Dillon said. "I really hate that mill, probably as much as Mom hates this place."

"Okay, but if you change your mind—"

Dillon shook his head, then looked at Trent. "Are you sure you want to stay in a one-horse town like this?"

"I've been looking for something Harper found years ago," Trent replied. "A place where I can belong, where I can fit in." He looked at Dillon as if he believed his son might understand that, but Dillon wasn't willing to give any sign that he did. "Even after thirty years, I still don't like the city."

"Collins is sure no big city." Dillon shifted his weight uneasily. "I have to thank you for helping Mom...us...out, but I won't pretend I'm happy about this marriage." Yet despite himself, Dillon felt his anger fading. Even a fool could see his mother was very happy. "When does the wedding take place?"

"This weekend. Trent and I don't see any reason to wait."

Dillon paused. "Do you plan to tell anybody he's my father?"

"We're leaving that up to you," Trent said. "We're happy for people to know, but if you'd rather, we'll kept it quiet."

"If he spends much time around here, they'll guess," Dillon mused, recalling that Christine had noticed the resemblance immediately.

"I hope once you get to know him, you'll want to tell people he's your father," Harper ventured.

"I expect Christine will announce to everyone in sight you're her new grandfather," Dillon said. "I won't deny it, but I don't aim to brag about it."

ANGIE WAS LOADED DOWN with illustrated books from both the florist and the caterer as she mounted the steps to the front porch at Weddington Farms. A part of her had been reluctant to come. She dreaded seeing the place, feared running into Christine. Or Dillon. But Harper needed her help with this hurry-up wedding, and Angie wanted to show her support.

Surely she could manage to hide her hurt for a few more days.

And maybe, if his confrontation with Trent was any indication, Dillon wouldn't even show up for the wedding. She almost hoped he wouldn't. When Trent's office assistant told her how Dillon had stormed Trent's office, she'd been hurt and angry all over again. She wasn't sure she could keep her anger in check if she saw him again.

The front door was ajar and she nudged it open. She called out for Harper but got no answer. She wandered back through the dining room, into the kitchen. Floretha would know where to find Harper.

But it wasn't Floretha or Harper she found in the kitchen. Shep stood in front of the open refrigerator, helping himself to a soft drink. Dillon stood at the back door, staring out.

Angie froze. As furious as she'd felt these past few days, seeing him still stirred a flurry of longing within her.

"Well, hello." Shep twisted the cap off his drink. "Say hello, Dillon."

Dillon turned. His curious expression grew guarded when he saw Angie.

"I'm here to see Harper," she said.

He looked at the books in her arms. His jaw tightened. "Come on, Shep." He gestured to the farmhand, who glanced at Angie apologetically.

"Nice to see you again, miss."

Angie tossed her books on the table, her emotions spilling out. "I'm sure it is if you have to put up with his sour moods the rest of the time."

"Oh, yes, ma'am. 'Bout every day. He's a trial, all right."

"Now, listen—" Dillon started.

"No, you listen, Dillon Winthrop," Angie said. "You're stubborn and mule-headed and you've ruined every chance we ever had for happiness."

"Angie, I—"

"But there's still hope for Trent and Harper. And if you have even a shred of compassion in you, you'll do what you can to support them. At least somebody will come out of this awful mess intact.''

Then she wheeled and stormed out of the kitchen, aware that her entire body was trembling with a firestorm of emotions. She heard Dillon's angry voice behind her, but she didn't want to listen to anything he had to say. It hurt too much. She had to face the fact that it was over.

THE FINALITY OF Angie's anger had shaken Dillon. He stalked out to the meadow where Duchess and a group of other horses grazed, hoping Shep had the good sense to leave him alone.

He should have known better. He seemed to be on everyone's list these days.

"You're acting like an ass," Shep said. "You know that, don't you?"

Duchess came up to the fence, nuzzled him. At least someone still liked him. "I know."

"Then what are you going to do about it?"

"What would you do?" Dillon demanded, just about to decide it was time he got a new best friend.

"Quit acting like you're getting such a raw deal, for starters."

Dillon mulled that over. He wasn't getting a raw deal, of course. He knew that. He owned Weddington Farms, free and clear. He had his daughter at his side and a mother who was truly happy for the first time he could remember.

He even had a father.

"You ever thought about how your old man might be feeling about all this?" Shep never did know when to leave well enough alone.

"No," Dillon snapped, but it wasn't true. Ever

since that day at the horse competition, he'd been unable to get Trent's reaction to Christine out of his mind. The man's gaze had been riveted on the child. His granddaughter.

An awful thought had occurred to him and hadn't let him go. What if Evelyn had never told him she was pregnant, if he'd never known about Christine? The feeling of loss nearly overwhelmed him. Was that how Trent felt?

In that moment, Dillon had empathized with the pain Trent must feel at being separated from his own flesh and blood. It made his father seem more human. But that had made it even more important, somehow, to hang on to his anger. He didn't want to sympathize with his father. He didn't want to understand.

"You know," he said, as much to himself as to Shep, "I used to think about changing my name. Legally. So I'd be a Weddington, too. And now it won't make any difference. Mom and I still won't have the same name. It's like no matter what I do, I'll never fit in."

"The only one who thinks you don't fit in is you, you stubborn cuss," Shep said. "I'd be glad to have even one parent. You've got two, and your old man is rich, you lucky dog. And you're not grateful for a bit of it."

Dillon knew his friend was right. His only problem was himself. Despite his resolve, all his anger and bitterness kept slipping away from him, bit by bit. He'd wanted to say that to Angie, but it was too late. All that was left was his pride and the knowledge that he'd made such a mess he couldn't begin to set things right.

CHAPTER TWENTY-ONE

A WEDDING WITH NONE of the trappings. That's what Harper had said she wanted, and Trent had to admit it suited him just fine.

No big fancy cake, no guest book, no march down the aisle. Just a parlor full of people, some of whom loved one another and some of whom hadn't yet made up their minds on that score.

Trent listened to the words of the service, Harper's soft hand resting in the crook of his arm. Words of love and commitment that he had spoken once before in a farce of a ceremony. The irony had been that the vows had taken hold of him, had ended up becoming the truth despite what had been in his heart when he spoke them.

For that, he was grateful.

He was even more grateful that this time he could say the words and mean them.

"With this ring, I thee wed," he declared, vaguely aware, as he slipped the simple gold band on Harper's finger, of his stepdaughter. Angie was wiping the corner of her eye. He smiled at her, then at Harper.

When the minister urged those in attendance to support the couple in their vows, Trent heard the restless shuffle behind him, where he knew Dillon stood.

Things still weren't resolved, but Harper had seen hope in his willingness to be there for the wedding.

Putting old problems out of his mind, Trent kissed the bride lightly and heard Floretha attempting to silence Christine's giggle. And then the minister from Harper's church said, "I now present Mr. and Mrs. Gordon Elliot Trent."

Floretha burst into tears. Christine looked up at her in alarm and gasped, "Don't cry."

The elderly woman replied, "Oh, heavens, child, I'm so happy these old eyes can't stand it. These are just about the happiest tears that have been shed in this house in a long, long time."

Then Harper burst into tears, as well, and Trent wished he'd had the foresight to invest in tissues.

ANGIE COULDN'T WAIT for it to all be over. She could leave this house, with all its reminders. She could have a good cry on the way home if she wanted, and no one need ever know. Her anger had vanished, leaving only grief for what would never be.

Trent and Harper would be leaving for the Charlotte airport any minute now. Everybody was waiting on the steps to shower them with rice as they made their dash for the car. Everyone except Dillon, Angie noticed.

Good. Maybe she could get out of here without having to see him again. It would be better that way.

Then, as Harper and Trent swept past, Dillon came around the corner of the house from the barns, leading two of Duchess's prize offspring. Festive velvet ribbons were draped around the horses' necks. Everyone stopped throwing rice.

"What's Daddy doing?" Christine whispered.

Angie put her hand on the little girl's shoulder. "I don't know."

She watched as he walked right up to the happy couple. He placed the reins in Trent's hands. "You'd better take good care of her," he said gruffly.

Angie took a step toward them. If he spoiled this moment, she might just kill him.

"You can count on it," Trent said.

"I know what everybody wants me to say," Dillon said. "But after hating you for so long, it's hard to start feeling the opposite."

"I understand," Trent said.

"But I'll try. I...I always wanted a dad."

Angie was close enough to hear the tears in Harper's voice when she spoke. "Oh, son."

"I want you to be happy, Mom. I really do. As long as Trent makes you happy, I *will* like him."

Angie felt tears of her own welling up. This was a side of Dillon she'd only seen glimpses of; a side he'd buried under anger and bitterness ever since Trent showed up.

"Anyway, I kept trying to think of a wedding gift. But I'm pretty selfish, and all I could think was that I didn't really want you to leave. So I thought if the two of you owned a couple of horses, we might see you out at the farm more often. So...congratulations."

Angie couldn't see the hugging that took place next for the flood of tears filling her eyes.

HIS LITTLE PRESENTATION hadn't been as hard as Dillon thought it would be. When the preacher pronounced his parents man and wife, his mother looked radiant. Somehow her happiness served to soften his feelings toward Trent.

Then he'd seen Harper and Trent standing next to each other at the reception, and his insides had turned to jelly. It gave him a weird feeling to see his mother and father as husband and wife. It was something he'd wanted all his life. And now he had it. If he had any brains, he'd forget the past and make the most of the present.

That's what he planned to do. The wedding gift to his parents was only the first step.

The car was heading down the winding drive to the highway now. Angie, Christine, Floretha and her daughter, Sandra, who had flown in from Kansas City for the wedding, continued throwing rice until they were out of sight.

"I hope they remember to call when they get there," Dillon said.

"They won't," Floretha said with one of the biggest smiles Dillon could ever remember seeing on her face. "Your mama's been waiting most of her life for this moment. You're going to have to forgive her if she forgets all about you for a few days."

"My stepfather will remember," Angie said.

"I wouldn't count on it," Sandra remarked as they all trooped back into the house. "He looked just as besotted as Harper."

"Mrs. Trent," Floretha corrected her. "Mrs. Gordon Elliot Trent."

"She'll always be Harper to me," Sandra said. "Now, before we see about supper, Mama and I have something we want to say."

"No, I don't," Floretha declared. "This is your idea."

"Okay, blame it on me," Sandra said. "I don't care."

"What is it?" Dillon asked.

"Mama's been working here for fifty years," Sandra said. "I've been trying to get her to quit, but she wouldn't as long as Harper was here. Well, with Harper married and setting up her own household, I think this is a good time for Mama and me to make some changes of our own. I'm moving back home and taking a job in Sumter. I found a nice little place in town. Mama can get to all the shops without having to wait for me to take her."

"This was none of my idea," Floretha insisted. "I don't want to leave the house I've been in over fifty years."

Sandra frowned. "It's time, Mama. Dillon, I didn't want to hit you with any more right now, but I thought this was the best time."

"Sure," Dillon said. "I understand." But he'd never known Weddington Farms without Floretha. It was as if he were losing all of his family at once.

"Come on, Mama. They've got things to talk about."

They left Dillon facing Angie. He was terrified of what would happen next. "I guess that just leaves us unsettled," he said.

"It seems that way."

"You waiting for me to start?"

"Yes."

"I can't say I like your stepfather—"

"Your father," Angie corrected.

"Okay, my father. But I'm willing to try. As much as you love him, he must be a pretty decent guy."

"He is, Dillon. I know you'll love him if you just let yourself."

"I'll give it a shot, but only if you'll marry me."

"Are you trying to blackmail me?"

"I'll try anything that works." He took her hand. She didn't pull away. It gave him hope that everything would be all right in the end. "You said I'd ruined any chance we had."

She smiled slightly. "Well, some of us get over our anger. If we see that people really want to change."

"I do." Dillon wasn't sure he had the courage to proceed, despite her nod. Maybe he could stall a bit longer. "Do you still want your equestrian center?"

"I'm not sure. I—"

"Would you if you could have it here? There's more than enough land for a farm and horses."

"Now you're trying to bribe me."

He smiled. "If Christine is going to be the best rider in the state, she's got to have the best training facilities around. And the best teacher."

"Are you going to work with Dad and Harper?"

"No. The mill is their baby. This place can be ours."

"Are you sure about all this?"

"The thing I'm most sure about is that I love you and want you to be my wife. Do you think you could be ready for another wedding by the time Trent and Mom get back?"

Angie smiled. "Is that an official proposal?"

"It's a repeat," Dillon said. "I made the official one at the competition with Mrs. Anthony listening to every word."

He held out his arms. Angie stepped into his embrace. "I wanted you to have time to reconsider. You were under a great deal of stress at the time."

"I've been under stress ever since I can remember," Dillon replied. "I'm counting on you to help me get rid of it."

"That sounds like an indecent proposal to me."

He laughed. "Considering what I've been wanting to do to you for days, it's damned decent." He sobered quickly. "You know I didn't mean what I said before. I was angry and hurt. I know that's no excuse. I can't promise I won't say something mean again— I've got a hasty temper—but I can promise I'll love you no matter what ill-considered words come out of my mouth."

Angie's smile told him he was forgiven. She kissed him lightly.

"I was thinking it might be a good idea for us to go away for a while. From what you said, everything here has been in a ferment ever since Christine came to live with you. Maybe going away would help relieve some of that pressure."

"How could I turn down an invitation like that?"

Dillon had almost forgotten how sweet it could be to hold the woman he loved in his arms. He could have sat next to Angie doing nothing more than holding her for a long, long time.

But he was grateful there was to be more.

HER INSIDES SHAKING with fear, Christine ran up to her room, grabbed Mrs. Stuart and dived behind the curtain. They were leaving her. Everybody was leaving—Grandma Harper, her new granddaddy and Floretha.

And now Angie was taking her daddy away from her.

They had all promised they loved her, that they would never leave her. But they were. Nobody loved her anymore, nobody except Mrs. Stuart.

After everybody left, somebody would come to take her away to a new place, someplace where she didn't know anybody, someplace where nobody loved her. She wouldn't go. She would hide where they could never find her. Then she would never have to leave the farm.

NIGHT WAS FALLING when they realized Christine was missing.

Dillon dispatched everyone to separate parts of the house in search of his daughter, but after every inch of the house had been searched, she was still nowhere to be found.

"She's just hiding," he said, trying to mask his uneasiness. "She does that when she gets upset."

"But why would she be upset?" Angie asked, worry clouding her face. "I thought she was delighted to have a new grandfather."

"I don't think she counted on Harper moving out."

"Then there's Floretha."

"I didn't even think about that," Dillon said. "I was so busy thinking about us—"

"Me, too," Angie admitted.

They left the house then. When he saw how dark it was growing, Dillon felt his first moment of real fear. What if they didn't find her before dark?

They saw the barn door standing open and the light on before they got there. The saddle lay on the ground and the door to Eddie's stall stood open, but the pony was still inside. Dillon closed the stall door and picked up the saddle, returning it to the rack almost without thinking. "Where could she have gone?"

"Let's check Duchess's pasture."

"Come on. I know a shortcut."

As long as he'd thought Christine was hiding in the house he'd been certain they would find her. But if she was upset enough to run away from the house in the dusk, she could have gone anywhere. There was no telling what could happened to her! There were several drainage ditches that were too deep for her to climb out of by herself. And some of them were full of water. They'd found a nest of water moccasins only last month.

It bothered him that he'd been so preoccupied with what was happening to him that he'd forgotten to look at all the changes from Christine's point of view. It was perfectly understandable that the child would be upset, and he'd never taken the time to even think about it.

He wondered if he was ever going to be a good father. Every time he managed to get something right, he stumbled into another big screwup. It just might be possible that Christine would be better off with her grandparents.

No. Whatever he had to do, no matter how he had to change, he was going to make damned certain the best place for his daughter was with him and Angie. He understood what it meant to be an only child. He was surrounded by them—Harper, Angie, Trent, Evelyn, Christine and even Sandra. They'd all gone through life holding on tight for fear they would lose the only person they had. He hoped he and Angie could have at least a half a dozen children. It would be wonderful to be able to pour his love into so many vessels.

"She must have been very frightened to have run away at night," Angie said. "We should have realized that—"

"*I* should have realized," Dillon stressed.

The pasture looked empty when they arrived. Duchess came trotting out of the shadows when she saw Dillon. The foal came trotting behind her, not at all sure that she wanted anything to do with these humans.

Dillon patted the old mare and talked to her in a soft, crooning voice, but he didn't slow his stride. Duchess and the foal followed, their eyes wide with curiosity.

They would have missed Christine if Angie hadn't thought to shine her flashlight up into the trees. Even then it was almost impossible to see her amid the many limbs branching off from the white pine. Dillon was surprised at the immensity of his relief. He hadn't known he could be so worried. Being a father could take an emotional toll he was only beginning to understand.

"Christine." Angie spoke first, but Christine didn't move.

"Floretha says it's time for dinner," Dillon said. "You'd better hurry before she puts it all back in the refrigerator."

"Floretha's gone," Christine said. "Everybody's gone."

"Floretha and Sandra are still at the house. They're going to move to a new house not far from here. I'll take you there so you'll know exactly how to find them."

"Grandma's gone, too."

"But she'll be back. She and Grandpa Trent will have a new house near your school. I'll take you there, too. You'll have houses with family in them all over town."

"Why can't they stay here?"

"When people get married, they like to have a house all by themselves."

"Like you and Angie? You're going away, too. I heard you say it. Then there won't be anybody here. It'll be just like when Mommy left me."

"We're not going to leave you," Dillon said, feeling guilty he hadn't thought of Christine when Angie proposed the trip. "We're just going away for a few days. We'll be back soon."

Why not take Christine? Dillon thought. She'd been under as much strain as he had. Besides, she would be a large part of his life with Angie.

"Would you like to go with Angie and me?" he asked.

Christine looked at Dillon and Angie, questioning.

"We wouldn't have much fun without you," Angie said.

"Can Mrs. Stuart go?"

"Of course," Dillon said. "Mrs. Stuart is part of the family, too."

"Are you and Angie going to move?"

"No," Dillon said. "All three of us are going to live here together."

"Always?"

"Always."

Until now, Christine hadn't moved. Dillon had

talked to the lacy hem of her pink dress. Now she peeped down from among the branches. "Is Angie going to stay?"

"Always," Angie replied. "I'm going to marry your daddy. I'll be your mother."

"Mommy left me all the time."

"Your daddy and I are going to take care of you. We won't ever leave you."

"Promise?"

"Promise. Now I think you'd better come down. It's hard to pack sitting in a tree."

"I can't. Mrs. Stuart is scared."

Dillon almost laughed with relief. Finally a fear he could do something about. "Stay right where you are. I'll come up and get you."

"Are you sure that tree will hold you?" Angie asked.

"It'll have to."

"I could go get her."

"No. This is something I have to do."

The limbs were flimsy, but Dillon placed his feet close to the trunk. The branches shook a lot, but they held.

"You're going to have to let Angie have your doll," Dillon said when he reached Christine. "I've got to hold on to the tree. You'll need both arms to hold around my neck."

Dillon was surprised at how readily Christine cast Mrs. Stuart to Angie. It didn't even seem to bother her that she bounced from limb to limb before hitting the ground. She reached out to Dillon and held him tight around the neck. For a moment he was too moved to climb down. He just stayed where he was, resting against a limb that seemed none too steady and holding on to his daughter.

For the first time, he felt that Christine *wanted* to be in his arms, that she *trusted* him. He knew he had a long way to go before she would love him with the kind of unrestrained love he had for Harper. But he'd made a beginning. His second of the day, actually. With Angie's help, he'd do much better in the future.

It would have been much easier if Christine had climbed on his back, but she only felt comfortable with her face buried in Dillon's neck. He got a few scrapes he wouldn't have gotten otherwise, but he figured they were worth it.

When he reached the ground and Angie threw her arms around both of them, Dillon knew he was on his way home at last.

EPILOGUE

Christmas Eve

CHRISTINE LAY IN HER BED and listened for the sound of reindeer hooves on the roof. Mrs. Stuart had told her in no uncertain terms that she wouldn't hear any reindeer because there was no Santa Claus.

Christine decided to take no chances. Mrs. Stuart had been wrong about a lot of things lately.

"Like Grandma and Grandpa Stringfellow," Christine whispered to Mrs. Stuart, who was snuggled under the covers with her. "You said when we went to visit at Thanksgiving that I'd never, ever want to come back."

But Grandma and Grandpa Stringfellow had said so many mean things about everybody that Christine had called Daddy and asked to come home early.

"And you were wrong about wicked stepmothers, too," Christine continued, mimicking Floretha's sternest voice to chastise the troublesome Mrs. Stuart. "Angie is the best stepmother in the whole world. She loves me like I've belonged to her always."

Christine never got tired of Angie's assurances. She waited for them every night when Angie tucked her into bed. And she got them, along with a hug and a kiss. She smiled drowsily and her eyes grew heavy as she remembered the ritual.

Noise from outside startled Christine to alertness. She wasn't sure if it was reindeer hooves she heard, but someone was definitely outside. She jumped out of bed and ran to the window. She saw Grandma Harper and Grandpa Trent get out of their car and walk toward the house, their arms full of brightly wrapped packages that made Christine's eyes grow wide in anticipation.

"Presents," she whispered reverently. "Lots and lots of presents."

She heard the greetings in the entrance hall, then the cheerful voices grew more distant. They had probably gone into the parlor where the giant Christmas tree twinkled and shone. Christine was too wide awake to go back to bed.

"Let's go watch," she said, taking Mrs. Stuart and tiptoeing to the top of the stairs.

If she leaned way over, she could see into the parlor. She watched everybody hug and laugh. Even Daddy and Grandpa Trent laughed together these days. She was never so happy as when everybody she loved was in the same house.

Then she saw them pour the glasses of eggnog. Daddy wrapped his arm around Angie and pulled her close. "Mom, Trent," he said, "Angie and I have a special present for you. It'll be a little late, but I hope you won't mind waiting for a second grandchild."

As everybody in the room exclaimed happily, Christine frowned, wondering what that meant. Then understanding dawned. "Oh, Mrs. Stuart, we're going to have a baby!"

A whole attic full of toys wasn't as nice as that.

She finally dozed off sitting right there on the stairs, saying her new name over and over again so she wouldn't forget it. Christine Trent. Christine Trent. Everybody she loved had the same name now. Christine liked that very much.

COMING NEXT MONTH

#758 BEAUTY & THE BEASTS • Janice Kay Johnson
Veterinarian Dr. Eric Bergstrom is interested in a new
woman. A *beautiful* woman. He's volunteered his services at
the local cat shelter she's involved with. He's even adopted
one of the shelter's cats. But he still can't manage to get
Madeline to go out with him. That's bad enough. Then Eric's
twelve-year-old son comes to town, making it clear that he
resents "having" to spend the summer with his father. Well,
at least Eric's new cat loves him....

#759 IN THE ARMS OF THE LAW • Anne Marie Duquette
Home on the Ranch
Morgan Bodine is part-owner of the Silver Dollar Ranch; he's
also the acting sheriff in Tombstone, Arizona.
Jasentha Cliffwalker is a biologist studying bats on Bodine
property. Morgan and Jaz loved each other years ago, but it
was a love they weren't ready for. *Are they ready now?*
They'll find out when a stranger comes to Tombstone,
threatening everything they value most.... By the author of
She Caught the Sheriff.

#760 JUST ONE NIGHT • Kathryn Shay
9 Months Later
Annie and Zach Sloan had married for all the right reasons.
They'd fallen in love and neither could imagine life without
the other. But those reasons hadn't been enough to keep
them together. Then—six years after the divorce—a night
that began in fear ended in passion. And how there's a
new reason for Zach and Annie to marry. *They're about to
become parents.*

#761 THIS CHILD IS MINE • Janice Kaiser
Carolina Prescott is pregnant. Webb Harper is the father.
After his wife died, he forgot all about the donation he'd left
at a fertility clinic. Due to a mix-up, Lina is given the wrong
fertilized egg—but that doesn't make her less of a mother!
Both Lina and Webb have strong feelings about the baby
she's carrying and the ensuing lawsuit. Can their growing
feelings for each other overcome the trauma of the battle
for custody?

Take 4 bestselling love stories FREE

Plus get a FREE surprise gift!

Special Limited-time Offer

Mail to Harlequin Reader Service®

P.O. Box 609
Fort Erie, Ontario
L2A 5X3

YES! Please send me 4 free Harlequin Superromance® novels and my free surprise gift. Then send me 4 brand-new novels every month, which I will receive before they appear in bookstores. Bill me at the low price of $3.71 each plus 25¢ delivery and GST*. That's the complete price and a savings of over 10% off the cover prices—quite a bargain! I understand that accepting the books and gift places me under no obligation ever to buy any books. I can always return a shipment and cancel at any time. Even if I never buy another book from Harlequin, the 4 free books and the surprise gift are mine to keep forever.

334 BPA A3UF

Name	(PLEASE PRINT)	
Address		Apt. No.
City	Province	Postal Code

This offer is limited to one order per household and not valid to present Harlequin Superromance® subscribers. *Terms and prices are subject to change without notice.
Canadian residents will be charged applicable provincial taxes and GST.

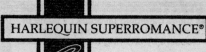

*Welcome—for the second time—
to the Silver Dollar Ranch,
near Tombstone, Arizona*

You may have met Morgan Bodine and
Jasentha Cliffwalker in *She Caught the Sheriff.*
Now this is their story—

IN THE ARMS OF THE LAW (#759)

by Anne Marie Duquette

Morgan Bodine is part-owner of the Silver Dollar; he's also
Tombstone's acting sheriff. Jasentha is busy studying the bats
that live in the caves on Bodine property. Morgan and Jaz
loved each other years ago, but it was a love they weren't
ready for.

Are they ready now? They'll find out when a stranger comes to
Tombstone, threatening everything they value most....

Available October 1997
wherever Harlequin books are sold.

Don't miss these Harlequin favorites by some of our most popular authors! And now you can receive a discount by ordering two or more titles!

HT#25700	HOLDING OUT FOR A HERO by Vicki Lewis Thompson	$3.50 U.S. ☐	/$3.99 CAN. ☐
HT#25699	WICKED WAYS by Kate Hoffmann	$3.50 U.S. ☐	/$3.99 CAN. ☐
HP#11845	RELATIVE SINS by Anne Mather	$3.50 U.S. ☐	/$3.99 CAN. ☐
HP#11849	A KISS TO REMEMBER by Miranda Lee	$3.50 U.S. ☐	/$3.99 CAN. ☐
HR#03359	FAITH, HOPE AND MARRIAGE by Emma Goldrick	$2.99 U.S. ☐	/$3.50 CAN. ☐
HR#03433	TEMPORARY HUSBAND by Day Leclaire	$3.25 U.S. ☐	/$3.75 CAN. ☐
HS#70679	QUEEN OF THE DIXIE DRIVE-IN by Peg Sutherland	$3.99 U.S. ☐	/$4.50 CAN. ☐
HS#70712	SUGAR BABY by Karen Young	$3.99 U.S. ☐	/$4.50 CAN. ☐
HI#22319	BREATHLESS by Carly Bishop	$3.50 U.S. ☐	/$3.99 CAN. ☐
HI#22335	BEAUTY VS. THE BEAST by M.J. Rodgers	$3.50 U.S. ☐	/$3.99 CAN. ☐
AR#16577	BRIDE OF THE BADLANDS by Jule McBride	$3.50 U.S. ☐	/$3.99 CAN. ☐
AR#16656	RED-HOT RANCHMAN by Victoria Pade	$3.75 U.S. ☐	/$4.25 CAN. ☐
HH#28868	THE SAXON by Margaret Moore	$4.50 U.S. ☐	/$4.99 CAN. ☐
HH#28893	UNICORN VENGEANCE by Claire Delacroix	$4.50 U.S. ☐	/$4.99 CAN. ☐

(limited quantities available on certain titles)

	TOTAL AMOUNT	$ _____
DEDUCT:	10% DISCOUNT FOR 2+ BOOKS	$ _____
	POSTAGE & HANDLING	$ _____
	($1.00 for one book, 50¢ for each additional)	
	APPLICABLE TAXES*	$ _____
	TOTAL PAYABLE	$ _____
	(check or money order—please do not send cash)	

To order, complete this form, along with a check or money order for the total above, payable to Harlequin Books, to: **In the U.S.:** 3010 Walden Avenue, P.O. Box 9047, Buffalo, NY 14269-9047; **In Canada:** P.O. Box 613, Fort Erie, Ontario, L2A 5X3.

Name: _____

Address: _____ City: _____

State/Prov.: _____ Zip/Postal Code: _____

*New York residents remit applicable sales taxes.
Canadian residents remit applicable GST and provincial taxes.

Look us up on-line at: http://www.romance.net

HBKJS97

Let's Celebrate!

LOVE & LAUGHTER™

invites you to
the party of the season!

Grab your popcorn and be prepared to laugh as we celebrate with **LOVE & LAUGHTER**.

Harlequin's newest series is going Hollywood!

Let us make you laugh with three months of terrific books, authors and romance, plus a chance to win a FREE 15-copy video collection of the best romantic comedies ever made.

For more details look in the back pages of any Love & Laughter title, from July to September, at your favorite retail outlet.

Don't forget the popcorn!

Available wherever
Harlequin books are sold.

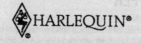

HARLEQUIN®

LLCELEB

As Seen on TV!

Free Gift Offer

With a Free Gift proof-of-purchase
from any Harlequin® book, you can receive
a beautiful cubic zirconia pendant.

This stunning marquise-shaped stone is a genuine cubic
zirconia—accented by an 18" gold tone necklace.
(Approximate retail value $19.95)

Send for yours today...
compliments of ✧HARLEQUIN®

To receive your free gift, a cubic zirconia pendant, send us one original proof-of-purchase, photocopies not accepted, from the back of any Harlequin Romance®, Harlequin Presents®, Harlequin Temptation®, Harlequin Superromance®, Harlequin Intrigue®, Harlequin American Romance®, or Harlequin Historicals® title available at your favorite retail outlet, together with the Free Gift Certificate, plus a check or money order for $1.65 U.S./$2.15 CAN. (do not send cash) to cover postage and handling, payable to Harlequin Free Gift Offer. We will send you the specified gift. Allow 6 to 8 weeks for delivery. Offer good until December 31, 1997, or while quantities last. Offer valid in the U.S. and Canada only.

Free Gift Certificate

Name: _____

Address: _____

City: _____ State/Province: _____ Zip/Postal Code: _____

Mail this certificate, one proof-of-purchase and a check or money order for postage and handling to: HARLEQUIN FREE GIFT OFFER 1997. In the U.S.: 3010 Walden Avenue, P.O. Box 9071, Buffalo NY 14269-9057. In Canada: P.O. Box 604, Fort Erie, Ontario L2Z 5X3.

FREE GIFT OFFER   084-KEZ

ONE PROOF-OF-PURCHASE
To collect your fabulous FREE GIFT, a cubic zirconia pendant, you must include this original proof-of-purchase for each gift with the properly completed Free Gift Certificate.

084-KEZR